Bad

CHLOÉ ESPOSITO

MICHAEL JOSEPH
an imprint of
PENGUIN BOOKS

MICHAEL JOSEPH

UK | USA | Canada | Ireland | Australia
India | New Zealand | South Africa

Michael Joseph is part of the Penguin Random House group of companies
whose addresses can be found at global.penguinrandomhouse.com

Penguin
Random House
UK

First published 2018

001

Copyright © Chloé Esposito, 2018

The moral right of the author has been asserted

Set in 14.41/17.5 pt Bembo Book MT Std
Typeset by Jouve (UK), Milton Keynes
Printed in Great Britain by Clays Ltd, St Ives plc

A CIP catalogue record for this book is available from the British Library

HARDBACK ISBN: 978–0–718–18571–8
OM PAPERBACK ISBN: 978–0–718–18572–5

www.greenpenguin.co.uk

Bad

Chloé Esposito grew up in Cheltenham and now lives in London with her husband and daughters. She has a BA and MA in English from the University of Oxford and has worked as a senior management consultant, an English teacher, and a fashion journalist. Esposito is a graduate of the Faber Academy, and this is her second novel.

Twitter @ChloeJEsposito
Instagram chloe.j.esposito
#BadAlvie

By the same author

Mad

For Lisa

Vengeance is mine, I will repay.

Romans 12:19, King James Bible

Though this be madness, yet there is method in't.

Hamlet, William Shakespeare

Love is my religion – I could die for that.

John Keats

Contents

Disclaimer

There's something you should know before we go any further: last week was mad. That's an understatement really. I had the best sex of my life. I discovered a penchant for guns. Now everyone thinks I'm my identical twin (because she died and I stole her life). Several people expired.

I wouldn't say it was *out of character*; it's not like I'm a fucking saint. But until last week I wasn't a killer. I was just like you. Sure, there were petty crimes: shoplifting, arson, embezzlement. But otherwise, I did what you do: I bottled it up and *drank*. I worked in classified advertising. I had a flat in N19. I hadn't murdered anyone (although it had crossed my mind). I wasn't involved with the Mafia. Interpol wasn't on my ass. But a lot can change in a few short days and I guess this is now the new me.

My head's still spinning. I don't know where to start. I should probably start at the very beginning, but all I can think about is the end and Nino breaking my heart.

It all began last week with an accident.

It wasn't my fault. Not really, you see. So do me a favour, don't judge.

My twin is the reason I went to Sicily. Beth was *desperate* for me to come. Paid for my flights and everything. She lured me with free champagne and the promise of some sun. I wouldn't normally have gone. I know better than anyone that hanging out with my thunder-twat twin is water torture at best. But I'd just been fired for watching porn and my dickhead flatmates threw me out. It was Sicily or a cardboard box. So stupidly I trusted her, and off I went.

Bad plan.

When I arrived at her villa in Taormina the place was magnificent. I'm talking *Condé Nast Traveller* porn. The most *fuck you* of *fuck-you cribs*. Sixteenth-century landscaped gardens, marble statues, fountains, flowers. And the swimming pool . . . you can't even imagine. Of course I was jealous. Wouldn't you be?

And then there was Beth's baby, Ernesto. The kid she had with Ambrogio. If only you'd seen him. He looked like me. He could have been mine. *Should* have been. 'Ma ma,' he called me. 'Ma ma ma.'

It was more than I could take.

My eyes turned monster-green.

Then Beth told me why she had invited me. She didn't just *miss me*. Ha. As if. She asked if I would swap places with her so she could go out for a night. She didn't want Ambrogio to notice. I knew something funny was up. I never should have agreed to it, but she bribed me with golden Prada sandals, so what's a girl to do? I waited and waited, all dressed up like Beth, until it was almost midnight. When she finally reappeared we had a terrible fight.

We were standing by the edge of the pool and somehow – I don't know how – she slipped.

She cracked her head on the tiles and disappeared under the water.

Air bubbles

and then

nothing.

I know.

I know what you're thinking.

I should have jumped in and saved her.

But you don't know how I've suffered.

So I let her die and stole her life.

I stole her clothes. I stole her son. I stole her fucking husband. I stole her millions and her villa. It should have been mine anyway. Ambrogio didn't notice a thing (at least not at first).

It was better than winning the lottery.

All of my wildest dreams had come true.

It turned out that Ambrogio was in the mob and had some interesting friends. His partners, Nino and Domenico, are hitmen in Cosa Nostra. They helped us bury my sister's corpse in a hole in a nearby wood.

Everything was looking peachy.

They all thought the corpse was me.

But the reason my twin had wanted me to swap places was so she could escape the mob. She didn't want her precious son to end up with a bullet in his head. She wanted to leave Ambrogio and elope with her lover, Salvatore. The two lovebirds were plotting to kill me and leave the island for good. Beth thought a body (*my* dead body) was the only way that they wouldn't come after her. What.

A. Bitch. What a fucking snake. But, at the very last minute, Salvatore refused to help her murder me.

Alvie: one. Beth: nil.

In your face.

But then I slept with Ambrogio and, reader, *I had to fake it*. It was like throwing a twig down the Channel Tunnel. 'Micro-cock' is kind. Oh, the years I'd wasted fantasizing about my sister's guy . . .

He knew it was me straight away.

He chased me through the night. I ran for my life. I thought he would kill me, so I did it first. I smashed in his head with a rock.

I ran to Salvatore's villa when Ambrogio died. I told him it was self-defence, and it kind of was, in a way. Salvo, thinking I was Beth, helped me dispose of Ambrogio's corpse. We lost him over the edge of a cliff. Made it look like suicide.

Then I slept with Salvatore. Two hundred pounds of sculpted muscle? I couldn't help myself. But he noticed I didn't have a Caesarean scar on my stomach like Beth.

Busted *again*.

I couldn't trust him to keep my secret. There was way too much at stake. So I went to Ambrogio's partner, Nino, and told him that Salvo had killed his boss. Nino was sexy. Nino was loyal. He said that Ambrogio was like a brother to him.

So that did the trick.

Nino murdered Salvatore and then I slept with Nino too.

I am going to be honest with you.

He was the best human man that I've ever slept with (and there have been a few). I dreamed of becoming an assassin at Nino's side. His partner. His bride.

I thought I'd found The One.

We came up with a plan to work together and make ourselves a fortune. We decided to flog a Caravaggio, some priceless art that Ambrogio had. The buyer was a dodgy priest who worked for the Sicilian mob. But the bastard claimed that the painting was fake. He wasn't going to give us the money.

So I killed him as well.

We escaped to London in Ambrogio's Lambo with two million euros in a suitcase.

It doesn't give me any pleasure to tell you that Nino was a mistake.

When we got to the Ritz he stole the car. He stole the fucking case.

I know I may never see Nino again. But, if I do, I promise you that all of hell will break loose.

YESTERDAY

Sunday, 30 August 2015
Tuscany, Italy

I watch the road through the rose-tinted windscreen. Tarmac shimmers in mirage-heat: a molten river of quicksilver. It feels like we're sailing, not driving. The sky is wide and impossibly blue, as blue as Damian Lewis's eyes or the Italian rugby team's home strip. I've never seen skies as blue as this, except for in movies. The olive groves, the rolling hills, the stunning Tuscan landscape, all dazzle as though they are freshly painted oils squeezed from the tube.

The hot leather seat sticks to my skin. These tiny Balenciaga hot pants barely cover my lips. A bead of sweat slides down my chest and snakes down in between my breasts. I take a swig of warm Prosecco. It's easily forty degrees.

'Want some?' I ask. I pass Nino the bottle.

He shakes his head, '*Niente.*'

I grip the steering wheel tightly and study my scuffed-up fingernails. I need a manicure. The baby pink has all chipped off and the dried blood underneath the tips has turned an ugly rusty red. My sister's fuck-off diamond ring glints like a tiny bomb.

TayTay's playing on the radio. 'Out of the Woods'. I *love* that song. I turn it up and sing along. The bassline feels like sex. I check my reflection in the rear-view. I look good in Beth's Gucci shades. I suit her clothes. I suit this life.

Nino passes me a cig and I sigh out smoke.

Now we're so fast we're not sailing, we're flying, speeding along at over 180. I watch the needle on the speedometer flicker, faster, faster. THIS IS THE FUCKING LIFE.

I blast the horn just for the hell of it.

'Betta, shut the fuck up.'

Betta, Betta, always fucking Betta.

I'm getting sick of being my sister, but Nino thinks I'm his dead boss's wife. If I tell him I'm the *other* twin, I'll risk everything. Risk my life. He might start asking difficult questions, like if I was involved in Ambrogio's murder. Better to keep on being Betta. Better to play along.

Oh, what a tangled web we weave when first we practise to deceive.

I'm a bona fide black widow.

We're heading north out of Tuscany. Towards the lakes and the Swiss border. Through Provence, Bourgogne, Picardy and, finally, London. Away from Taormina. Away from my sister. Away from the cops and the copious corpses. Away from the guilt. The fear. The sleepless nights. So. Many. Dead. I stretch my arms up overhead, love that delicious release in my shoulders and neck, the sweet drugs coursing through my veins, that feel-good glow in my head. The aftertaste of coke drip-dripping down the back of my nose to my throat. I smile at Nino, lick numb lips. I can still taste him from our last kiss: his salty tongue, the Marlboro Red. I can smell the aftershave he's wearing and his sexy sweat. I can smell the money, stashed away in the priest's old leather suitcase. I get a rush just thinking about it. It makes me so wet . . .

'Do you know how *rich* we are?'

'Two million euros,' Nino says. He grabs the worn brown Gucci case and smooths the cracked leather. '*Allora?* How long is that gonna last?'

'We can make some more,' I say. 'Nino, baby, we are *immortal*. We make a great team. Don't you think?'

We're leaving the cops and the mobsters behind us, our future before us, bold and bright. Alvie and Nino together for ever, killing and fucking and fucking and killing.

'Hey,' I say, 'do you wanna pull over? I feel like some roadside fun.'

He nods.

I turn down a country lane and kill the engine dead. Nino gets out and opens my door. Offers his hand for me to take. We walk round to the front of the car then Nino undresses me.

My cheek slams hard into hot metal, singeing on the bonnet. My hot pants are down around my feet. Nino's hands are on my tits. God, I love my badass boyfriend. I know it's only been a *week*, but I feel like I've known him *for ever*. I stretch my arms up over my head and claw the shiny scarlet paint. His body's heavy, pressing down into my dripping, naked back. I feel his heart pound through his chest, his stubble sharp against my neck. His skin is scorching, sizzling. I can taste salt and sex.

He pounds me pounds me pounds me.

'Nino, Nino, Nino,' I say.

I wish he would say 'Alvie'.

We come together. I see red. Our bodies jerking, shaking. For a split-second we're not here – we're in a different universe. I have no sense of who I am; Nino and I are one. The French call this *la petite mort*, 'the little death' or something. Like part of me has died inside. But I've never felt so alive. So what the hell do they know?

Then we crash back down to Earth. Back to reality. But you know what? That's pretty cool. Right now, I dig being me. Nino pulls out and I stand up, dizzy, spinning and light-headed. I hear his boots crunch into gravel. I hear him sighing, '*Betta.*' I reach down for my hot pants and pull them back up sticky legs. I lean against the Lambo and watch him spark up a fag.

'Where have you been all my life?' he says.

'Waiting for *you*,' I say.

His fingers brush my bottom lip.

I look into his eyes.

All this . . . all this feels like a dream. I feel safe. I feel wanted for the first time in my life. Being here right now with him . . . I've never felt like this before. It's almost too good to be true.

DAY ONE:
The Traitor

Chapter One

TODODAY

TODAY

Monday, 31 August 2015
Ritz Hotel, St James's, London

I can just hear Beth now:
   'Alvie? Why are you vomiting in the sink?'
   Because I'm shitting in the toilet.
   'What, at the same time?'
   Yeah, at the same time. It's called alcohol poisoning. It's super exciting. You should try it sometime. Bitch.
   I crank my heavy eyelids open, just a crack. I'm blinded by Daz-ad brilliant white: the porcelain bowl. I close them again; that hurt. I rest my cheek on the cold, hard rim and ride the waves of nausea. I am a surfer acing barrels in Hawaii, gliding over swell and crashing into white water. Oh no, here it comes, *again*. I vomit what's left of my dwindling stomach acid again and again and again.
   'I'LL GET YOU FOR THIS, NINO. THIS IS ALL YOUR FAULT.'
   Gin, wine, vodka martini, carrots (weird, I didn't eat any carrots?). My breath echoes around the inside of the bowl. My head pounds and spins.

'I'm never drinking
Ever again. This time I
mean it.' Whatever.

My first haiku of the day . . .

Genius, Alvie, you've still got it. Who cares if no-one likes my poems? Keats wasn't appreciated in his lifetime. Beth always said I was wasting my time, but I don't do it for the critics.

I finally flop face down on the floor. The bathroom tiles rise up to meet me and smack me – *WHACK* – on the side of the head.

Did I actually just fall off the toilet?

My mouth floods with blood from a cut on my lip. I feel like death, but at least I'm not *dead* – eating burgers on the john like Elvis Presley. My body shivers on the black and white tiles. Urgh, what's that? Oh, it's me. BO mixed with Toilet Duck or ocean-breeze bleach. I'm naked apart from Beth's diamond necklace. I crawl, commando, like an infantry soldier, on to the warm and fluffy bath mat: my desert island in a hostile sea. I'm in a slick-looking en-suite bathroom made entirely of marble and glass. Everything's shiny. Everything's new. There's a hot tub and a walk-in shower big enough for two. I lie on my back and stare at the shower. I'd like to get in, but I'm not sure I'd make it . . .

There's a hiss as a tiny white plug-in air freshener spritzes the room with synthetic magnolia. My eye is caught by the widescreen TV hanging up on the wall. I grab the remote and turn it on. I have a vague feeling I should check out the news, a strange sensation in the pit of my stomach that isn't alcohol-related; let's just call it a hunch . . .

An unflattering picture of me at Beth's wedding.

I turn up the volume to max.

'The body of a woman, believed to be that of British citizen, Alvina Knightly, twenty-five, was discovered this morning in a wood near Taormina, Sicily. Our Italian correspondent, Romeo D'Alba, reports.'

> *Fuck, fuck, fuck, fuck, fuck,*
> *Fuck, fuck, fuck, fuck, fuck, fuck, fuck,*
> *Fuck. THIS. SHIT. IS. BAD.*

Technically that's still a haiku. It's not *Shakespeare*, but I'm really hungover. You can't expect me to do my best work at a time like this.

My cigarettes are by the sink; I spark up and suck on a Marlboro. I didn't think they'd find her body, at least not so soon. Am I screwed?

But they don't know who it is.

A balding man in a beige suit stands among oak trees and chestnuts, holding a microphone just below his wobbly double chin. (How the hell did *he* get on TV? He looks like a Scotch egg.) He gestures behind him to a clearing in the woods, waving a white flabby hand. A hole in the ground cut off by police tape, a heap of earth and a ton of bricks, piles of rubble, smashed-up concrete: my twin sister's grave.

'The property had no planning permission. The unfinished building was poorly constructed, hidden deep in the

Sicilian woodland. But it was an unusual scent that alerted the attention of Antonia Ricci's Alsatian this morning. Signora Ricci, please tell us what happened when you took your dog, Lupo, out for a walk.'

The camera pans out to reveal a woman standing at Romeo's side. Antonia is small and anorak-clad, her golden hair a frizzy halo. Her face is long with an aquiline nose. She looks a bit like her dog, I suppose. Lupo stands, panting, between her legs, his great, pink tongue lolling floppy and wet, his ears pricked up stiff and pointy. Romeo thrusts the microphone in Antonia's face. She looks fucking terrified.

'Lupo . . . he sniff . . . he bark at the building. He is upset. I try to pull him . . . to pull him away, but he no move. He is a very good dog.'

Lupo barks.

'Shh. Lupo.'

She gives him a treat.

'He dig and dig and dig. He want to catch something under the building. Me, I think it is a *topo,* a . . . squeak-squeak?'

'A mouse?'

'A mouse. But I scared. The house, it look *strano* . . . strange . . . and then I discover a long blonde hair here. Here. It is here.' She points at the ground. 'I hear the stories. I know. I know Cosa Nostra . . . So, I call the police.'

Romeo nods and reclaims the microphone. He eyes the dog now sniffing at his crotch.

'No. *Basta,*' says Antonia, tugging hard on Lupo's lead. '*Mi dispiace.*'

'The police arrived at seven thirty this morning. They recognized the site as typical of the infamous Sicilian Mafia, the Cosa Nostra. They were unsurprised to find a dead body hidden within the concrete foundations.'

The camera pans out to Sicilian woodland. The dog lifts up one of its hind legs and pees on the rubble.

'LUPO. NO.'

'The discovery of Alvina Knightly's body and her suspected murder call into question the apparent suicide of her brother-in-law, Ambrogio Caruso, twenty-nine, who died only three days before. The police are investigating evidence that Ambrogio Caruso was, indeed, murdered too. This is Romeo D'Alba, BBC News, live in Taormina.'

Great.

I turn off the TV with the zapper.

They've got my body *and* Ambrogio's. It's just a matter of time. They'll be after Beth. Hopefully only for questioning, to see if she can shed some light. But Beth's *twin* and her *husband* have snuffed it. Is she going to be their number-one suspect? What if they think Beth's their guy?

Beth. Oh God, that's *me*.

Unless . . . Can I be Alvie again? Even if I've officially croaked? URGH. This is a *mess.*

I stagger up and off my bath mat. The toilet flush sounds like a tsunami. I lean over the sink and run the cold water and splash some up into my face. I glance in the mirror. Bad idea. I look like the one that crawled out of a graveyard, like Uma Thurman in *Kill Bill 2*. Blood on my lips and smudged mascara, wet hair messy and matted and limp. My skin is kind of grey. I'm Morticia Adams or the undead. It reminds me of the state I was in a week ago back in Archway.

Awesome.

Fucking fabulous.

All the way back to square one. No money. No job. No home. No boyfriend. I needn't have bothered in Sicily. All that time and effort *wasted*. Seven days of damned hard work. Why did I even go to Taormina? All I wanted was a holiday. A bit of sun to work on my tan. Beth practically begged me to get on that plane and it's not like I had a choice. I had hit rock-fucking-bottom. There was nothing in London for me, just a deluge of debt and a scratch card habit. The threat of herpes and STDs. I lived in a vermin-infested cesspit, a natural breeding ground for scabies, while my perfect twin had married *my guy* and moved to the Burj Al Arab.

No, you know what? This is square *minus one*. I took one step forward then two steps back. Now 'Alvie Knightly' is counting worms and Italian cops are on my ass. What do I do? Look on the bright side? That I don't even fucking exist? I need to find Nino and get my moolah then disappear . . . to Monaco. But how the hell am I going to find him if I'm stony broke?

I thought my life was already a train wreck, but now, I guess, it just got worse.

I peer into bloodshot eyes and sigh. Come on, Alvie.

Think. What would Beyoncé do? Nino's out there running free. He's got the Lambo and the suitcase with the money. But I'm Gloria Gaynor: I'm a survivor. I'm going to make him pay. I'll get my revenge, just like Hamlet. (But a girl – Hamlette? No, that sounds like omelette.) I'll find him and I'll kill him. Just watch me. If only he wasn't so fit . . .

I tiptoe through the lounge like I'm walking on eggshells. Miniature bottles litter the carpet: Smirnoff, Glenfiddich, Jack Daniel's, Pimm's. Half empty, topless, sad. I down 50 ml of Bombay Sapphire, the lone survivor in the fridge. I sucked the rest of the minibar dry before passing out late last night. Hair of the dog, that's what they say. It burns my insides just like paint stripper.

There's a complimentary chocolate shortbread perched on a tray by the teacups and saucers. Chrome silver kettle. Sachets of Twinings. I pop the biscuit in my mouth and chew. It seems to relieve the bitter taste of betrayal, sweeten the heinous stench of treachery. *Et tu, Brute?* It's like he stabbed me in the back with my own damn knife.

> *Nino, oh, Nino,*
> *I'm coming for you. Nino,*
> *Oh, Nino, you worm.*

I see his black fedora hat abandoned by the armchair. I pick it up and try it on. Marlboro Reds, leather, sex – I close my eyes and breathe his scent. I remember the first time I saw him at Beth's villa and the way the whole world seemed to stop. Nino driving his people carrier with my twin sister wasted in the trunk, Metallica blaring on the stereo. His muscular forearms inked with tats. His naked body. The chiselled abs. The perfect twelve-inch dick. I frown. No, I don't miss Nino, just his cock.

I can see him now, the back of him anyway, speeding away in Ambrogio's car, racing off down Piccadilly, red tail lights on the Lambo flashing. Man, I loved that ride. Screw you, Nino, you thieving dog. That car was the love of my life.

'If you expect nothing from somebody, then you're never disappointed . . .' I should have listened to Sylvia Plath. I should have been a nun.

I whip off the hat and chuck it on to the sofa, catching the scent of a bouquet of roses standing tall in a vase by the door. How did *they* survive my late-night rampage? The raping and pillaging like a Viking. I was Keith Moon or Keith Richards or some other rock star trashing my room. I was a typhoon, a tornado: Hurricane Alvie.

It's going to take me all week to recover. I'd kill for some coke. Or a Lemsip.

Right. I've had enough of this. Where the hell is Beth's iPhone? It's got to be here somewhere.

I search the scarlet-velvet crumpled curtains in a pile by the wall. Candelabras, crystal ornaments and copies of glossy magazines are all sprawled across the living-room floor. At least there's no chicken. Or tiger. Or baby. I feel like I'm filming *The Hangover Part IV*. Man, I wish this *was* a movie, then I'd press pause or hit rewind. I'd go right back to the beginning and strangle that bitch in the womb.

Finally I find the phone poking out from beneath a rug. I grab it and open the app I downloaded, the one that tracks Nino's mobile phone. That was a stroke of genius, Alvie. One of the best tricks I know. I took Nino's phone while he was in the shower. He'd just been on it, so it was unlocked. I installed the software just in case. Man, it's lucky I did. Somehow I knew not to trust him. Somehow I guessed he was full of shit. I could have waited for him all night downstairs in that bar drinking vodka martinis. Now Nino's location will show up whenever he has signal. I check the app for the first time. The last place that cockwomble showed up was somewhere inside Heathrow Airport. But that was *hours* ago. I click refresh once, twice, three times, four. Nothing. It's not fucking working. His GPS isn't showing up.

Right. That's it. I'm totally screwed. I'm never going to catch him now. That app's my only viable lead. I kick the kettle into the fireplace and throw a teacup at the door. It cracks and breaks into two pieces, like my stupid heart. How the hell am I going to find him?

That I, with wings as swift as meditation or the thoughts of love, may sweep to my revenge.

I take another look at the screen. He could be on a plane by now. Maybe his phone's on airplane mode. I'll check again later. It'll be OK. Relax, babe. Take a chill pill.

There are eight missed calls and one new email from my mum to Beth. I click into the message and read.

From: Mavis Knightly
MavisKnightly1954@yahoo.com
To: Elizabeth Caruso
ElizabethKnightlyCaruso@gmail.com
Date: 31 Aug 2015 at 09.05
Subject: Where are you?

Elizabeth, darling, where on earth have you got to? I'm
out of my mind with worry. I'm here in Taormina with
your son and the nanny and nobody knows a thing.
The police are crawling all over the place, asking
questions about your sister. There seems to be a bit of
a hoo-ha because she was buried in that wood. I told
them what you said on the phone about how it was an
accident, but I don't think they believed me . . .

I called my mother up last week and told her that Alvie
was dead. I said she was a terrible swimmer and fell into
the swimming pool, drunk. She didn't seem at all surprised. *Relieved* more like . . .

Anyway, enough about that. I was so sorry to hear
about Ambrogio. What a shock. You poor, poor thing.
I can only imagine your suffering. He really was the
most wonderful husband. The perfect son-in-law. So
rich. So dashingly handsome. I'll never forget the sight
of his backside as he waited for you to walk down the
aisle. I told the police, there's no way it was suicide. A
man as good-looking and wealthy as that does not go
killing himself willy-nilly. I showed them a photo of you

on your honeymoon, that lovely shot of you both on the beach enjoying a sunset daiquiri. 'Ambrogio Caruso,' I said to the officer, 'is married to my daughter, Beth. Would you kill yourself if she was your wife?' He agreed you were something else. He even went as far as saying you got your good looks from your mum. I didn't deny it, I have to admit. If he had seen your father, Alvin, there wouldn't be any doubt in his head. They're very flirtatious, Italian men. I must say it makes a nice change. In Sydney, women of a certain age are simply invisible. But I'm still a woman. I still have needs. And I appreciate the compliment. You make an effort to look after yourself . . . the chemical peels, the regular waxing, the colonic irrigation. One tries to maintain one's appearance. I'm not going to the knacker's yard yet.

Anyway, do come and see me, my dear. All this stress isn't good for my nerves and I can tell the cortisol's interfering with the HRT.

Yours unconditionally,
Mummy xxx

PS I did try calling you on your mobile, but there seems to be some kind of technological malfunction. It just rings and rings and then goes to voicemail? Will you call me back, angel, please?

I delete the email. Shake my head. She's unbelievable. There's a knock at the door.

What's that? *The police?*

'Who is it?' I say.

I eye the window. I guess if I had to, I could climb out. What floor is this? Oh, the penthouse . . . *Genius.* That's a great plan, Alvie. You're stark bollock naked. It's central London. Middle of the day. No one's going to spot you up there on the roof running around in the buff.

'Sorry, madam, midday check-out was, erm, well, at *midday.*'

'Right. I see. And what time is it now?'

'One thirty.'

Shit. 'I'm coming.'

I've got to disappear before they see this suite. Nino and I have paid the bill (in cash last night with a fat wad of euros), but that covered our stay, not a full fucking refurb. I'll have to do a runner.

But I don't have anything to wear. Nino's fucked off with my clothes in the suitcase. Along with all the cash. What's *he* going to do with my sister's dresses? Gucci, Lanvin and Tom Ford. I doubt they'd suit him, honestly. Ha! I want them back. And my Channing Tatum picture. I can't believe he took that too. It isn't like he needs it.

I grab my dirty dress from yesterday (Beth's little black Chanel) and head into the bathroom for a shower. I step into the steaming water. Sing 'You Oughta Know' by Alanis at the top of my lungs. I wrap my hair up in a turban, pull on a robe and head into the suite. I light myself a cigarette and then pace up and down the room like a lion in a cage at the zoo. I need some wonga to go and find

Nino: flights, hotels, vodka, etc. But all my own cards are maxed out and I can't use Beth's without drawing attention. What am I going to do?

I catch a glimpse of Beth's diamond necklace sparkling round my neck. Beth's diamond earrings. Beth's Omega watch. I've still got her wedding and engagement rings on . . . They all worked a treat last week, when I was posing as my twin. I fooled almost everyone, but now I guess I don't need them.

I wonder how much I'd get if I pawned them.

I'll do it. Right now. I'm *gone*.

I'm about to open the door and run downstairs out into Mayfair when I stop – my hand on the doorknob – and freeze. What the hell am I thinking? Seriously? Poor little darling unarmed Alvie against that vicious monster Nino. He's a professional mobster hitman. He's got *twenty years* of experience. God only knows how many people he's killed. *Definitely* more than me. It could be in the hundreds. Or thousands. Come on, what chance do I have? I must have lost the plot.

I release the doorknob and slump down in a heavy heap on the floor.

I could have had it all.

I was *this* close. *This* fucking close. The villa. The car. The yacht. The baby. The priceless Italian Renaissance art. I was living the life. *La dolce vita*. Two million euros was just the start. He took *everything* from me when he left me here last night. Hot tears pool and spill from my eyeballs. I blink, blink, blink them away.

What's that smell? Miss Dior Chérie? That's strange, even after my shower I can still smell Beth's perfume: saccharine, sticky, sickly sweet. I must have put too much on.

My sister's voice whispers in my ear. '*I'll get you for this.*'

Say *what*? Is that *Beth*?

I open my eyes and sit up. I look around, but the room is empty. There's nobody here except me.

'*You killed me.*'

'Not really. You kind of slipped.' Do I really have to listen to this? 'You are no longer my problem.'

'*Ha. I will be. Just wait.*'

'What the fuck? Are you *threatening* me? You're dead. I saw it with my own eyes . . .'

'*I'll get my revenge.*'

I stand up and lean against the wall, a cold sweat breaking on my face, my breathing short and ragged. I turn on all the lights in the room: the glittering golden chandeliers, the standing lamp on the writing desk, the light on the coffee table. I grab an ivory letter opener.

'*I'm going to make you pay,*' she says. '*You killed my husband in cold blood, you had my lover murdered . . .*'

Damn, she's right. I did do that. I guess that's why she's cross.

'OK. Just wait. Just wait,' I say. The 'dagger' quivers in my hand. My voice is faint and quiet.

'*Oh, I can wait. I've got nowhere to go. You stole my life, remember?*'

She laughs a cruel and joyless laugh, like the nightmare clown in *It*. Where the fuck is it coming from? I stand in the middle of the room and turn round 360 degrees. She isn't in here, is she?

'Firstly, you're *dead*. You're *dodo*. Get it? You're just a stupid voice in my head. Secondly, what are you going to do? *Talk at me?* Terrifying.'

Silence. Nothing. Not a peep. Not a laugh. Not a sigh. Not a sneeze.

'Beth?' Where did she go? I creep towards the mirror. 'Beth, it's not funny. Are you still there?'

I step in closer, peer into my eyes. I'm so close now that my breath fogs the glass. 'Beth? Beth. BETH?'

'"*Vengeance is mine, I will repay.*"'

'ARGH. Shut up, you zombie cunt.'

I flop back down on the floor.

'*You're going to let Nino walk all over you, just like Ambrogio did. They fuck you, then they leave you. You can never make them stay.*'

'No. There's no way. I am *not*.'

'*Look at you. You're so pathetic. You never could get it together.*'

'I'm finding Nino if it's the last thing I do.'

I sit up a bit taller and sniff.

I spot the bouquet of roses, laughing, taunting, mocking me. Nino never bought me flowers. Come to think of it, no one did. I spot a small white envelope tucked away inside the vase. I jump up and seize it.

OMG. They're from *him*.

What does he want? What does it say?

CARISSIMA ELISABETTA, IF YOU CAN CATCH ME,
WE CAN WORK TOGETHER.

That's it. No kiss. No 'Darling, I'm sorry'. No 'My love, I made a mistake', or 'I want you back', or 'I'm a terrible person'. *If* I can catch him? *If? If?* There's no fucking 'ifs' about it. I'm his *nemesis*. I'll do more than *catch him*. Ha. I'll murder him in the fucking face. Seriously? How patronizing. I don't need to work with him. That fuckturnip ruined everything. Does he think I'm going to *let it go*? Roll over like a poodle and let him fuck me? Lie down flat like a welcome mat? No.

I am ALVINA KNIGHTLY.

He'd better be *terrified*.

O, from this time forth, my thoughts be bloody or be nothing worth . . .

Revenge should have no bounds.

I grab the flowers in thick, fat handfuls, the thorns on the stems all digging in, scratching, piercing and drawing blood. I hurl the roses down on the carpet, petals flying in every direction, water spraying, my thumb dripping blood. I jump up and down in Beth's Prada sandals, up, up and down till they're mush.

Chapter Two

Burlington Arcade, St James's, London

'How much?'
'Two hundred and twenty-six thousand pounds and ninety-eight pence.'
The man has a singsong Scottish accent, like Ewan McGregor in *Moulin Rouge*. The jewels sparkle on a black velvet cloth that's spread out on the walnut table.

'And again. I didn't catch it.'

'Two hundred and twenty-six thousand pounds and ninety-eight pence.'

'Fuck.'

'Bless you.'

I'd thought maybe fifty or sixty thousand. *Seventy* at a push. But this is amazing. This is a fortune. Perhaps *today* is my lucky day?

'Would you like me to write it down?'

He produces a Mont Blanc pen from his pocket and scribbles the sum on a piece of white card. He draws an extravagant, curling pound sign – larger than necessary, with a flourish – as if to make a fucking point.

I'm going to push him, hold out for more. I'm not letting

any more men screw me over. I've learnt that the hard way from Nino.

'Three hundred thousand.'

'I beg your pardon?'

'Let's call it three hundred and we have a deal.'

I spit on my palm and stick out my hand, ready for the man to shake. The old guy scratches his balding head. The fine white hairs are frizzy and dry; he needs to buy some conditioner. (I know there's more to life than hair, but it *is* a good place to start . . .) Flecks of dandruff land on his shoulders like a sprinkling of snow on Christmas morning. I wish he'd stop scratching. Now it's a blizzard. I could build a snowman.

'I'm afraid that figure is too high, ma'am. We make very, *very* precise calculations whenever we conduct a valuation . . .'

Blah, blah, fucking blah.

'You want the diamonds? You give me the money. Otherwise I'm leaving.'

Nice.

I'm getting better at negotiating. It's all about leverage and balls.

The man peers over the top of his half-moon glasses and leans in towards me. 'In that case, madam, I wish you good day.'

He folds tweed arms across his chest and taps his brogue on the wooden floor. Oh, I think he wants me to leave. The bastard's calling my bluff.

'*Nice one, Alvie,*' says Beth.

I look around his jewellery shop. It sells antiques as well as watches, vintage brooches and diamond rings. There are paintings on the walls and sepia photos. Victorian lace. An ivory box. There's a human skull, which looks quite fun, with a creamy pate and broken teeth. *Alas, poor Yorick.* I don't want that, though (not if it isn't Nino's.) And it looks kind of bulky to carry around.

I spot an ancient cuckoo clock sitting on a dusty shelf.

'Two hundred and twenty-six thousand pounds and ninety-eight pence *and I want that clock.*'

I point at the shelf. The man turns to look. I don't know why I said that really. I don't even like it to tell you the truth. It's ornate and carved and far too fussy, with annoying Roman numerals and stupid leaves stuck all around. It's varnished wood with copper chains and pendulums all hanging down. There's a little door at the top for the cuckoo bird to pop its head out. It looks like something my gran would have bought on a trip to the Schwarzwald in 1928.

'You've got yourself a deal,' he says. 'I'll transfer the money right this minute, directly into your account.'

I hand the man Elizabeth's jewels and slap him hard on his shoulder.

'No, I'm going to need that in *cash.*'

A cloud of dandruff puffs up from his jacket. I wipe my hand on my dress.

After a while, the man comes back with a dozen or more thick rolls of banknotes. I count every single one. It's right, down to the very last penny. I open the clock and shove the money inside. Spark a celebratory fag. Whoop! Whoop! I can't believe it. *Two hundred and twenty-six thousand pounds and ninety-eight p all for me.* I stride out of the pawn shop, beaming, into the Burlington Arcade. I practically skip my way past the shops. Ooh, look, I like that bracelet . . .

But now is *not* the time to shop.

No, I need that money for Nino, the vodka, the flights. Etc. Etc.

I need to find Nino and the rest of the cash. Two hundred bags of sand ain't bad, but it isn't *justice*. Just a start. Who gives a shit about Beth's stupid villa? Who cares if I burnt it down? I'll buy myself another one. I'll get another classic car.

I burst out of the arcade and on to Piccadilly. Car fumes and coffee from a nearby Caffè Nero. The scent of caffeine reminds me of Nino. He used to like it strong and black. No milk. No sugar. (I don't know how he could drink it like that.) The memories come flooding back and I close my eyes. I can almost *taste* him, the bitter espresso hot on his lips. The earthy tobacco. The smell of worn leather. His horseshoe moustache scratching rough on my skin.

No. No. He's gone. He's gone. I shake my head to throw his image out of my brain. I swear to God: *I swear off men.* I have had enough. I'm going to be a born-again virgin. (Hmm, is that an actual thing? Perhaps my hymen will grow back? I'll be as tight as a weasel's ass.)

I glance again at the iPhone app, but it still says the air-port. Now that I have got some cash I can be on my way.

'TAAAAAAXIIIIIIIIII,' I say, sticking out my arm.

No. Fuck you, Nino. You're dead to me now. I can taste *the money* — and the little bits of chocolate still stuck in my teeth from that complimentary shortbread I ate at the Ritz.

Chapter Three

Heathrow Airport, London

I slam the flute down on the bar and scan the heaving crowds. Nino could be *anywhere* by now: Bali, Fiji, Mississippi . . . Or, even worse, he could be *here*. He could be hiding in the crowds watching me get drunk on Bolly. Waiting till I'm comatose and he can make his killer move. I narrow my eyes and scan the hordes of really badly dressed tourists. Nobody is looking back. No one notices me.

The waiter pours me some more fizz. I take a big gulp and I shiver. It's cold and crisp, just the right side of bitter. The pale gold liquid sloshes around inside the tall cut-crystal glass. I watch the bubbles rise. How many is that? This should be my last. I need to keep my wits about me. I need to be ready like Freddy.

I grab Beth's iPhone from inside my tote and swipe to refresh the tracking app again and again and again and again. But no, it still says the same thing. He was *here* at Heathrow Airport, right here at Terminal 5. But it's been hours now. Oh man, why hasn't it changed? Fucking technology hates me. Always has and always will. Clocks and watches stop in my presence like I've got some magnetic field that interferes with the maths. I bet the stupid app is broken. That's it. He's gone. It's *over* . . .

I chuck the phone back on the bar and down the rest of the champagne.

'Why do all the guys leave me?' I say to no one in particular.

'*Because you're a psycho?*' offers Beth.

'Oh cheers. Yeah. Really helpful.'

'*Nino's not the first, you know. There was Alex, Ahmed, Simon, Richard, Michael . . . need I go on? Bradley, Jamie, Stewart, Hamish, Norman, Humphrey, George, John, Paul, Mark, Clark, Madhav, Mohammed and Daniel and Patrick . . . But you know what? It all started with Dad. He left you when you were one.*'

'Shut up, Beth. Pipe the fuck down. Dad left *you* as well.'

She's right, though; Dad was the first to leave. He couldn't stand the sight of me. He only managed twelve short months before taking off for ever. Nino managed less than a week. I must be getting worse.

I call up YouTube on my phone and search for 'self-defence'. The first hit is 'Five great self-defence moves'. Apparently 'strong' is the new 'skinny': #GirlsWhoLift. I'm going to go Hilary Swank on his ass. I'll get as buff as Rich Froning. I need to be ready for a fight. He could strike at any second. I'll have to learn some killer moves, some judo or ju-jitsu. The guy on screen demonstrates what to do if some lying Sicilian bastard attacks you. He shows how to respond to a punch or a head-butt, a kick or

a knee in the groin. I watch the clip again and again, trying to learn the moves by heart. He keeps on saying, 'Keep
it simple.' He says, 'It's easy.' *Bollocks.* He's going too fast
and I can't follow. I'll need to practise to learn.

Ping.

What was that?

The app is flashing with a new notification. I click the
tiny icon and hold it close so I can read. I can't see very
well and my eyes are all blurry, but that looks like Bucharest, Romania. Yes. I've got him. He's there. If that dead
shit's in Romania, then that is where I need to go. You
can do it, Alvie baby. You're Wonder Woman. A Jedi
knight.

*Hold, hold, my heart. And you, my sinews, grow not instant
old, but bear me stiffly up.*

It is fucking *on.*

Hmm, Romania. Interesting choice. I wonder why
Nino went there.

I need to go and book a flight.

I pay the bill. *How* much? Who cares. I'm rich now, I
can afford it. Champagne is one of life's essentials, like
Pop-Tarts or Pringles or coke.

As soon as I get on the plane I start to regret moving so
quickly. What am I going to do if I find him? I haven't
practised my self-defence. I haven't got a plan.

I bang my forehead hard against the back of the seat in
front of me.

It doesn't really help.

The stupid drop-down plastic tray falls into my lap. I slam it back up again: whack.

'Are you all right there, madam?'

The air hostess has a matron's voice: strict and stern, no nonsense.

'*No.*'

Cuckoo. Cuckoo.

'Oh for fuck's sake.' If it isn't Beth, it's that stupid clock.

'Hey. Do you mind?' comes a voice from ahead. It's the guy sitting in the chair in front.

I say, 'What's up, babe? Wanna join the mile-high club?'

He makes a face and turns round.

I snap my head towards the aisle. The hostess looks distressed. Upset. She peers along my row of seats, her forehead crinkled with concern.

'Madam?' she says *again*.

She shakes her shiny chignon at me, her tangerine lips a thin orange line. She wears a stiff navy cravat and a starched white-cotton dress shirt. She has a tiny wasp-like waist. I read her name badge: 'Gertrude'.

'When the fuck do we land in Romania?' I cannot take much more of this.

I rest my cheek on the back of my seat and breathe into the foamy cushion; it smells of other people's hair.

'We land in Bucharest in three hours, madam. We've only just taken off.'

'Can you bring me some more wine?' I say.

'I think you've had enough. I can't serve you any more.'

I roll my eyes. I raise my voice. 'I have had *enough*? Are you kidding me? I've had *one* teeny, tiny, minuscule bottle of cat-piss Chardonnay that was almost too nasty to drink.' I'm not counting the stuff I had at the airport; that was in a different time zone.

I lean back in my chair and close my eyes. It's quiet now. There's no one around. (The next-door passenger got up and left to sit somewhere else. Don't know why.) I just want to sleep. I'm sick of this shit. If I pass out, then I won't have to think about it. Dreaming has got to be better than this. This is a *nightmare*.

Bubbles rise to the surface of the water. The pool is bottomless and black. Her body sinks, bright white in the moonlight, as pale as a ghost's. The night is dark. The stars have gone and the full moon hides behind a tree. A thick and opaque silence swallows us up like a cloud. I search for her face in the darkness.

Pop.

Pop.

Pop.

Pop.

Then no more bubbles.

She's dead.

I lean further over the edge. I look, but there is nothing there. Beth's corpse has vanished. Gone. I peer into the abyss. Two bright lights flash on. Her eyes? No way. What the actual fuck? What is going on? Her arms reach up from the water towards me. They're long and white and endless, just like eels or cooked spaghetti. Her hands grip tight round my throat. I can't breath. I'm choking. Her fingers curl tighter. She pulls me down. My feet slip on the tiles and I crash into the water. Liquid closes overhead. I gasp and gasp for breath.

I can't see anything – but then – two bright light bulbs blinking, shining. Her face is no longer hers, but a clown's.

'Who are you?' I say.

'I am Mr Bubbles,' says Beth.

Bitch, she knows I have coulrophobia.

The water sucks me down like a vortex. I'm spinning around and around. All I can see is the clown. A round red nose, two yellow eyes. Red blood is smeared around her lips.

She laughs. Her laugh turns to a scream. But it's me who's screaming.

DAY TWO:
The Thief

TEN YEARS AGO

Saturday, 7 May 2005
Lower Slaughter, Gloucestershire

Beth bangs on the bathroom door.
'Alvie? Are you throwing up again?'
'No.'
I flush the loo.
She bangs again. 'Let me in.'
'Fuck off.'
'I'm worried about you.'
I roll my eyes. 'OK, I'm coming.'
Stupid sister. Nosy brat. Now she's got braces and a training bra, she thinks she's the boss, all grown-up.
I glug the mouthwash. Spit it out. It's extra-strong spearmint. It stings my mouth.
I wipe my face dry with the towel and study myself in the mirror. Two new spots. No sign of vomit. I unlock the door. *It's showtime.*
Beth pushes in. Bolts the door behind her.
'Sit,' she says.

I frown. Concern is written all over her face like she's someone who gives a shit.

She points at the toilet. 'Sit. *Please.*'

I close the lid and then sit down on the cold hard plastic seat. Great. Here we go *again* . . .

'Alvie,' she says.

'Before you begin, I *was not* throwing up.'

I cross my arms and sit up tall. There's no evidence; it's all gone.

Elizabeth raises a perfect eyebrow then takes the lavender air freshener and spritzes every inch of room. Tiny droplets flood my face. I choke on chemicals. She stands up high on tippy-toes to open the little bathroom window. A blast of cold air rushes in.

'All right, I get the point.'

'Alvie,' she says in that whiny voice. 'I saw three empty Pringles tubes and five packets of strawberry Pop-Tarts in the bin.'

'So what?'

'Yesterday was bin day.'

'And?'

'You ate them all today.'

Damn, she's good. Like some kind of spy. She could work at MI5.

'Why was it me? Maybe Mum had some?'

'You're the only one who likes Cheese and Onion.'

Beth holds my gaze. I can read her mind. She thinks she's got me all figured out.

'You know, there's a name for what you've got.'

'Oh yeah? There's a name for you too . . .' I say.

'Alvie, it's called bulimia. And this isn't funny.'

'It is not *your* life. It's *mine*,' I say.

'What does that even mean?' She looks at me and cocks her head. Bites her lip with worry. 'Alvie, please, you have to stop. I'm serious. It could *kill* you.'

I rest my head on the cool white tiles on the bathroom wall.

If I just sit here and stay quiet, perhaps she'll go away?

'Why won't you let me in?' she says. 'I'm your sister; I love you. I spoke to your counsellor at school yesterday –'

'You fucking what?' How dare she? How could she? Talking about me behind my back to that four-eyed fuck, Lorraine?

'I had to, Alvie. You're so thin.' She looks my body up and down. 'I don't know what to do.'

WTF? She's thinner than me.

'Why do you have to do anything? Why can't you mind your own damn business?'

'This is getting ridiculous. I hear you after every meal. It sounds so disgusting.'

'I'm sorry if I gross you out. It's not my fault Mum's cooking stinks.'

'I followed you at school,' she says. 'You do the same thing there.'

'School dinners are even worse,' I say to the floor.

Beth's voice changes. Softer. Quieter. 'It won't change anything, you know.'

I snap my head up. Glare at her. She's wearing a new

pink sparkly T-shirt with '90% ANGEL' written on it. I need to go and get myself one that says '90% DEVIL'.

'What's not going to change what?' I snap.

'Throwing up . . . Getting so thin . . . Mum's not going to love you more. Dad isn't going to come back.'

Hot blood flows to my cheeks. That was cruel. Below the belt. How dare she bring up Dad like that? What gives her the right? That subject is way off limits. It's an unspoken rule between us: we never, ever mention him. I feel like punching her. Or I could grab the loo's ceramic lid and smash her pretty head in?

I think of the photo tucked away inside my Primark wallet; it's the only picture I have of Dad. I stole it from Mum's wedding album. She didn't notice it was gone. It's dog-eared and worn along the creases. But at least I get to see his face every time I take it out. I look at it and dream about how very different life would be if my dad had stuck around instead of taking off. I wasn't even a year old and then – poof – he was gone, like Houdini. He disappeared off the face of the Earth without a trace or an email address. The only proof that he ever existed are me (and my sister), my stupid name and that faded photograph.

Mum said he'd moved to San Francisco, something about an accounting job, but I know he didn't. She made it all up. I've searched San Francisco high and low. Not the *place* (I've never been to America); I looked on the internet. Everyone has an online presence. We all exist on there, in the ether. There's no Alvin Knightly in S. F., or anywhere in California. I checked and rechecked every couple of months, just in case he showed up on a bowling team or a company bio, on LinkedIn or a poker account, but he never did.

I wasn't giving up. I extended my search to other countries, went Lisbeth Salander on his ass. *Alvin Knightly*'s an unusual name; surely, if I looked hard enough, eventually he'd show up? I called the Institute of Chartered Accountants, but they had never heard of him. I thought about hiring a private detective, but I couldn't afford the fees.

I finally came to the sorry conclusion that there weren't any stupid Alvin Knightlys anywhere in the whole damn world. Unless (and I know this is a long shot) he'd changed his name to Alvin Knightley. (I found one of those in 2003, but it's highly unlikely, honestly, because the guy in the photo was black.) I've been looking since I was eleven, when I first had access to a PC, and there's never been any sign of my father. I'm not dumb. I know what it means. It means he's fucking *dead*. Or if he's off the grid, it's on purpose. That kind of thing takes cunning. Planning. You have to really fucking mean it. Have to *want* to disappear. It once crossed my mind that he might be a spy, like Austin Powers or John le Carré (which would explain where Beth gets it from: Miss Spanish Inquisition), and the government might have swapped his name for a code, like 007. But then I thought, *don't be an idiot*. This is real life, not the movies. He's not Jason Bourne; he's a bookkeeper.

Beth reaches out and touches my arm, breaking my train of thought.

'DON'T YOU FUCKING TOUCH ME.'

I jump up and unlock the bathroom door, but the metal bolt catches. It pinches my skin. I force it and slam the door shut behind me. I sprint down all fifteen stairs.

My sister's voice calls after me. 'Alvie. I'm sorry. Come back. Please.'

Whatever, bitch.

Too late.

Chapter Four

TODObody

TODAY

Tuesday, 1 September 2015
Henri Coandã International Airport,
Bucharest, Romania

'Wake up please, madam, we're here.'
'No, no.'
The clown. Where's the clown? The seat is wet from where a little bit of dribble ran out of my mouth and formed a pool. I feel a hand shaking my shoulder.

'ARGH. Get off,' I say.

'Excuse me, but you need to get up. Everyone else has alighted the plane.'

'Plane? What plane?'

I open my eyes. It's that infuriating air hostess, Guinevere or Geraldine or something. And this is clearly a plane.

'Where are we again?' I try to sit up.

'Henri Coandã International. We've landed in Bucharest.'

I rub my eyes with both my hands. I really need to go back to sleep. I roll over on the seat and curl into the cushion.

'Just five more minutes,' I say.

'Madam? Madam?'

'I don't want to go. Just leave me alone,' I say.

'Would you like me to get a mobility cart?'

'No. Yeah. Fine. Whatever.'

She disappears, leaving only the scent of too much ylang-ylang in her over-perfumed wake. I close my eyes. Everything's quiet, apart from the hum of the air-conditioning. There's nobody around. I sink into synthetic material. This is beyond shit. I'm far from home, wherever *that* is. All I want to do is sleep. But now that we've landed I can turn on my phone (without risking almost certain death). I need to check on Nino. I reach for my phone in the little net pocket at the back of the seat in front of me. I stare at the screen. Current location: 'Bucharest, Romania. Henri Coandã International Airport.'

My shoulders tense.

He's here.

'Here we are. We got you a cart.'

I look up and see the air hostess accompanied by a couple more stewards. They arrive at my row and peer in. They study me cautiously, as though I were an escaped meerkat on the run from London Zoo, one that's frothing at the mouth and highly likely to be rabid.

'Are you ready, my love?' says one of the stewards. 'We'll just lift you up and into the cart.'

'One, two, three, lift.'

Oh man, here we go.

Beep.

Beep.

Beep.

The mobility cart crawls slowly along, the orange light on the top flashing bright. We clear passport security and head out to arrivals. I close my eyes and rest my head against the cool white metal bar. My brain is woozy from the wine.

Cuckoo.

Cuckoo.

Cuckoo.

Shut up, *birdbrain*.

Fresh air. That's what I need. Something to wake myself up. I spot a green-lit 'Exit' sign and grab my bag and jump off the cart.

'I'm going now then. Cheers,' I say.

The little old man who is driving the cart has a hearing aid on that doesn't seem to be working. Or maybe he can't hear me over the hum of the battery-powered engine. I walk towards the double doors and they swish wide open. I stumble outside.

The night is black and the air is crisp. There aren't any clouds and the moon and the stars are bright and defined as though someone has drawn around them in biro. I look both ways down the silent street. Nobody here, just me. Oh man, I'm in no state for Nino. He'd take me down in two seconds flat. I can't just wait here in plain sight. I know he's around here somewhere . . . somewhere . . . skulking about like a bat. I take a side street, quicken my pace, leaving the lights of the airport behind me. I'm in a residential area on the outskirts of town. My breath fogs into a cloud. I wrap my arms round myself. Oh my God, it's freezing. I'm wearing my sister's skimpy dress with no socks or underwear on. It probably looked great on Beth. She was always slimmer than me.

I'll find a cab. Get a hotel. Sort myself out for tomorrow. Yes. Yes, that's what I'll do. A weapon. A plan. A *strategy*. I'll pull myself together.

Someone grabs my bag.

'Hey. No. What the . . . ?'

Someone's nicked my handbag.

My phone.

My money.

My cuckoo clock.

I stop dead in my tracks and look around. What just happened? Who was that? A man's dark figure turns a corner and his footsteps fade. A sick feeling spreads from my stomach. Adrenaline floods to my head. *Fuck*. Was that Nino?

'HEY,' I say.

He's not getting away.

I sprint after the thief.

A misty drizzle that isn't quite rain fills the air with eerie grey. Tiny droplets chill my skin. I wish I was wearing more clothes. Sharp night air hits my bare arms and legs and sends a shiver down my spine. I turn into a gloomy alley; surely he's down here? A pair of streetlights cast long shadows. The pavement's slippery and wet. Overflowing rubbish bins and refuse sacks are strewn around. I smell the putrid stench of rotting. Something's died. A bird? A rat? A cat with only half a tail meows and bolts when it sees me coming. It dives into a rusty bin.

'Nino? Is that you?' I say, but it's too quiet. A whisper.

Cold and dirty puddle water splashes up my feet and legs. Urgh, so gross. On my Prada shoes. This place reminds me of Archway.

That's when I spot him up ahead – and my skin breaks out in a cold sweat. Footsteps echo off the walls.

'Hey, you. Come back. Come here.'

He's dressed all in black with his back to me. A silhouette like a giant spider. He turns round and I take a sharp breath. For a split second I think it's Nino. But it's just the dark playing tricks on me. Horrors haunting my subconscious. My imagination running wild. I study his face, as white as a mask, inhuman, almost demonic. His nightmare eyes are fixed on mine. Why is he staring like that?

'Give me my bag,' I call into the darkness. I try to sound tough, but who am I kidding? My voice is thin and too high-pitched, trembling like a leaf.

The man begins to run again.

I start sprinting, my stupid shoes rubbing and ripping into my skin; my feet are aching, blistering. My thighs are fucking on fire. Come on, Alvie. You can do it. He's just some guy; he's not Usain Bolt. I'm closing in: three metres, two metres, one metre away. Shit. What if he has a weapon? What if he has a gun? Fuck it, I'm here now. It's too late. I jump on my handbag and grab it.

'Hey, you bastard, that's Hermès.'

My fingers grip the leather. The bag alone is worth a

grand. He reaches out a dirty hand. He has bitten-down nails. A scar by his thumb. Everything's moving in super slow motion. He pulls down hard on my arm.

'Urgh. Get off. This dress is Chanel.'

My handbag crashes down to the ground.

Did he just break my cuckoo clock?

We slam into each other. I dive for the bag, his foul-smelling body up against mine. I stumble against the wall and rough bricks scrape along my arm and hack off a stinging lump of skin. I feel the warm blood sliding down all the way to my wrist. I'll get him for that. I will. I hear his breathing, heavy, rasping. Feel his hot breath on my ear. A sudden WHACK.

No.

Not the face.

The world goes black beyond the man.

All I can see are those eyes . . .

He seizes my bag and I come to. Come on, Alvie, you've got shit to do.

'Didn't Mummy ever tell you? Don't hit *girls.*'

I reach for a strap. It's tug of war. I swear to God, if he breaks it . . .

He turns and pins me to the wall. His rough hands grip around my throat.

'*Ciao*, Elisabetta,' he says.

He knows who I am? I mean, who I'm pretending to be? But how? Is he working with *Nino*? The app said he was around here somewhere. My eyes flick up and down the alley. His fingers tighten round my neck. I can't breathe. I try to scream, but there's no sound. He holds my hands above my head. I struggle, but he's stronger than I am. I gag. My lungs are burning. I'm squirming, but his grip is tight. Shit. Fuck. I'm stuck.

'*Ha ha. He's going to kill you,*' says Beth.

I stamp my heel into his foot with all my might. Six inches of killer Prada. He screams. Releases his grip. Now's my chance. He's distracted.

I shove his head against the wall. My hands are shaking, but my aim is good. His skull makes a heavy clunking sound like a sledgehammer on a rock. A dull thump, but nice and loud. The man collapses to the ground, his body slumping in the dirt like a rag doll. He is as limp as a sack of potatoes, as heavy as a bag of manure. I squat down on to his chest, panting, gasping, out of breath. My throat is burning. Shit. That was close. I peer into his face. Another guy trying to screw me like Nino. Take that, motherfucker. A pool of blood starts to spread from his head, as slick and shiny as oil. Oh my God, have I . . . have I killed him?

Cuckoo.

Oh, look. The clock's still working.

I slap him. Hard. He doesn't move. He doesn't even flinch.

'Come on. Wake up. WAKE UP,' I say.

'*You won't get away with it this time.*'

My heartbeat quickens. I'm shaking. Sick. What have I done? *Who am I?* I lift my hand towards his face. His neck is thin and sinewy, skinny like a turkey's. I feel for his pulse at his jugular. The feeble trickle seems to wither with the slightest bit of pressure. There's nothing there. Not even a flutter. He's quiet. He's still. He's dead.

No, no, no, no. What have I become?

'*I thought you liked killing?*' says Beth. '*I thought you were a "natural"?*'

'I *do* like killing. But this wasn't *the plan*.'

'*You could never do anything right.*'

OK. OK. Chill out, Alvie. It's the middle of the night. The middle of nowhere. I can just disappear.

I pick up Beth's battered Hermès tote and head back down the empty alley. I check the walls for CCTV cameras. Look back at the corpse getting wet in the rain. Who the hell was he anyway? And how the fuck did he know my name? I stop. I can't go till I know. I have to turn back. Just for a second. Then I'm out of here. I run back towards the body, crouch down low right next to him. I reach inside his jacket pocket and find a leather wallet.

There's a Romanian identity card. It says his name was Dragos Gabor, but that means fucking nothing. Did Nino send this guy here to mug me? Or hunt me and lure me away somewhere quiet? I peer into his ugly face. Was he in the mob as well?

I chuck the wallet in a bin. There's no cash in there anyway. I check his other pocket. Two mobile phones. That's weird: *two* phones. One for the wife and one for the girlfriend? One of them looks like Nino's. He had one of these, a battered old Sony. Black, with a crack down the screen. It could be a coincidence . . .

But then I get it.

Nino isn't here, is he?

Just his stupid phone.

That fucktard set me up. I knew it. He must have known about the app. I bet Nino paid him to lead me here. What else does that assgoblin have planned?

I feel like I'm underwater, drowning, sinking, searching, lost. I glance again up and down the alley, but there's nobody here, at least not yet. I've got to get out of here.

I scroll through the contacts on Beth's phone, my fingers shaking, slipping and sliding. The screen shines wet with the rain. Eventually I find 'Nino Brusca'. I press call and wait.

A split second later, the Sony starts buzzing. I pick it up and stare at the screen: 'Elisabetta Caruso'. That was my sister's married name. That proves it; this is Nino's phone. I hear his voice on the answering machine – '*Ciao, sono Nino Brusca . . .*' – and I cut him off. I can't listen to him speak. It sounds like he's right here.

I shove the phone inside my bag and look down at the man. What was I thinking? I can't leave him here. I've got to act fast. There's not a moment to waste. I grab him by the ankles and drag him, my tongue sticking out of the corner of my mouth. I have to walk backwards and lean away to counterbalance his great weight. But even then, it's fucking hard. Urgh, why are corpses so heavy? I kick off my heels. That's better. He's medium build, average height, but somehow heavier than he looks. I yank him and his body drags on the ground like his bones are made of lead piping. His face is twisted into a grimace. His pockmarked skin is dirty-white. I shove some bin bags out of the way — there's a crunching sound of broken glass — and haul the body against the wall. Every muscle in my body is straining. Lactic acid. Burning pain.

I grab a sack and heave it on his face. Put another bin bag on his chest. I dump another couple on his legs. That will do, at least for now. He won't start to smell for a couple of days. But I'll be long, long gone by then. And it stinks enough already.

I stand back and study his makeshift grave. There's no sign of the body, just piles of trash. Not bad, nice work. I think I'm done. It's good, considering.

The rain is really falling now, and cool drops kiss my burning skin. I take a deep breath, feeling better now. Calm, composed. Well done. See that, Alvie, you're a pro. No need to freak out. I study my battered Hermès tote. It's covered in muck. Dirt-black. I sling it over my shoulder and light myself a fag.

I trudge through the empty airport, yawning, carrying my dirty shoes on a hooked-up index finger. I need to buy another ticket. Back to London. Unbelievable. Such a fucking waste of money. I've only just got here. I had hoped to be in Monaco any day now. Sipping Negronis in Monte Carlo and splurging all my new-found wealth on Dior and YSL. But no. Not yet. No rest for the wicked. So it's back to Blighty, I guess. None of the desks are open yet, so I can't buy my one-way ticket. I slump down in a seat in the lounge. I'm going to have to wait. I can't believe

Nino tricked me, the bastard. Now I'm really, *really* mad. What the hell is he playing at? Sending me flowers, a romantic note, and then hiring some nutjob to kill me? Did you ever hear anything more schizophrenic?

Oh man, he's worse than Beth.

The chairs are hard and plastic and I'm right in the blast of the air-conditioning in front of a wide-screen TV. The telly's showing Romanian news with the sound turned off and the subtitles on. I doubt that mugger would make the news, if/when they find him. He wasn't young and blonde, like Beth. He wasn't very pretty (a one or two out of ten). I hope I've covered him up enough. Perhaps I should go back again and check? But no. Use your head, Alvina. You should never return to the scene of a crime; that's textbook lesson number one. They'll never find a murder weapon (my hands are attached to my arms). No known motive. No CCTV, I checked. I'm leaving the country in a matter of hours. I'm getting pretty good at this. I stretch my arms up over my head, yawn again and relax.

I pick up Beth's iPhone, and click into the apps.

I wonder if Beth has Tinder.

Chapter Five

I delete that stupid tracking app. I've got no use for that any more. How am I going to find Nino now? What am I going to do? I could be sitting here for *hours* before the next plane to London leaves. I scroll through Beth's mobile phone. No Tinder. That wasn't her scene. I doubt she even knew it existed. Or Happn or Hinge or Grindr or Bumble or any of those things. I upload Tinder. I'm just *curious*. I want to see what the locals look like. Do I have time for an airport quickie? I could have a holiday fling. Some dashing Romanian heart surgeon could come and whisk me off my feet . . . I download the app, find a picture of Beth and create an account as 'Beyoncé'. So what? Who cares if I'm a catfish? That's my whole life now.

Right.

Right.

Right.

Right.

I want a date.

I salivate.

Stefan.

Cristian.

Mihai.

Nicolae.

Boy, you've got a lot of meat.

That's someone I need to meet.

Male model?

Body double?

Batman.

He-Man.

Ripped like fucking Superman.

Sexy smackers.

He's a cracker.

Nice chest.

He's the best.

Trouser snake.

My heart breaks.

Hmm, I wonder if Nino's on Tinder. Of course he is. He's a Tinder*beast*. Why is anyone *ever* on Tinder? To meet their future husband/wife? For a long and fulfilling relationship?

OH MY GOD.

I CAN USE TINDER TO FIND HIM.

I can use Swipebuster to track him down. Alvie, you're a fucking genius. This has to work. It's gold.

The only possible *minor* flaw is the fact that I have Nino's phone. But I'm willing to bet on two probabilities:

1. He already has a new mobile.
2. He's uploaded Tinder.

(With a libido like that the man needs sex *at least* two or three times every day. I bet he's on there right this minute. There isn't a second to waste.)

Now, where the hell would Nino go? I'd hazard a guess at Italy. Not Sicily, that's far too risky. The cops and the mob are after him. So Naples? Didn't he mention that when we were planning our escape?

I tell Swipebuster I'm looking for someone who is called 'Nino Brusca' and that the last time he showed up was somewhere in Naples. I set up a fake email address to get the results. A message pings into the inbox:

Nope. Nothing. They can't find him. There's no one in Naples with that name. Perhaps he's used *Giannino* Brusca? Perhaps he's used an alias?

Urgh. I can see this getting frustrating. There must be an easier way.

I google 'How to find someone on Tinder'. Albion Services comes up. It uses facial-recognition technology. All I need is a photograph. Perhaps there's one in Beth's phone? I scroll through her gallery. Thousands of pictures of baby Ernie. Some selfies of Beth in a new dress. Some arty snaps of the amphitheatre in Taormina. And, ooh, what's that? A birthday bash. It looks like it's Ambrogio's party. And there is Nino. Yes, that's him without a doubt. He's standing right next to Ambrogio as he blows the candles out. It's a bit dark and his face is small but it might . . . it might just work. I crop the photo and zoom in on Nino's criminally handsome face. I upload it to the tracking bot and take a guess at the town. I try Naples again just in case. I enter the email address and wait . . . Come on, come on, come on.

A message pings into the inbox.

No. He isn't there.

Shit. Fuck. Damn. Bugger.

What about London? He could still be there?

I type it in. Upload his face. A face to shame the angels . . . Sigh. It's such a shame I'm going to turn it into foie gras. I click go and bite my nails. This had better work.

Another message pings into the inbox.

Nothing. I'll try again.

Rome? How about there? That's Italian.

OH MY GOD IT'S HIM.

It looks like a brand-new picture of Nino without his hat (which is in my bag). 'Nino Brusca, 39, Rome.' This is beyond awesome. I've always wanted to go to Rome. It's definitely top of my bucket list. (Rome, Havana, Las Vegas, Bangkok.) I've heard they have awesome sex clubs. This is all working out rather nicely.

The desks are open now at last. I buy myself a one-way ticket to Rome and wait at the gate. I am travelling as my sister, since Alvie's officially dead. They might have put a block on my passport. It isn't worth the risk. The plane is leaving in fifteen minutes and I cannot fucking wait. I sit and fidget and watch the news.

WTF is that?

I gawk at the TV screen.

That woman is my *mother*.

What the hell is she doing on telly? Is it *The Antiques Roadshow*? No, it's not. The camera cuts to a close-up of my mother's perma-tanned face: perfect make-up, voluminous blow-dry, three strings of pearls. I can't hear what she's saying. I try (and fail) to lip-read. She reminds me a bit of a blonde Margaret Thatcher; there's an identical diabolical air . . . She's cradling a sleeping baby Ernesto, looking straight at the camera, almost, it seems, looking straight at me. I stare right back, unblinking, unbreathing, as tense as a stalking cat. It's the first time I've seen her in a couple of years. She hasn't aged a bit, like one of those radioactive apples you get from the supermarket. Perhaps she's been cryogenically frozen and only just thawed out? Behind her, the remains of Elizabeth's villa, blackened and broken by the fire, smoulder and smoke like the scene of a plane crash. The palm trees, the flowers, the frangipani, all burnt to a crisp and crumbled to dust. The swimming pool sparkles beyond her right shoulder. I shiver in my chair.

A picture of Beth on her honeymoon in Kenya appears on the screen, with 'ELIZABETH CARUSO' in capital letters. My stomach sinks. Shit. Now it's official. The cops are looking for my twin. I bet she's wanted for questioning in my supposed murder. Which means, of course, that *I* am. My mother's appealing for help to find her, hence the desperate look on her face. I bet the cops think I know something. They think I'm a witness or worse. Do they suspect it was *me* who killed my sister? No, no, no, this is all messed up. Now they'll trace her fucking mobile. Why me? Oh what a mess.

Ping.

What now?

An email from my mother. I click into the text.

From: Mavis Knightly
MavisKnightly1954@yahoo.com
To: Elizabeth Caruso
ElizabethKnightlyCaruso@gmail.com
Date: 1 Sep 2015 at 08.56
Subject: RE: Where are you?

Elizabeth, angel, did you receive my last email? I'm getting really rather stressed. No one here has a clue where you've got to. My anxiety levels are through the roof. I have barely slept a wink, and it's not the jet lag, I can assure you. Migraines. Dry mouth. Itchy skin. Eczema behind my knees. I've developed a stomach ulcer. It's psychosomatic, of that I'm sure. A stabbing pain in the mid-abdomen, two inches above the navel. Very uncomfortable. I'm bent double with the pain. I manage to go about two or three feet before I need to sit down again. It's an excess of stomach acid. I need to eat some chalk. Of course, my doctor is in Australia, and the man in the chemist here doesn't speak English. I'm getting tired just writing this. Will you please call me back?

PS The police are looking for you. They want to ask you some questions about your sister.

I roll my eyes and delete the message, then switch off my sister's phone and shove it in my bag.

If the police are looking for Beth, then I am going to have to be Alvie. I'll need to use Alvina's passport when I get to Rome. Beth's ID got me through security, but that was before the news broke. Unless . . . unless . . . Oh God. The police are sure to block Alvie's passport. But how long does it take to do the admin once someone has popped their clogs?

They call my flight and we board the plane. I stand in line and start to sweat. What will I do when we get to Italy? Who the hell am I? Alvie or Beth?

Chapter Six

Leonardo da Vinci–Fiumicino Airport,
Rome, Italy

'*P*assaporto,' the official says, his voice muffled by glass. I study the palm of his outstretched hand, the deep grooves of his heart line, his lifeline, his whatever-the-fuck line.

My fingers clutch the passports in the bottom of my bag. I should just turn round and get back on the plane. Or live here for ever in the airport, like that guy at JFK. A lifetime of duty-free shopping and vitamin D deficiency. But no, I can't. That's ridiculous. Nino's in Rome. That's where I need to be. I try an unconvincing smile and take out my own passport. I hand it to the man. He's chatting with his colleague in Italian. Be cool, Alvina. Be breezy. I hold my breath and watch him as he leafs through the burgundy book. I've got serious heart palpitations. My chest is tight. The fake smile cracks and I bet my forehead is shiny.

I study the picture in the passport and read the details upside down:

KNIGHTLY
ALVINA

BRITISH CITIZEN
10 OCT 89
CIRENCESTER

(Ooh, that's a Roman town. He'll like that.)

I eye the back of his computer. Is there something flashing on the screen? What's taking him so long?

'*Benvenuto*,' he says with a grin. He hands me the passport and winks.

'Oh. Right. *Benvenuto*,' I say.

I snatch the book and leg it out to arrivals. I can't believe he let me through. Perhaps the airport staff don't know I'm dead? Or was he too busy laughing and joking to notice his monitor flashing red? Either way, thank fuck for that. I made it to Italy.

I run into the nearest loo and peer at the girl in the mirror. My sister's face stares back at me. Those are her eyes and that is her mouth. That's our nose with the sprinkling of freckles, slightly turned up at the end. I look like Beth, but hugely hungover. I am a wanted woman. That was my face up there on TV (Beth's face, but you know what I mean). The cops are going to recognize me. What am I going to do? I need to get a nose job or something. I need a master disguise. I should cut my hair, but I *really* don't want to. It took me an age to grow it out. (An ill-informed crop back in 2011 resulted in years of an 'in-between' length.) I could change the colour, but brown is too obvious. Blue, green, yellow, red, pink? They'd expect me to cut it, so I could get extensions. Wear a large, distracting hat. Buy some mirror

68

sunglasses. Perhaps some piercings? A tattoo? But a nose job, yes, that's just the ticket. It would totally transform my face. Jennifer Grey from *Dirty Dancing* never looked the same again. I need a teeny, tiny button nose that's really nothing more than a pimple. I want the conk of a Manga star. The snout of a Disney princess.

I head out of the airport and hail a cab.

But first, I need a place to stay. I'll find a flat on Airbnb. I prefer that to another hotel. No room-service maids. No prying receptionists. Windows that you can climb out of. I'll book a month, but we shall see. If I like it here, who knows? I could stay indefinitely. (If I survive, that is.) But a month should be long enough for now. I'm here for one thing and one thing only: to exterminate that *stronzo*. And shopping, obviously. I'm sure they have great shops out here. I have €200,000. All I've bought so far are flights and champagne. I want to go to fucking Prada. I'm going to buy the whole shop.

Trastevere, Rome, Italy

I am so excited to be here I write a haiku in my head:

Rome. You sexy son
Of a bitch. Where have you been
All my life? Kiss, kiss.

This city is fucking spectacular. It's even better than in the movies. I thought *Angels and Demons* was photo-shopped, but no, this place is BOSS. Oh, eternal city.

Caput Mundi. Capital of the whole damn world. City of Cicero, Virgil and Ovid. The streets are a Latin love elegy. The buildings are marble cum-shots. Rome. The home of Fendi, Bulgari and Valentino Garavani. The Colosseum. The Roman Forum. Frascati (that fizzy wine). Isabella Rossellini. Pizza. Pasta. Sex and fashion. Francesco Totti (fit).

I wind down the window in the taxi and stick my head out in the breeze, my hair streaming out in a banner behind me, the hot sun burning my skin. I can smell the sultry stench of sex and taste the summer heat. The thick, black, crack-cocaine-strong coffee wafting from the terrace bars. I watch the men in Ferragamo suits ride too fast on wasp-like Vespas, swerving in and out of the traffic and BEEP BEEP BEEP BEEP BEEP. They have black-out shades and fags in their mouths and tans to rival David Hasselhoff's. Damn, I love Italian men. I'd sleep with any one of them.

'Hey, have you got any other music?' I say to the comatose cabbie.

His eyes flick up in the rear-view mirror. 'Is Ligabue. Is great.'

'I don't know what he's saying,' I say. 'Blah, blah, blah, blah, blah.'

The cabbie sighs and presses some buttons on his retro digital radio. He finds a track in English.

'Awesome. Can you turn that up?'

He cranks up the volume. It's 'Wrecking Ball'. I nod my head in time to the bass and dance a bit in my seat. I love Miley; she is *badass*. She has a tattoo of an avocado.

I'm going to get a tattoo while I'm out here. I'm thinking 'DIE NINO' or perhaps just 'FUCK YOU'. I'll see how I feel when I get there.

I flick fag ash out of the window. The air is dusty and dry. The traffic seems to crawl along the choked-up city streets. The skyline is crowded with domes and columns, spires and towering pine trees. It's beautiful. Man, I already love it. It's fucking poetry. Is that St Peter's Basilica? We must be near the Vatican City. Oh my God, I'll have to go and visit John Keats's grave. That's one dead guy I actually like. Seriously, what a legend. 'Thou wast not born for death, immortal Bird!'

There's a statue of the Virgin Mary, her halo lit up with LEDs. Her painted dress is chipped and blue. She always reminds me of Beth.

'Is Trastevere,' calls the cabbie, shouting over the pounding bassline.

Miley's on about starting wars. I think I know what she means.

The car pulls up next to the kerb and I pay him. I'm about to get out.

'You go now, crazy English girl.'

My hand is on the door handle, but I don't move. I stare at the street outside. Nino is somewhere here. Tinder said. It doesn't lie. I remember the chainsaw. The bodies. The blood. I remember that hole in the ground in the wood. 'IF YOU CAN CATCH ME, WE CAN WORK TOGETHER'. But what if *he* catches *me*? A single bullet between the eyeballs? A clean slit across the throat?

The pavements are crowded with dark-haired men. Any one of them could be him . . .

'*Allora?*' the cabbie snaps. He swivels round in his seat and frowns.

I can't stay in here all day.

I take another look up and down.

He wouldn't do it here in broad daylight, not in front of all these shops.

I jump out of the cab and slam the door shut. '*Vaffanculo,*' I say.

I'm about to call up Airbnb and find myself a new flat, when I remember the cops are looking for my sister. I can't use her phone. They'll be tracking that. I still have my old Samsung, but I can't risk turning that on. No, there's only one thing for it. I'll buy myself a burner. There's an Italian version of Carphone Warehouse over the road. I sprint across the busy street and head inside.

The flat is tucked down a winding side street. Pot plants. Ivy. Balconies. It's quiet here. Private. Secluded. No one to hear you scream.

I meet my new landlord (a two out of ten. Not *all* Italian men are fit then. I take that comment back). He gives me some keys and I give him some money. Then he fucks off again.

You have got to be kidding me: *five* flights of stairs? It's murder. No sign of a lift or an escalator. Now I am all hot and sweaty. I hope it was worth the effort. I guess it's safer on the top floor, so that's a plus, I suppose. I push through the door and OMG. It's an actual *palace*. Screw the Ritz. This is all mine and it's fit for royalty. I dump my bag in the entrance hall and float through the rooms and endless halls, my fingers trailing the dado rail and my feet barely touching the floor. I glide across the marble tiles and twirl around the rooms in awe. Prelapsarian landscapes are painted on the wooden walls: lush green grass and sunny skies, cherubs and forests and flowers. The ceilings are high and painted gold. There are crystal chandeliers. It's gorgeous, better than Beth's old villa. Four-poster beds and French armoires. The scent of beeswax and jasmine. I love it. I am going to stay here for ever (or at least until I'm dead).

I fill the bath with steaming water and too many bubbles and sink in deep. I'm finally here. I deserve a treat. My hand slides down between my legs. I'm wet. I touch myself . . .

Nino. Nino.

But I can't focus. I'm distracted. I turn on Beth's mobile phone for *half a minute*. I doubt that's long enough to track. I need to see if there's any more news. I might have missed something important.

Ping.

A text from an unknown number.

'WHAT THE FUCK? DID U KILL MY GUY?'

Ha. It's Nino. He must have noticed his man's disappeared and put two and two together. You know what? I'm not going to reply. Let him work it out himself. Let him worry about it . . .

I put down the phone and then pick it up again. Put it down. Then pick it up.

I can't text Nino from Beth's phone, the cops might trace the signal. My new burner is on the side. I type in Nino's number.

'YEAH I DID AND UR NEXT.'

Send.

That should freak him out.

'IT'S ME BY THE WAY. I HAVE A NEW PHONE.'

I send that as well.

I delete his text and scowl, then turn off my sister's phone. I'd better not turn it on again. That was already too long. I stub out my fag in the scalloped soap dish, then download Tinder on my new phone. I scrub off the blood from under my nails. My toes stick out from the mountain of bubbles. I emerge from the bath in a cloud of steam, perfumed and powdered and sparkly clean. No mud or blood on my face or legs. No leaves stuck in my hair. I check myself out. Divine as a goddess. Why hasn't he texted back? Nino's an *imbecile*.

Another ping.

Ah, there he is.

'I LOVE IT WHEN U TALK DIRTY.'

Barberini, Rome, Italy

'But how can it be an *emergency*?'

'All right, fine, so it's not an *emergency* exactly, but it's definitely urgent.'

'Urgent?'

'Yes.'

The receptionist crinkles her tiny nose and looks me up and down. She has flawless features and perfect skin. No, I mean *a hundred per cent perfect*, like some kind of alien. It isn't normal. I've never seen skin as perfect as hers. Not even Beth's. Not even baby Ernesto's. It's like she was made out of some kind of plastic, spray-painted, perhaps, like a shiny new car. Her skin is so radiant I'm momentarily distracted. What does she do to it? How does she get it to *glow* like that? Perhaps she gets unlimited Botox because she works in this clinic? Or what's that funny one, microdermabrasion, when they scrape off your top layer of skin like a snake? Vampire facials? Mud masks? Lasers? I wonder if they're recruiting.

'Helloooooooooooo?' she says.

I think I was staring. Possibly drooling. What was I saying? Baby-soft skin.

'Oh. Yes. I'm in a hurry, you see. I'll need to leave at any minute, but I have to get this procedure done first.'

'Right. I see. And where are you going?'

'I don't know yet.'

Where the hell is Nino?

'So let me get this straight,' she says. 'You want me to ask Dr Pirandello if she's free to perform an *emergency* rhinoplasty operation?'

'No, I told you. I want a *nose job*.'

'Rhinoplasty *is* a nose job.'

'Then why the fuck didn't you say that?' English is clearly not her first language.

She sighs. 'This afternoon?'

'Yes, that's right.'

I need to get going. I can't hang around. Every second counts . . .

She looks at her watch. It's an Omega, like Beth's. (My wrist feels suddenly very naked. I sold Beth's watch, but it's OK. Now I've got this cuckoo clock and, you know what, it's growing on me.) I can tell she's confused, but it's really quite simple.

'Can't you just call her and ask?'

She looks at me with deep blue eyes, as azure as Sicilian skies: coloured-contacts. 'I've checked her schedule. It's not really that easy. We usually recommend one or two consultations, and then patients wait *at least* a couple of weeks to ensure they haven't changed their minds. That they've thought it all through . . .'

'Uh-huh. It's fine. I won't change my mind.'

'And then there's the theatre; we need to book the room, the nurse, the anaesthetists . . .'

Her breath feels cool, like peppermint chews. When she said that word 'anaesthetists' it was like stepping off the plane in the icy tundra. It was like an Arctic breeze. I don't want to think what my breath smells like. (I want to get an electric toothbrush, a nice one, like Ambrogio and Beth's.) I hope she hasn't noticed the wine. I can still taste blood from when I fell off the toilet: a deep gash in my lower lip. I'll have to talk with my mouth half shut. I'll buy some Hubba Bubba. I lean in closer over the counter so that I'm a few inches away.

She winces. To hell with it.

'How much do you want?'

'I beg your pardon?'

'Just name a figure. How much do you need?'

'Are you trying to *bribe* me?' she says.

Someone give her a prize.

'Dear Lord Jesus. I'm in a hurry. How much to do the thing today?'

I drum my fingers on the counter . . . *Drum, drum, drum, drum.* Ooh, that sounds like the intro to 'Firestarter'.

'It's really not about the money.'

I can see I'm getting nowhere fast.

'All right then. Fuck it. I'll go somewhere else.'

'Try Dr Baldassini? Over the road? He did my nose,' she says.

I storm out of the door and fly down the stairs, out into the beating sun. Urgh. This is ridiculous. I am getting burnt. I wish I had an umbrella or a parasol. Umbrellas always remind me of him. No, not of Nino, *Ambrogio*. They remind me of the night we first met. We listened to 'Umbrella' by Rihanna, but I bet he wouldn't remember that (and not just because *he's dead*). It was only a one-night-stand, but I wanted more than that. I popped my cherry and got pregnant all in one night. Not bad. Pretty efficient. But I lost the kid and my twin stole my guy. I told you she was a bitch. Oh, Ambrogio, *bello mio*. He was such a disappointment. If only he'd had a bigger dick, then none of this would have happened.

I sprint down the road past the Fiats, Ferraris and Maseratis that line up by the kerb. I can hear the traffic bumping and grinding. The buzzing of Vespas. The honking of horns. I pass tall, white, elegant houses, all converted into surgeries, private hospitals and shrinks. 'Dr Baldassini' is engraved on a shiny brass plaque on the wall. Ooh, this place looks promising. It has a sign outside with a picture of a girl who looks a little bit like Beth. I scale the steps and slam the buzzer. Push through grand, imposing doors. Inside, it's cool with nice high ceilings. The scent of Madagascan vanilla. A yucca in a pot. I march across the black and white tiles to the woman at reception.

'Hello, can you help me?' I say. 'This is an emergency.'

'Come in,' says a male voice in an Italian accent.

I glance at the platinum blonde at reception. She nods her head and smiles.

I open the door and step inside, inhaling the clinical medical air. It smells like too much Mr Muscle; it seems impossibly clean and bright.

'How can I help you, Miss Err, Miss?'

I take a sharp breath. 'Beyoncé.'

I close the door behind me.

Wow.

Dr Baldassini is *way* too hot to be a surgeon. He stands before me dazzling, blinding, like some kind of god in his crisp white coat. Spotlights shine down from the ceiling. A stethoscope hangs round his neck. It looks quirky, cool, satirical, like some kind of fashion statement. I'm sure I saw accessories like that on the runway last spring at McQueen. His shirt is undone at the top (two buttons) and I catch a glimpse of hair on his chest. His designer stubble is sculpted and perfect. There are dimples in his cheeks when he smiles. He is well built. The ideal height. (I guess I must have a *thing* for Italians.)

It is such a waste.

I picture his lonely life in theatre, hidden away behind white gauze, surgical masks and funny blue scrubs. Waterproof boots. Do surgeons wear *hairnets*? A face like that should be plastered on billboards for women all over the world to see. I wonder if he was born with that all-American jaw. Is that his real chin?

He looks into my eyes; his gaze is sublime. I go all warm and gooey inside like a Swiss cheese fondue with white wine. He extends a hand for me to shake. His grip is firm like he really means it; his skin is warm and smooth. I step in a bit closer and breathe him in. His aftershave is something spicy: Neroli Portofino by Tom Ford. Bergamot, amber, rosemary, lemon . . . (My nostrils are wasted as a layman. I should have been a professional nose, a perfumer for Yves Saint Laurent or perhaps a *nez* for Chanel.) This surgery had better not ruin my excellent sense of smell.

'Please, take a seat?'

I sit on a futuristic chair that could have been stolen from a spaceship and examine the table strewn with strange round blobs: they're clear, translucent, like jellyfish bodies (without the stinging tentacles). It takes me a minute to work out what they are.

The doctor sees me staring. 'Here.'

He reaches towards me over his desk and hands me a squidgy silicone ball.

'They're top of the range Allergan implants. That one's 450cc.'

I pick it up and give it a squeeze. It feels a bit like Play-Doh.

'Oh.' I put it back on the table. 'Right.' It's all a bit weird to be honest.

'So, what can I do for you today?'

S&M? Anal? A bit of light bondage? Perhaps a nice threesome: you, me and George Clooney? You could get naked and I could watch?

He leans back in his leather chair and folds his hands behind his head. 'And please, you can call me *Leonardo*.'

Leonardo? Nice.

His voice is salted caramel: deep, low, smooth. I bet he has good bedside manners. That's important for a doctor: a soothing voice. Great pillow talk. He could tell you you've got a week to live, but with a voice like that you'd just think, *Fine*.

Leonardo smiles. He reaches for three of the silicon balls and begins to juggle. He's *good*.

'My receptionist mentioned *emergency* surgery? It's not usually something we do here at the clinic, but I'm sure if we can agree the right figure, to cover unavoidable extra expenses, we could work something out.'

'Really? You could?'

'Of course. It is a little last minute but, I'll see what I can do.'

'Awesome. That's brilliant. That's great.'

I knew I'd find a cowboy doctor somewhere if I looked

hard enough. Who cares about ethics? The Hippocratic oath? Everyone has a price.

I look at his hands, now clasped on the table; his nails, filed and polished, are naturally shiny, and his skin's a creamy pinky-white. He looks like he gets professional manicures. I guess he has to look after his hands. He is a surgeon after all; they are his trade. I bet they're insured for a *bomb*. I imagine his hands on my naked body. His palms massaging my shoulders, his fingers closing round my throat. He'd slide his hands down to my chest, teasing my nipples, cupping my breasts. He'd smooth his hands along my stomach, right down to my hips and part my thighs. He'd rub my clit. Go knuckle-deep. I want his fingers inside me.

'Beyoncé?'

'Oh yes? Where were we? Um . . .'

Leonardo, Leonardo, Leonardo. I like it. It rolls off the tongue like fellatio. Perhaps he's a Renaissance man, like Da Vinci? An artistic genius? A mastermind? He's clearly a heart-throb like DiCaprio. My first ever crush was Jack in *Titanic*. (He should have kicked Rose off that raft.)

Leo pulls on latex gloves. I shift a bit in my chair. Now I'm wet and my pussy is aching. I fantasize about sex on his desk.

'Oh God, Alvie. You can't sleep with your doctor. It's unprofessional, or something . . .'

What *is* that annoying voice in my head? The voice of reason? Sensible Alvie? My conscience in overdrive?

There's no way it's fucking *Beth*. Anyway, I don't have time for sex. Nino's out there waiting, *gloating*. I need to get a wriggle on.

Didn't I just swear off men? I've got a memory like a goldfish. And didn't I just swear off men?

'I'd like a nose jo— I mean, a *rhino* operation. ASAP today,' I say.

'And what kind of look were you after?'

'Well, I was thinking a cross between Heidi Montag and Madonna circa 1994.'

'Hmm. I see.'

'The smaller the better really,' I say. 'Like a Russian hamster.'

I draw the shape in the air with my index finger. It looks a bit like a comma: ,

Leo nods, but I'm not sure he gets it. His eyes linger on mine, searching, reading: a puzzled look on his handsome face. Why is staring at me like that? I'm sure he gets this all the time, twenty times a day at least. Ah, I know. He's imagining me naked. He's got that glazed and faraway look that guys get all the time . . . Perhaps he fancies me as well? I bet he does. I can tell.

'Hello, *Elizabeth*.'

Mr Bubbles stands over me. I stare up into his face. Bloodshot eyes glare down at me from a chalk-white face. I am strapped to a gurney. I struggle and strain, but I can't move a muscle. My ankles and hands are bound too tight. I wriggle and writhe. My eyes sting with the stench of whisky. His rasping breath lands on my cheeks. His mouth is just an inch away. He's getting closer, moving in. There's something stuck between his teeth. I think it's human flesh.

'Please, I want to be Alvie again.'

He laughs and laughs, a mad sound like a siren.

'Please, please, please, please.'

His face turns into Beth's.

I open my eyes and look around. What's all this? Where am I now? Why am I connected to all these tubes? Is this a *hospital*? Clinical curtains. Bare white walls. The smell of industrial disinfectant. What the fuck am I doing in here? Have I been in an accident? Has someone tried to kill me (again)? I can't feel my face. I can't feel my head. Am I paralysed? Am I dead?

'Help. Help.' What's happened to me? 'Nurse? Nurse? NURSE.'

There's a red emergency cord by the bed. I give it a yank and a light flashes on. I hear a ping somewhere out in the ward. Breathe, Alvina, just breathe. It's all all right. You'll be OK. You probably drank too much again and passed out on a zebra crossing. I close my eyes. Something about the Ritz Hotel? Something about some Martini? Think, Alvina. Think. Did *Nino* do this? I scrunch up my eyes and furrow my brow. No, I know. I've had major surgery. The light bulb in my brain flashes on. A rhino job. A master disguise. Now I remember; it all makes sense (kind of). I'm on the run. I'm undercover. I need to find that twatwaffle. There's no time for waiting around.

83

'*Buona sera, come stai?*'

I open my eyes and glare at the woman now approaching my single bed.

'And who the hell are you?' I say.

The woman smiles. She looks like my gran: short, styled hair in a light dove grey, a wide, inviting smile. Laughter lines spread out from her eyes. She'd be good in the adverts for Bisto.

'My name is Sister Romano. I looking after you today.'

Sister? Urgh. I don't like *sisters*.

'And what is this shit?' I say.

I yank the needle out of my hand and the sticky tape catches. There's a stinging pain and a globule of blood oozes out from my skin. I lick it; it tastes nice.

'These are your painkillers,' she says. She eyes the needle now dripping on the floor. 'You don't want it, the morphine? OK. No problem. I take it out.'

Morphine? Ooh, I *do* like morphine . . .

'How do you feeling today?'

'I'm feeling *fine.*' *I want to get out of here.*

She flicks a switch on the side of the bed and the mattress moves. It whirs and groans under the strain of my weight as I inch up to sitting.

Holy shit.

'What is that?'

I cross my eyes and look down at my nose. I can see some kind of white plaster . . .

The nurse peers into my face and beams a radiant smile.

'*Sì*,' she says. 'Have a look.'

84

She hands me a mirror and I hold it up. She peels off the plaster.

'*You look like Pac-Man*,' offers Beth.

'Oh sweet Jesus,' I say.

My nose is *gone*. This is insane.

'Isn't it . . . too small?' I say.

'No, is nice. I want to see . . .'

She gives it a squeeze. I can't feel anything.

'Hey. Hands off. *It will snap.*'

I'm still staring at myself in the mirror. Leonardo, *you miracle worker*. The man's a bone fide genius. A saint. A magician. (And he's *fit*. Damn my sister and her voice in my head. She wouldn't let me shag him.) There's no way the cops will recognize me. I don't look like Alvie.

'You are in theatre for three hours and now you must to relax.'

'*Three hours?*' Shit, that's ages. What about Nino? 'I've got to go.'

She bites her lip. She looks upset. She reapplies the white bandage. I glare at her face.

'Where are my things? I'm leaving,' I say.

'*Signorina*, but you just wake up.'

'I've got to get out of here. Where is my phone?' I open the drawer by the side of the bed. Found it. Back of the net. I grab it and slam the drawer shut.

'You can't leave now. *Mamma mia.* You don't want Doctor Baldassini to check you first?'

Mmmmm, Dr Leonardo. Yes, I would. But not right now. I don't have time. Not even for a quickie. It's a race against time, like *The Crystal Maze*. And anyway, *I have quit guys*. Now I remember *everything*. The money. The vengeance. The plan.

I jump out of bed and nearly fall over. Wobble a bit and grab on to a rail. It must be all that anaesthetic. Or maybe with my tiny nose I've lost my centre of gravity. When my head has stopped spinning and the floor is still I look around for my clothes. I fling open the cupboard and spot the Chanel hanging on a little hook. I take it and pull it on. I find my shoes and slip them on, but there's no way I can walk in these six-inch heels. I take them back off and carry them. It hurts to move. It hurts to walk. I already had the *mother* of all hangovers, and now it feels like my nose is alight. I want some more of that lovely morphine. Some horse tranquillizers? Some gin?

'You need to wear that,' says the nurse, pointing at the splint on my nose. 'Keep it on for six weeks. Night and day. No take it off.'

'Of course.' *Not a chance in hell.*

I see Beth's battered Hermès tote in the cupboard and shove in my phone. I check for the money. Yes, it's still there in the cuckoo clock. I guess that's it: my whole world in a handbag. At least I'm travelling light . . .

'And these pills are for you. Four times a day.'

Ooh. *Drugs* ♥ ♥ ♥

'Great,' I say.

She gives me a paper bag bulging with packets of medicine. I stuff the pills inside the tote. It's so full now, I can't close it.

I pull the blue curtain aside and limp away across the ward with my cold, bare, icy feet. I spark myself a Marlboro Light. The nurse calls after me.

'They very strong painkillers. Codeine and paracetamol. Be careful not too much.'

'Yeah, yeah, yeah, whatever.'

'OK. *Ciao*, Beyoncé.'

Trastevere, Rome, Italy

I push inside the chemist's. My face feels like it's been run over by a speeding double-decker. I grab another fistful of pills and swallow them one by one. I rub my eyes. They're all puffy and swollen. My throat is sore and dry. I can't breathe in through my nose. I can't move my face. I grab a bottle of Lucozade. I need a drink before I crack like a Patagonian salt plain. My nose had better look bang tidy when these bandages come off.

I browse the aisles. Now, what do I need? I'll buy myself some essentials. I find some hair dye (fuchsia pink), a cock ring, some Durex Play lube and some flavoured condoms, a hairbrush, some toothpaste, a toothbrush (electric), some lipstick, concealer, mascara and – YES – some seriously cool mirror shades. I pay the girl with some cash from my clock and then head out of the shop.

I climb up the stairs to my flat and make my way to the bathroom.

I dye my hair over the sink. Pink water twists and swirls down the plughole as I rinse it all out with the mixer tap. I wring out my locks in the red-stained sink, then dry my hair with the dryer. I style it in the brightly lit mirror. Candyfloss locks swish down my back. I look like that Troll, Princess Poppy. I peel off the plaster over my nose and check my hooter out again. DAMN, THAT'S FINE. I mean, hell yeah. *Who's that?* Neon pink hair and a beak as sweet as a Maraschino cherry. I am a strawberry whipped-cream sundae. I am Angel Delight. I plaster concealer over the bruises starting to purple over my nose. It hurts a bit, but it could be worse. The pills are working. I'm feeling all floaty. I slap on some lipstick. Slick on mascara. Slip on the shades and you know what? It's an awesome disguise. I'm a *twelve* out of ten. I swallow some more of the painkillers. I'm ready to fucking rock.

Chapter Seven

I'm hungry after the anaesthetic. I take my new nose out for something to eat. This place looks nice: Taverna Trilussa, an old-fashioned Italian restaurant. Ivy climbs up painted walls. There's a canopy and a pretty terrace. Wooden shutters and candle lanterns. I'm going to check it out. I push through the doors and step inside. The room is crowded with diners, eating and drinking and talking. Shouting. Arguing over their Bolognese. The air is heavy with sensual smells coming through the kitchen door. Oh my God, my mouth is watering. I'll eat anything. Everything. A waiter comes over and smiles at me. He's cute, like a young Matt LeBlanc.

'*Buonasera, signorina.*' He looks me up and down.

'Chow,' I say. 'A table for one?'

'Of course. Please, follow me.'

I let him lead the way. Tight black trousers. Taut glutes. Buns like a nutcracker.

We cross the teeming restaurant, squeezing past the tables and chairs to a little spot in the corner. He pulls out a chair for me to sit down and drapes the napkin over my lap. His fingers brush my inner thigh. On purpose? An accident?

'An *aperitivo* for you, *bella*? A glass of Prosecco? An Aperol Spritz?'

'I'll take a vodka, straight up,' I say.

He nods and licks his lips. '*Sì, bellissima.*'

I pick up the extensive menu and study the endless lists of dishes. I have no clue what I should choose. I usually order margheritas from the local Holloway Domino's.

I scan the room instead. This place is ancient. There are dark wooden beams across the ceilings and framed oil paintings hang on the walls. There are barrels and lamplight and Renaissance murals, wrought-iron grills and shelves lined with books. It's cosy. Authentic. Traditional. Not as glam as that place in Taormina I went to with Ambrogio and Beth. But it's cool. *Anonymous.*

The waiter returns with my drink on a tray.

'Your vodka,' he says with a wink.

I take a sip through the plastic straw. It's cold and crisp with a knock-out kick. Mmm, that's nice. Refreshing. I neck some more painkillers.

'So, what's good to eat?' I ask.

I look into amaretto eyes.

'This place is famous for *cacio e pepe*, pasta with pepper and cheese.'

'Awesome. Cheese is good. I'll have that.'

'An excellent choice. Fantastic.'

He smiles and reaches for the menu. His fingers brush my hand. My wrist. *A mistake?* No, I don't think so.

I watch him as he walks away. He's hot: an eight out of ten. He's definitely the fittest guy in here. All the other waiters are passes. Then it hits me. I know why I like him. He looks a bit like Nino. Black hair, dark eyes. Lean.

90

Mean. Trim. Perhaps Nino looked like that twenty years ago, when he was a young hitman?

Urgh. Right. Nino. So. How am I going to kill him? I need to think. Need to work on my plan. I'll make a list. Draw a diagram. I need to brainstorm or something. I'll write down every crazy idea. Do some blue-sky thinking. Everything I come up with counts. Nothing is off limits. I reach into my bag and find a red pen. But I don't have any paper. I look around for a napkin or something, but no, there are just cloth serviettes. Whatever, they're white. They'll have to do. I spread one out on the wooden table and write in capitals at the top:

ALVIE'S VENGEANCE ♥

I draw a picture of Nino in the middle. It's just a stickman. I'm not great at art. It doesn't look a thing like Nino, more like Tom Hiddleston. I draw the hangman's noose round his neck, then the rest of the gallows like I'm playing that game. Then, in thought bubbles all around, I write an extensive list: shoot him, stab him, run him over, push him off the edge of a cliff, learn martial arts and karate-chop him, whack him over the back of the head, strangle him, lock him inside a car and asphyxiate him with carbon monoxide, douse him in chlorine trifluoride so he spontaneously combusts.

'Your pasta, *signorina*,' says the waiter, whispering gently in my ear.

I whip the napkin off the table and shove it back on to my lap. Hopefully he can't read English. I smile up at him and ask, 'Do you know where I can find a hardware store? A B&Q? Something like that?'

'No, I'm sorry. Not in this area.'

'I need to buy some rope and a hammer . . .'

I take a look at the dish.

I prefer extra-large as a general rule. But oh my God, it's *massive*. The waiter places a *frying pan* in front of me on the little table. It's filled with a creamy mass of spaghetti; the sauce smells like cheesy heaven. The waiter produces a pepper mill that's almost as tall and broad as he is. (It does not escape my attention that this thing is totally phallic.)

'Would you like some?' he asks.

'Uh-huh,' I breathe. 'I like it extra-hot.'

The waiter stands right next to me and grinds the pepper on to my plate. His hip is pressed against my arm. His cock is at eye level. There's a definite bulge where his penis must be. I'd hazard a guess at nine inches? I'm overpowered by Lynx Apollo. The pepper mill goes *GRRRR*.

'It's OK?' he says.

I say, 'Yes.'

'*Buon appetito.*'

I shove a forkful in my mouth. This stuff is better than sex. The pasta's perfectly al dente, firm and stiff to bite. The sauce is creamy and salty and dangerous. *Oh fuck, that's good. Oh God, that's great.* Within two minutes I finish the plate.

'*Urgh, you're such a pig,*' says Beth. '*Are you going to throw it all up now?*'

My sister thought gluten was the devil and carbs were the Antichrist.

'No. I want some more,' I say. I'm comfort-eating. Sue me. I need something warm and gooey inside. Something that feels like a hug. I used to eat to forget about Dad. To distract myself from Beth and Mum. I smile and look up at the waiter. 'I'll have another one.'

The waiter's eyes are wide.

'Oh, and another drink.'

He clears the frying pan away.

'Another *tonnarelli con cacio e pepe*?'

'Another one just like that.'

I watch him run back to the kitchen, slouching in my wooden seat. I finish off the rest of my drink and slowly lick my lips. That dish was *unbelievable*. The ultimate in food-porn. I think of the Mac 'n' Cheese Pot Noodles I used to eat back home in Archway: they don't even compare (the Bombay Bad Boy flavour was nicer. Or the Original Curry one).

I drum my fingers on the table. I'm not *Beth*. I'll eat what I like. I might even have pudding.

The waiter comes back with my drink on a tray.

'Your vodka, *signorina*.'

I take a big swig. He watches me swallow.

'You know, I've worked here seven years and you're the most beautiful lady I've ever served.'

'Oh yeah?' I say.

I'm sure he says that every night, but you know what? I'll take it.

'And you're the only one who has ever ordered *two* pans of *cacio e pepe*.'

Now that I can believe.

'Yeah, well. It's really good.'

'I like a woman who can eat.'

'Uh-huh? *Fucking watch me.*'

I could eat him alive, don't try to stop me. Lips like wild strawberries . . . creamy skin like panna cotta. Perhaps I'll take *him* home for later in a doggy bag?

He disappears to fetch my food. I slurp up my drink. Whoop! Whoop! That vodka's gone straight to my head. I giggle for no reason.

So, where did I get to with that plan? I yank my napkin off my lap and spread it back out on the table. I read through all the different ideas, then write some other ones: feed him a lethal dose of drugs (ricin? heroin? cyanide?). I wonder if Nino's at supper right now. Some little place around here, maybe? Poor bastard, he doesn't know it, but he fats himself for maggots. I have another scan through the napkin. It's almost a comprehensive list. I draw another thought bubble: drown him in a swimming pool/bathtub/lake.

'Your pasta,' the waiter says with a smile.

There's a strange look in his eyes. Is that fear or admiration? I think I'm freaking him out. Another frying pan appears with another mountain of spaghetti. 'Eat me, eat me,' it seems to beg.

'*Greedy cow,*' says Beth.

I grab my fork and stab the pasta, scooping a load into my mouth.

'You don't want pepper?' asks the waiter.

'S'OK.' My mouth is full of food.

I cannot eat this fast enough. I shovel pasta faster and faster, fork after fork after fork. It's far too hot, but I don't care. I want it in my face. I swirl hot sauce around my mouth. *Oh my fucking God.*

I didn't know that I was starving till I tasted *that*.

'You know,' he says, looking into my eyes and leaning in towards me, 'I finish my shift in forty minutes.'

I wonder what they do for dessert.

'Maybe you come back to mine? We drink some wine. Listen to music. I live just round the corner . . .'

Actually, I'm pretty full.

'I can't eat anything else,' I say. 'Can I just have the bill?'

'OK, no wine. Music? Romance?'

I shake my head. Look down at my belly. But then I get a better idea. I cock my head to the side and smile.

'Meet me *here* at my apartment.'

I give him the address.

'I want you to run at me and punch me.'

Diego looks blank. He stares at me.

'I want you to try to jump me. *Attack* me. But don't touch my nose.'

He shakes his head. 'I don't understand.'

'Look,' I say. 'Diego, this is *foreplay*. It's *sexy*. It's how I get off.'

I roll my eyes. He still doesn't get it.

I call up YouTube on my phone and show him 'Five great self-defence moves'.

'Oh. You want to wrestle?' he says.

'Yes. Yes. Wrestling.'

I push the sofa out of the way and move the armchair and coffee table. Table legs scrape across the floor. I shove it up against the wall. Ace, that's better. Now we have space to roll around. I need to practise some killer moves and I can't do it on my own. It takes two to tango.

'So, I'll stand here and look that way . . . and you come at me from behind.'

'OK. *Va bene*,' Diego says. '*Non c'e problema*.'

It's good he's doing it in Italian. Authentic. Just like Nino would. His accent's cute. The same as Nino's. Perhaps he's from Sicily too?

'Ready?' I say. I face the wall.

'*Uno, due, tre* . . .'

'No, no, no. I don't want a countdown. It's important that it's a *surprise*.'

'But you know I'm coming?' he says.

'But I don't know *when*.'

I stand and study the living-room wall. The wallpaper is a pretty magnolia. I trace the pattern with my finger: a fleur-de-lys design. Silence. Nothing. No attack. After a while, I turn back.

'Are you coming or what?'

Diego takes a run-up and jumps me, leaping on to my chest like horny Lab. We crash to the ground. He pins me down, his heaving body crushing mine. Oh my God, my stomach's exploding. Too much spaghetti. I need Gaviscon.

We roll around and around and he hits me. Whacks me hard in the side of my neck.

'OW. That hurt. Get off,' I say. I'm panting, wincing, throat aching, head spinning. 'What the hell was that?'

'You say you want me to attack you?'

He sits and cradles his throbbing hand.

'Not like *that*. For fuck's sake,' I say.

'*That was shit*,' says Beth.

We stare each other out.

'So . . . what now?' he says. 'We have sex?'

I get up and rub my neck. 'No, not yet. No way,' I say. 'I haven't finished with you.'

Diego stands in the middle of the lounge and I watch my YouTube tutorial. You have to go for the eyes and the groin. You have to jab with your elbow.

'OK. OK. I'm ready,' I say. I chuck my phone on the coffee table. 'Are *you* ready?'

'*Sì.*'

I take a run up from the far side of the room and knee him in the balls.

'RAAAAAAAAAAAAAAGH.'

'AAAAAAAAAARGGGHHH.'

He doubles over.

'What? Was that good? Did it hurt?'

Diego looks at me with tears in his eyes. He flies out of the front door.

'Hey, where are you going?'

★

I make my way to my bedroom and jump into the king-size bed. I lie spread out like a roadkill octopus, staring up at the tassels on the lamp. All of that eating and fighting have *killed* me. I feel like a beached whale. Not a regular one, like a blue whale or a killer, an obese whale that died of heart failure on the beach on its way to Weight Watchers. The one the other whales took the piss out of. The one that couldn't get a date. They'll have to knock a hole in the wall and lift me out with a forklift truck. Then I'll be all over the news and everything will be fucked. Oh why did I eat all that pasta?

'*I won't say, I told you so,*' says Beth.

I wish I could be more like Gwyneth and survive on berries and pollen.

The sheets feel cool and silky smooth. Someone's left a mint chocolate square in the middle of my pillow. I tear off the tinfoil and eat it. (I didn't have dessert.) I study the carvings on the ceiling. Angels and roses and swirling seashells. It's made of crumbling white plaster. The style is Renaissance, antique. There's a gorgeous fireplace in the corner. A polished marble mantelpiece. Chandeliers with fake wax candles cast a warm, inviting glow. Ancient glamour. Golden age glory.

'Cuckoo,' says my clock.

It's 1 a.m. At least in London. It's probably two (or three?) out here. That could get confusing. I should probably wind it forward an hour (or two?). It's not much use carrying that thing around if it's fucking *wrong* . . .

I know I should be out there now, scouring the Piazza di

Santa Maria. Running around central Rome and executing my plan. But I'm knackered. Drained. Beyond exhausted. It's been a long day. A long couple of days. I'm still recovering from surgery. I had to kill that mugger in Bucharest. I've eaten three kilos of cheese and pasta. I'll get up and find Nino later. I'll find him before he finds me.

(I'm not *lazy*. I'm energy-efficient, like a German car.)

Ah, Nino, I can almost taste you. I know you're around here, somewhere. I can feel it in my bones . . .

I stretch out across the bed. The fan is on right overhead, the breeze caressing my hot skin. I pull up my dress and spread my legs. Fingers slide along my thighs. I'm still not wearing any pants. I need to buy some new knickers. I wish he were here, right here, right now. I really want to kiss him. Oh what I'd give to sit on his face. To ride him until sunrise. I'd bite his lip so hard it split. I'd suck his soul inside me. *I am Nino. He is Alvie.* We're like Cathy and Heathcliff; I want him to haunt me (when I finally kill him that is). I can still taste that chocolate I found on my pillow; I wish it was Nino's blood.

Why do I desire the things that destroy me?

I close my eyes and sigh.

My fingers trace around my breasts. I massage their soft circumference, my nipples hard, erect. I tease and squeeze them with my fingers. First I'd fuck him, then I'd kill him. It would be so fucking hot. My fingers stroke my parted lips. The skin is sleek and wet. I touch myself and push inside. I'm aching. Longing. Desperate. I arch my back and stretch it out. Oh yeah, that's good. That's great.

Oh man, I want to come. I picture Nino deep inside me, his big hard dick throbbing, erect. I want his cock against my G spot. His hot breath on my neck.

'I never knew you were so bad . . .' That's what he'd say to me.

Perhaps I'll strangle him in bed? Snap his neck with just my thighs like some kind of Russian Bond girl? But Nino's strong. He's stronger than me. I need something quick. Quick and deliberate. Something guaranteed to work. I push my fingers deep inside. I feel like blancmange. I could hide a razor in my bra? I could whip it out and slit his throat. I'm breaking out in a hot sweat. My mind's a foggy, woozy mess. I'm panting now. I'm short of breath. It's building, harder, stronger. Where is Nino when you need him? I want to fucking come.

I sit up in bed and look around. Dizzy. I need something else to tip me over the edge. My favourite dildo, Mr Dick, is still in Taormina. He probably melted in that fire. But I have that new electric toothbrush. Maybe *that* would work? I leap up from the bed and run into the bathroom. I pull it out and switch it on. It vibrates, whirs and buzzes, the handle jumping in my palm. I can smell the Colgate spearmint toothpaste. Can really feel those batteries work. I jump back on to the bed and feel that *bzzzz* between my legs. Ooh, that's fresh. Electric. Minty. The bristles chafe, but it's OK. Alvie Knightly, you're a genius.

I'm going, going all the way.

Waves of pleasure

build

and
build.
I see that man lying dead in the alley,
but this time he has Nino's face.
Empty eyes.
A strangled scream.
'YES. YES. I've got him, the fucker.'
My body tenses then releases as I come free as the rain.

I roll over and snuggle down. I'm too tired to brush my teeth (plus I know where that toothbrush has been). I close my eyes and yawn. I'm just drifting off to sleep when I hear a clunking noise. A sound just like a window closing. The creak of a rusty hinge. I sit up in bed and flick on the light. My heart pounding. What the fuck? I'm on the fifth floor. No one can get up here. But perhaps there's a fire escape? Has that sexy waiter come back? Is it . . . could it be Nino? Shit, shit. Please, God, *I don't want to die.* I still don't have a weapon. I need to find something and fast. I fling off the sheets and jump out of bed. Sprint into the hall. The window is open. I close it again. Not cool. I run through the dark.

A knife. I'll find a carving knife. There has to be one in the kitchen. The drawers crash and bang and metal clangs as I rifle through them all. I can't see what the hell I'm doing, but I'm too spooked to turn on the light. I'm short of breath and not thinking straight after that codeine mixed with vodka. I don't know how many pills I had. It's amazing I'm thinking at all. My fingers fumble. Come on. Come on. A butter knife, a serving spoon, a wooden rolling pin. I empty the drawers. Fling open the cupboards. There's got to be something in here. A knife or some scissors? A potato peeler? A skewer? A pestle and mortar? But no. There's nothing. Not even a corkscrew. (I really need to get a gun. Or a roomful of guns like in *The Matrix*. A never-ending supply.) I really don't have time for this. Why was the window open?

I feel a wooden block on the sideboard; inside are five assorted knives.

HELL YEAH.

That's what I'm talking about.

Perhaps there is a god?

I choose the longest and biggest. Perfect. That's just what I need. Good for carving turkey or chicken or oven-roast beef. It's heavy, solid. My heart skips a beat. I press my thumb against the tip; it draws a drop of blood.

If he comes in here, I'm ready. I'll get him.

'*He'd still win*,' says Beth.

I cradle the knife like my long-lost son.

The readiness is all.

What was that? A floorboard creaking? Was that a knock at the front door? I strain my ears to hear. I need to get a guard dog or something. Or a tiger like Mike Tyson? A dragon like that little kid? I creep back down the hall to my bedroom, the knife clutched in my shaking hands. Why did I come here? What am I doing? Why did I think I could take on a mobster?

'*You don't stand a chance*,' says Beth.

'Fuck you, I'll see you in hell.'

I tiptoe back into my bedroom. I can't see anyone in here. I walk over to the unmade bed. Where the hell has that toothbrush gone? It was here, I swear to God, right here on the sheets. Did someone take it? Is Nino here? Was he spying as I got off? (Actually, that's kind of hot.) Is he still hiding in here? I press my back against the wall. My eyes are wide with fear. I hold my breath so I can hear.

Not a sound. Not a creak. Not a footfall.

I fling open a wardrobe and jump inside. I pull it shut and peer out through the crack between the doors. Well, this is shit. Now what do I do? For the very first time I wish that I was back in my old flat in Archway.

DAY THREE:
The Puppy

TWO WEEKS AGO

Wednesday, 19 August 2015
Archway, London

I give Mr Dick a peck then tuck him back inside his drawer, roll over on my futon bed and pull the duvet up. For years he has been my favourite sex toy. More than a sex toy, a lover, a *friend*. He was there when I needed someone to talk to or someone for an all-day shagfest in bed. He never cheated or walked away. He never said no. Never left me for dead. We developed a special bond; we were closer than twins. Sure, his batteries run out sometimes and that's a pain, but I don't complain. He is always a pro. Always does the job. The perfect gentleman.

Do you remember the time when I bought you four new Duracell Plus Power batteries? You gave me that legendary multiple orgasm and I came for all of five minutes. Or the time when we stayed at the Wembley Travelodge and watched Brad Pitt movies back to back? I liked *Thelma and Louise* and you liked *Snatch*. I'll never forget the day I found you hanging on a hook in that Soho store. It was love at first sight. You were so pink and shiny, luminous in the neon light. Eleven glorious inches of rubber. Anatomically perfect. You smelled so fresh, like a brand-new eraser. You were the very last one in the shop. I couldn't wait to get you home and rip you out of your packaging, to let you loose between the sheets. You know the rest, the fun we had. I know you would never leave. Ha. Unlike some people . . .

I reach inside my Primark tote and grab the pack of Marlboro Lights. Shit, there's only one fag left. I'll have to find some more. I rummage around for my purple Zippo. Somewhere, somewhere. Where? Where? Where? I find it underneath my purse and, finally, light up. I hold the smoke in, close my eyes, then let it out again slowly. I wait for the nicotine rush to come, like that will make it all all right. Like it's some magic potion.

And I can't help myself.

I open my purse and pull out the photograph. It's folded up behind the old bus tickets, loyalty stamps for coffee shops and vodka bar receipts. I open it up on my lap and study the crumpled photo. The picture was taken in Lower Slaughter in December 1987. My mum and dad are standing by the church in the heart of the village. It is quintessential Cotswolds. Picture-perfect. Chocolate-box. Honey-coloured limestone cottages, bowling greens and millponds. Alvin had looked so smart on his wedding day: a black tuxedo and top hat and shiny patent brogues. He had looked so handsome, like Prince Charming. He was the ideal groom. I guess my mum looked OK too, but he was in a different league. His hair was slick and black and thick. His figure lithe and slim. It's been twenty-five years since I saw him. Twenty-five years ago today . . . at least that's what my mother says. I don't remember it.

I stub my fag out in a mug.

You know what? Fuck it. Fuck *him*.

I'll find someone who'll never leave. I'll find somebody loyal.

I rip the photo up into hundreds of tiny pieces.

They fall through my fingers like sand.

Chapter Eight

Wednesday, 2 September 2015
Trastevere, Rome, Italy

I fall out of the wardrobe, out through the wooden doors, and crash on to the bedroom floor. The light streams in through half-drawn curtains. I drop the knife, which glints in the sun, and I rub my elbow. Ow. That's going to bruise. I fell slap-bang on the funny bone. I crawl on my hands and knees back towards the unmade bed. Oh. There's my electric toothbrush underneath the table. Nino didn't steal it then. I pick it up and chuck it back on to the bed. I've got a terrible crick in my neck. I fell asleep in that goddamn wardrobe and slept all night sitting up. He isn't here. I'm going out. I need some coffee. An Espresso Martini. I grab Beth's golden Prada sandals and that's it; I'm dressed, I guess. Still no pants, but what can I do? At least in Rome it's hot. I shove the knife inside my bag and sprint down all five flights of stairs humming 'Bad Blood' by Taylor Swift.

There's a café on the square, on the Piazza di Santa Maria. I find a table and pull up a chair. Order some coffee and a croissant. I rub and rub at the back of my skull and roll my head from right to left. It's windy. The wind must have opened the window. And I guess the noise was just 'house sounds'. Old places do that sometimes.

I reach into my wallet to find some cash so I can pay the bill. My fingers hover over the pocket where that photo used to be. I open it up, although I know too well it isn't in there. I ripped it up and I'm glad I did. I'm over it. Over *him*. I can still see the photo in my mind's eye; I didn't need a hard copy. My father's face on his wedding day was the picture of optimism. For the first time it crosses my mind that he looks a little bit Italian. There's something about his face, his figure. Shit. He reminds me of Nino. That's not *gross*, it's biology. My dad could be *Sicilian*, with the dark eyes, the bronzed skin. Not with a name like 'Alvin Knightly', but still, to *look* at him . . .

'Nino,' comes a voice from behind me. I swivel round in my plastic chair. My knee catches the edge of the table, making the whole thing tip up. Nino? Now? Where? Here? I finger the blade in my bag.

'Nino, *amore, vieni qui.*'

There it is *again*.

The voice belongs to a young woman. She's sitting at the next table along, leaning over and talking to the floor. I bend over slowly to see who she's talking to. Is *Nino* down there? Why?

Oh, it's just a *dog*.

For a minute then I thought I'd found him. Right outside my new flat. But no, that would have been too easy. Of course it's not him; it's a sausage dog. I pop the tail end of my croissant into my mouth and chew. It's filled with tangy marmalade: a bittersweet apricot goo. Unless Nino's morphed into a dachshund? Like that boy in *Metamorphosis*, that weird novella by Franz Kafka. But that was a beetle, I suppose. Still, stranger things have happened. *Nino. Nino.* They have the same name, otherwise that's it. The similarities end there. It did confuse me briefly. I'm hungover and sleep-deprived.

'*Bravo*, Nino,' says the woman.

The puppy sits and extends a paw. (He's better trained than the other Nino.) She shakes his furry hand. I watch the tiny sausage dog; his fur's a glossy chocolate brown. His ears look so soft and silky. He wags his stringy puppy-dog tail and looks up with bright, shining eyes that could break the hardest heart. Oh my God, he's really cute. I could eat him up. Shame, I've just had my breakfast. But, seriously, he's edible.

'*Bravo*, Nino. *Bravo*,' she says and tickles him under his chin.

'*Alvie, no. Don't get distracted.*'

Shut up, Beth. Get out of my head.

'*You don't need a stupid dog.*'

Actually, Beth. I do. A guard dog, remember? A trusted hound. A loyal friend. Something to be my eyes and ears while I am asleep. I'll buy this dog. He's perfect. I'll keep him with me at all times. He's nice and compact. It's an excellent plan. He'll keep me safe and sound.

I stub out my fag and wave at the waitress. Do the squiggly sign for the check. The woman pushes back her chair; I hear the legs go *scrape*. She drops some money in a silver dish, then stands ready to leave. My God, she's tiny.

Really small. Only just bigger than the dog. I'd say she's about five-foot tall, and that's *with* the patent wedges. She takes the dog's red-leather lead and says, '*Vieni. Andiamo.*'

'WOOF. WOOF. WOOF,' says Nino, excited. *Bless his cotton socks.*

He leaps up high into the air and runs round in a mad circle, chasing his little wiggly tail round and round and round. He's nuts, this dog. He's cool, like me. We're made for one another. ♥

'No, wait,' I say, jumping up quickly. My plastic chair tips over. I look down at the little dog and he looks back at me. He licks his nose and blinks. *Take me home,* he seems to say. *I want to come with you.* 'How much for your puppy?' She looks back and frowns. 'Your dog. I want him. How much?'

We both look at the tiny puppy. He is no bigger than a mole. His body stretches like a spring, impossibly long, between four paws. He'd fit inside my handbag, easy. Or I could buy a new baguette? I can see him now with his head poking out, watching the world go by. Perhaps I'll buy him a little jacket and a matching baseball cap? Tartan? Or leather? No, I know, *sequins*, in a Union Jack. Paris Hilton has a chihuahua, but Adele has a sausage dog. I can train him to attack and kill, just like that awesome widow did in 'A Vendetta' by Maupassant. (That's another method to add to my list. Death by dachshund. Ha. *As if.*)

'I want to buy your dog.'

'Ah,' says the woman. 'No *Inglese, mi dispiace.*' She smiles and turns away.

'A hundred euro? A thousand? Ten thousand?'

I grab a fistful of cash from my clock.

'No, no. *Mi dispiace.*' She pulls the lead and walks away. I stare at her glossy hair. It's the same chocolate brown as the dog's. '*Andiamo*, Nino. *Vai.*'

I watch his diminutive legs scurry away. He scales the cobblestones like boulders. He's surprisingly quick, like a millipede on speed. Milli? That's a thousand, isn't it? Centi's a hundred and milli's a thousand. *Centi*pede, *milli*pede. Is that Italian or Latin?

'Milli euros? Milli? Milli?'

I sprint after the young woman. (Oh my God, what am I doing? Chasing this woman through central Rome. This is ridiculous even for me. But I want that sausage dog.) People sitting on the terrace are pointing and whispering; there's a real crowd over there in that bar. Everyone's staring at me. It's hard to run in high heels on cobbles; my stupid shoes keep getting stuck. I need to buy some more sensible footwear if I'm going to go on this man-hunting chase. Perhaps I'll buy some nice ballerinas, some pretty flats in which I can *run*? You don't see James Bond messing around in sandals. I've never seen Jeremy Renner in *heels*. No, I need some more sensible footwear to stand half a chance.

I kick off my shoes and shove them under my arm. (The first thing I'm doing is buying some flats and a dress to replace this beat-up Chanel.) I point at the puppy. 'Milli euros? Milli? Milli? Milli?'

The lady stops and turns round.

'*Per* Nino? *Ma no. Non vendo il cane.*'

I'm not giving up just like that. I follow her on to another square. She quickens her pace (and so do I), but the puppy can't keep up. He's running, running as fast as he can. Now she's dragging him by the collar. He's just lying on his side with his feet in the air.

The ancient square is almost empty; it's still early: eight o'clock. I hear the clock tower dong-dong-donging. Then some cuckoos from my clock. A baroque church towers high above us. There's a painting of the Virgin cradling the infant Christ. The colours are muted, weathered pastels: pinks and yellows, dusky blue. The baby reaches up for Mary. I think of Ernie back in Taormina. I really fucking want that dog.

The woman walks towards a butcher's. She ties him up outside the shop, his lead attached to a metal rail. She turns and glares at me. I pretend that I'm not looking, walk a few steps the other way, then turn and make for the dog. I sprint over to the store, bend down and grab the wriggling pup. I yank his leash from where it's tied.

'It's not my fault. I did try to *buy* you,' I whisper in his ear.

I pick him up and race away. It's so much better with no shoes on. I sprint back across the square, past a fountain spewing water, past a man selling selfie sticks and a Peruvian pan-pipe band setting up for the new day. I race past the café, people pointing and staring.

'Hey,' shouts the waitress. 'Your check? Your bill?'

Oh shit. I didn't pay her.

'Later. I'll come back later,' I call.

I run and run and run. I'm back on my winding side street when I hear the woman calling, 'Nino?'

Finally I reach my door. I scrabble around in my bag for the key, my heart pounding in my chest, the puppy wriggling in my arms. I find the key and burst through the door. I slam it closed – BANG – behind me.

'*I can't believe you just stole a dachshund . . . Actually, yes, I can,*' says Beth.

'WOOF. WOOF. WOOF,' says the dog.

The dachshund sits at one end of the bed and I sit at the other. We stare each other out. He rests his head on his tiny paws and I rest my chin on my hands. Now that I've got him I don't know what to do with him. I can't take him to Prada. He'll pee on the floor.

'Hello, Nino. My name is Alvina. I'm your new mistress,' I say.

He licks his nose with a long pink tongue, but he doesn't reply.

'We're going to have lots of fun together. I'll take you out on some crazy adventures.'

He scratches his ear with his hind leg. I hope he doesn't have fleas.

'It's nice to find someone who's a good listener. It's been pretty tough these past few days . . .'

His ears prick up and he cocks his head. He whimpers a little bit.

'But you and me, we'll be great buddies. You can be my sidekick.'

I pick him up and hold him on my lap. I stroke his silky head.

'I used to have Mr Dick before, but he burnt to death in a house fire. Don't worry, I won't let that happen to you. You'll be safe with me.'

I grab Nino's old fedora from out of my handbag and sniff it. It's all crumpled and folded funny, but it sure as hell still smells like him. I shove the hat under the dog's nose. 'Nino, *kill*,' I say.

The puppy sniffs and then looks up. He doesn't look impressed. I need to teach him how to kill. How to go for the jugular. I'll give him a taste for human blood like the hound of the Baskervilles. I look at the tiny creature and sigh. He's as lethal as a slug.

I don't know where *my* Nino is and I've got no way of finding him. I've been chasing him for three whole days and all I have is this mutt. It's all a mess. And I'm a mess. I look down at my crumpled dress. *Man, I really need to shop.* No bra or pants. A filthy tote. It's getting kind of urgent. I'll go and buy a whole new wardrobe. Something nice to cheer me up. Yes, yes, that's what I'll do. Shopping will be fun. This is *Rome* after all. Italy = fashion. What does Alvie Knightly wear now that she's a kickass killer? I want to look super hot when I find him. He's going to realize his mistake. Sizzling. Smoking. Fucking explosive. I need a cool new look. Something to go with the fabulous hair and my designer nose. Shopping then killing. My perfect day. It's all part of my cunning plan. My foolproof disguise.

'Right. Well, you stay there,' I say.

Nino looks up and cocks his head.

I leap off the bed.

I want to go to Via Condotti. The internet says that's the best place to shop. I'll buy a whole new badass outfit. I'm thinking *leather*. Skin-tight. Hot. Black for autumn/winter. Sexy. And I need some more sensible footwear for sprinting. And a new handbag. Obviously. I glance at the cuckoo clock: Greenwich Mean Time is eight thirty. I guess that means it's 9.30 a.m.? We've been hiding out for nearly an hour. I hope that woman has gone. I walk over to the kitchen window and peer out through the half-drawn curtains. People bustle on the square below. It's starting to heat up. I can't see her down there now. And – no – I can't see my Nino.

'Nino,' I say, grabbing my bag. 'You be a good dog. Don't chew anything or trash the apartment.' Ha ha. No, that's *my* job . . .

Nino whimpers. I open the door. The puppy runs out after me. He whips through my feet as fast as a whippet and squeezes past me into the hall. Before I know it he's run down all five flights of stairs.

'Bad dog, Nino. Stay there.'

I run downstairs and pick him up and run upstairs again.

'Sit,' I say.

He doesn't.

He flies through the door and back downstairs, all the way down to the bottom. I don't know why I'm wasting my breath. He speaks *Italian*.

Chapter Nine

Via Condotti, Rome, Italy

I walk into Prada and everyone stares. The store is spacious and sparkling. Gleaming tiles and bright white light. The floor shimmers, as slick as an ice rink.

Other shoppers turn and gawk. I ignore them and march right in.

'Fuck are you looking at?' I say.

Maybe they think I'm famous?

There's the sound of people muttering. An old lady sees me and kind of chokes. The sales assistants gawp. I know I'm in a bit of a state: dirty dress, no underwear, no shoes on (because they hurt), my Hermès tote is covered in mud and – oops – some of that mugger's blood. At least my nose and hair look ace: it was worth that thirty grand.

A shop assistant approaches me. Nino growls at him.

'GRRRRRRRRRRRRRRRRRRRRRRRRRRR RRRRRR.'

That's my boy. Go on. You fucking tell him.

Fierce as a sabre-toothed tiger.

'*Ciao*, can I help you, *signorina*?' He looks me up and down.

'Chow. Chow. Chow. I need some new clothes. My ex-boyfriend stole all my dresses.'

'Ah, *sì*?' he says.

'*Black* clothes. They've got to be black, so that I'm hard to see in the dark.'

He looks relieved; I'm here to shop, not rob him or eat him. 'Is for an occasion *speciale*?'

Nino snaps and leaps out of my bag. The man jumps out of his skin. I let Nino run around. He needs to let off steam.

'Something durable. Hard-wearing. Got to be good for fighting in.'

'Fighting? Is "*litigare*" . . . no?'

'And it has to be sexy. Super hot. I'm thinking skin-tight leather onesie. You know, like Catwoman?'

'Leather. *Certo. Sì*. Of course. Please, come this way.'

I follow the sales assistant; he leads me to the back of the shop. The other shoppers turn and stare. I think they like my rock-chick hair. I look like Pink or Nicki Minaj. They covet my neon locks. I follow the man across the store until we reach the new collection. There's a rail with some black leather trousers and matching jackets on. Nino runs in and out of the clothes. He rips a jacket off the rail. The store guy doesn't notice.

'We have these jackets. They are new. They look *molto bello*. See, the leather is very soft.'

He hands me the sleeve to touch: it's as soft as baby Ernie's skin. I take a deep breath; it smells like Nino. Dead cow, but really nice.

'Yes, but is it *durable*?'

'I think for you, extra long. Also, look.' He shows me

the trousers. 'Is very nice. Italian leather from Toscana. You want you try on?'

'Yes. These too. I'm a UK size ten.' I think about last night's pasta . . . At least, I *used* to be.

He grabs the garments and leads me to a stylish fitting room: sumptuous, spacious, with floor-length mirrors. Glossy black velvet curtains are draped across the doorway. There's the scent of lily of the valley. (I'm pleased to see my nose still works.)

'You want I get for you some shoes? A top to try on also?'

'Yes, yes, a *leather* top. *Flat* shoes. And a handbag. And bra.'

'*Certo, signorina. Un momento.*'

'And a G-string,' I add.

He goes to fetch the other clothes. I light myself a fag. Nino climbs back into my handbag. I think he wants to go home.

I suck and suck on my Marlboro. I hear footsteps as the man approaches. I stub out my fag. It burns a hole in the carpet. Oops. I cover it up with my bag. I pull the thick curtain aside and take the pile of clothes.

'Oh. Do you smell smoke?' he says.

'Could be a BBQ?'

I try on the trousers with a skin-tight shirt, the jacket and lingerie. I run my fingers through my hair and pull on my mirror shades. I apply some purple lipstick from inside my battered tote. I open the curtain and step out.

'Ta-da.'

'Ooh, *fantastico.*'

I spread my arms out to the sides like a glorious, murderous butterfly. I'm a dangerous death's-head hawkmoth.

'*To be fair, you do look hot,*' says Beth.

Damn straight, bitch. 'Are you being *nice* to me now?'

I could floor *anyone* in this outfit, take on Mayweather with my own bare hands.

'Awesome. I'll take three of each,' I say to the man.

'Three?'

'Yes, *three.*'

'You want *three* of everything? You buy *three* exactly the same?'

'Yes, I do. It's my new look. One washing, one drying, one on,' I say. 'I want to wear it all the time, you know, like a uniform?'

'*Sì,*' he says.

He doesn't get it.

'A costume . . . like *Deadpool*?'

'OK. *Va bene.*'

I twirl round and check out my bum. 'And I want to wear it *now.*'

I twizzle in the full-length mirror. Swish my Rita Ora hair. I take several hundred selfies, till I get the perfect shot. I pout into the camera and strike a pose, then I update my photo on Tinder.

Chapter Ten

I pay for the clothes and the shoes and the handbags. Ping. Ping. Ping.

OH GOD. WHAT'S THAT?

I grab my phone and stare. It's Tinder. I have a 'Super Like'. I know it's from him before I even look. I check. It is. I was right.

'Nino Brusca, 39, from one mile away, *Super Likes* you.'

Shit. Fuck. Shit. Fuck. Shit. Does he know I'm *Beyoncé*?

Great. Now Nino has found me on Tinder. He must have seen through my fake name. It says he is *a mile* away. But it could be less, couldn't it? That's the *minimum* fucking distance. It could be a hundred metres. Or six. A chill runs up and down my spine. What the hell is he doing so close? Nino's around here somewhere. Is he . . . is he following me?

I hide behind a mannequin in the window of the store. I peer out at the crowded street, but I can't see him on Via Condotti. Perhaps he has gone shopping like me? He's the one with the two million euros; he's got money to burn.

I grab the six Prada shopping bags and run out of the shop and on to the Piazza. I climb the endless Spanish Steps two or three at a time. (The shoes are great, black-leather pumps, flat and good to sprint in. I love the bags;

they're bling baguettes, the ideal shape for the puppy. Cream leather. Golden chains. Nice gold Prada logos. The jacket and the matching trousers are a little OTT. Too-tight smooth Italian leather. Sure, my ass looks phenomenal, but I'm getting really sticky.) The midday sun is glaring down as I huff and puff up ancient stairs. It must be forty degrees.

I push past tourists, swearing under my breath. But finally I reach the top and get an awesome view. I can see everything from here. The busy square down there at the bottom. The whole length of the high street. Ooh look, there's Dolce & Gabbana. I'll pop in later (when he's dead). Over there is Moncler. And Gucci. This is even better than Westfield. Like Bond Street, but continental. Like Oxford Street, but with some class. I scan the heaving crowds for Nino.

I flop down on the uppermost step, the Prada bags scattered around me. I push my shades back on my head. I'm still catching my breath. This isn't easy with all these bags. Those stairs were really steep. Where the hell is he? He can't be far. I need to spot *him* before he sees *me*.

Tourists taking V-sign selfies. Honeymooners holding hands. Kids licking vanilla gelato. What will I do with him when I find him? I pull out my list: shoot him, stab him, run him over, push him off the edge of a cliff . . . I feel for the blade tucked away in my bag. Thank fuck for my big knife.

I strain my eyes and scan the busy Piazza di Spagna down below. Is he somewhere near that marble boat?

There's a fountain in the square. The Keats museum is to my left, and to my right there's a tearoom called Babington's. Did he pop inside for afternoon tea? Could he be in there drinking oolong?

Then – I can't believe it – I spot him.

YES.

That's him.

Down there on the square. Black hair, black leather jacket, horseshoe moustache. (No hat, but then I have got that squished inside my bag.) Oh my God. I've finally found him. *Oh villain, villain, smiling, damnèd villain.* I pull out the knife. I grip it tight. THIS IS FUCKING ON.

I pick up my shopping bags, run down the stairs and push through the crowds. Panting, sweating, swearing, tripping. This is it. My only chance. One shot, like Eminem. I might not get another opportunity. I can't let him get away.

I finally reach the marble fountain. He was here. Right *here* by this boat. But now where has he gone? Cool water droplets splash my face. I spin round 360 degrees and spy the back of Nino's head. He turns and we make eye contact, just for a split second; I forget to breathe. The world stands still. So does my heart . . . He turns and walks away.

Shit, now what?

That *stronzo*'s seen me.

Now he knows that I'm in Rome, there's no question *he'll* be after *me* as well.

'NINO. NO. WAIT,' I say. I reach out my hand . . .

He disappears into the metro station. Oh no, not the

Tube. I'll never find him down there. I race across the cobbled square.

Hang on, where's the dog?

I stop. Look around. Where is my puppy? I spot him drinking from the marble fountain, his little pink tongue going lap, lap, lap. *Oh for God's sake. I can't just leave him.*

'Nino.' I whistle. 'Come here, boy.'

He jumps up, his tail wagging. He runs towards me across the square, his floppy ears flapping, his black eyes sparkling, darting through feet and legs. I put down all the shopping bags. He leaps up into my arms and licks my face. I wipe it off and pop him into my Prada bag.

'Ready? Come on, let's go.'

I pick up my shopping and run inside. Shit, I need to buy a ticket. I don't have time for that. I climb over the barrier and head down the escalator. I think I see him at the bottom. My shopping bags slam into children and tourists. It is way too busy in here. My muscles burn with lactic acid. My breathing is heavy and loud. I'm running, running, running, running. I think I'm losing my mind.

'Move it. Hey. Out of the way.'

Why won't people *move*, goddamnit? Can't they see I'm in a hurry?

I finally reach the lower level. Hordes of people are queueing up. Someone with a parrot. A wheelchair. A pushchair. A tree in a pot. Some guy with a backpack that's bigger than he is. A woman carrying a cardboard box; on the side it says 'Fragile'. Yeah, good luck with that. I shove past her and scan the crowd. Every other guy looks like

Nino. Black hair. Black jacket. Kind of *Italian* . . . Oh no. No, wait, that is actually him.

I hear myself screaming, 'NIIIIIIIIIIIIIIIIIIIINOO OOOOOOOOOOOOOO!'

It echoes off the walls.

He turns and dives into a tunnel. Disappears among the mob.

Where does that subway lead to? *Linea A* or *Linea B*? Fuck, fuck, fuck, fuck, fuck.

I sprint into the crowded tunnel. It's sticky. Humid. Hot. Steamier than a tropical brothel. No air-conditioning. Graffiti covers curving walls. Someone's spray-painted a heart – '*I love you*' – just to piss me off. I hear the roar of a passing train. The high-pitched shriek of skidding brakes. The distant hum of metal rails.

I reach the end of the narrow tunnel. Now there are two sets of stairs going down . . . which one? They both look the same. I study the poster on the wall. It's a multicoloured map. It makes no sense to me at all. The trains all go in different directions. North or south or east or west. I look around, but I can't see Nino. I don't know which way to go.

'*RAAAAAAAAAAAAAAAAGH*,' I say.

Somebody is going to die.

My blood bubbles and boils.

Left or right? I have no idea. Nino (the dog) barks in my bag. He can sense the tension rising. Animals are good like that. He's going completely mad in there. Jumping around like a Mexican bean. I unzip the bag and go, 'SHHH.'

'WOOF. WOOF. WOOF. WOOF.'

I take out the knife and hold it tight. Zip the bag and sprint down the stairs (I pick the left, but it's anyone's guess). I reach the bottom, crash on to the platform and skid towards the edge. The doors swish shut and the train pulls away just as I reach it. *Damn.* The platform's deserted. I'm all alone. I shake my head in disbelief. I must have only just missed him.

I stand and pant and sweat.

I'll just have to catch the next train then. One will be here any minute. I study the ripped-up posters and the bare black brickwork. The bright strip lighting hurts my eyes, too white against the gloom. We're a hundred metres underground. It feels apocalyptic. Soon the platform begins to fill up. I stand at the edge of the tiles. I hide the knife under my arm and keep my eyes glued on the tunnel. Come on, come on, come on.

I feel a rough hand on my neck. I'm about to scream when I'm totally winded. An arm grips tight round my waist and the knife falls on to the metal rails.

Oh my God, it's *him.*

He whispers in my ear. A hissing sound and too-hot breath.

'*Shhh.*'

I can't turn round. Can't move my head. I smell the leather of his jacket. Can feel the heat rise from his chest. His body, lean and taut as barbed wire, presses up against my back. I feel his heart BU-BUMP, BU-BUMP. Can feel his heavy breath. There's the deep, low hum of a Tube approaching. The platform rumbles.

JESUS FUCK. He's going to push me in front of the train. I struggle and strain, but I can't move a muscle. He's got me in a vice-like grip.

'*He's going to kill you*,' says Beth.

I break out in a cold sweat, my vision blurring, my mind a mess. The front of the train emerges from darkness, speeding out of the pitch-black. Noise. Wind. I can't speak or breathe.

'*He's going to turn you to jam.*'

He holds me over the edge of the platform, dangling me into the path of the train.

'Please. Please,' I want to beg him. '*No*,' I want to scream. I open my mouth, but no words come out. Feet kicking. Heart racing. Life flashing.

Three metres, two metres, one metre away . . .

I look up and see the train driver; his eyes are white and wide with fear. This is it. I'm fucking *dead*. I close my eyes and hold my breath . . .

Beth laughs in my ear.

WHOOOOOOOSH.

He pulls me back at the very last second. The train has missed me by a couple of inches. Stale air blasts into my face. I get a bit of grit in my eye. Holy fuck, that was *close*. I taste the dust and the salt from the sweat and tears now streaming down my face. I collapse on the floor and sob and sob and sob and sob. I wipe my eyes and look around. But Nino has gone.

People are staring and crowding around me.

'*Tutto bene?*'

'*Stai bene?*' they say.

'I'm all right. I tripped.'

I try to get up. Somebody helps me. I glare at the gathering crowds. They get the message and leave me alone. My heart beats in my throat. Pounding, pounding, like a gang bang. I've never been so scared in my life. Two more inches and I'd be pesto. Every inch counts.

'*Why did he let you go?*' says Beth. '*He should have let you fall.*'

'How the hell should I know? Oh and thanks for the moral support.'

By the time I'm able to breathe and see, the train has pulled off and the platform is empty. There's nobody here except me. That's it. He's gone. I'm all alone. Alone with a sausage dog . . .

What is Nino playing at? First the mugger and now *this*. That assclown is playing dirty. There's no doubt about that. I thought maybe if he saw me in person, he would realize his mistake. Come crawling back – 'Oh, baby, I've missed you' – with his tail between his legs (tail/trouser snake). But there's no sign of an apology. Not a hint of shame or remorse. I swear to God, the next time I see him it's over. RIP.

I find a bench at the back of the platform and sink down, shaking. Spent. My handbag's warm against my ribs. I catch a whiff of something gross.

'NINO? WHAT THE FUCK? GODDAMNIT.'

The dachshund has taken a shit.

★

I emerge from the gloom of the underground station, blinking in the Roman sun. My phone goes ping with another message. I find it inside my new bag. The phone's a bit sticky, but it's OK. I wipe it on my shirt.

'UR CHASING ME WITH A FUCKING KNIFE? U TRY THAT AGAIN UR DEAD,' it says. 'I LIKE UR SEXY NEW HAIR.'

Chapter Eleven

Trastevere, Rome, Italy

I chuck my new handbag into a bush. Fucking Nino. Fucking fuck. So gross. *Seriously?* Two thousand euros of new-season Prada. Less than three hours old. I transfer the phones and the cock ring and wallet and condoms and make-up and cuckoo clock into one of the other new handbags. It's lucky I bought some spares. At the rate I'm going, I'll get through one bag a day.

I drag the dog on his lead and stomp along the city streets. What the hell was my psycho ex doing? Why didn't he kill me when he had the chance? I cross the square by my flat and do a double-take. It's that woman, the one who owned my dog, sitting outside the café. She's drinking a large glass of white wine and eating some Kettle crisps. She sees Nino and he sees her. The dog goes bat-shit crazy.

'WOOF. WOOF. WOOF. WOOF.'

I march over to her.

'Take him. Just take him. You can have him,' I say. 'He ruined my new Prada bag.'

I let go of the leash and Nino runs over.

She shrieks with delight. 'Nino, *amore.*'

I skulk down my narrow street. I can't stay here. Not now.

I push through the door to my apartment and trudge up all five flights of stairs. I don't feel safe. Not without a guard dog. For all I know that *stronzo* followed me. I bet he knows I'm living here. Perhaps it *was* him here last night, lurking on the fire escape and watching me get off with my toothbrush. He 'Super Liked' me, the dick. I pack my new clothes, the two new handbags, the cuckoo clock and everything else. I stomp back down five flights of stairs and call up Airbnb.

I find myself a new apartment, a two-bed flat in Trastevere. It's on the fifth floor, *again*. It's a bargain at seven grand. It looks more like a gallery than someone's flat. The walls are crowded with paintings and photos. There are sculptures and carvings on the shelves. There's art everywhere you look: modern, abstract, impressionist. That picture looks just like a Warhol. A tin of Campbell's tomato soup. I check, but it's not an original. It's just a *print*, so who cares?

I go back and make sure the door is locked. I pull the chain across the gap. Double-bolt it. Double-check it. I look through the spyhole, but no one's there. I run my fingers through my hair. I take a deep breath and exhale. At last, I feel safe. Kind of. *Nearly*. I study my hand; it's still trembling, shaking. I need a drink. Something fucking strong. A whisky or vodka or maybe a brandy. A Blow Job. A Flaming Lamborghini. Something to take my mind off that bellend. My nerves are shot. I'm stressed out, like my mother. I can't believe I just had to *move house*.

I draw all the blinds and then pull the curtains and shutters closed, just in case he's spying on me through the windows and taking aim with his big gun. I head into the open-plan kitchen. It's full of overgrown pot plants and flowers. It's as wild as a rainforest jungle, a luscious garden indoors. I find myself another knife. It's the only one there is, but at least it's bigger than the last one. I'd guesstimate about sixteen inches, like the knife in the shower in *Psycho*.

I sit down in the lounge in a comfy chair. The knife rests on my lap. It's stainless steel. Black plastic handle. Nice and sharp serrated edge. It should do the job. But that is what I thought last time and that knife fell on to the tracks. Nino's so strong. He could have killed me. I've got no muscles. No stamina. No strength. No killer moves. It was *lucky* I killed that man in Romania. And I cannot rely on *luck*. I need to train. Train *hard*.

I lie down on the floor and do a press-up. A couple of sit-ups. A star jump. A lunge. I'll get myself fit. I'll do a boot camp. Just a few more days of this and I'll be Serena Williams. You watch.

Right. That will do for now. I reach for my fags. Now I've worked on my physical fitness, I need to get strategic. Smart. I flop back in the chair and grab my phone. I call up YouTube and 'Five Great Self-Defence Moves'. Yeah, yeah, yeah, OK, I get it. You've got to bridge. You've got to block. I watch it three or four more times and then I turn it off.

I switch on the TV news. I need to know what's going on. Are there any new developments on my sister's case? Are the cops still looking for my twin? Is Alvina Knightly still dead? I flick through the TV channels. Is there any more evidence? Are there any more leads? On screen there's some footage of policemen. A scene of chaos on a road. That looks like the motorway outside Rome, but I could be wrong. Motorways all look the same. They're long and grey with a ton of cars. That could be anywhere.

Of course the news is in Italian, so I don't understand a word. But now the scene flicks to a different story and Salvatore's on TV. Salvatore, my sister's lover, the sexy sculptor from next door. That's his face up there. And that's a picture of his villa. There's another image of his car. The boot of the Beamer is wide open. The TV camera zooms inside. I flinch, but it's empty. That's where we chucked Ambrogio's body. Salvo helped me lose his corpse when I killed him last week. We drove it up to the top of a cliff and then dropped it in the sea.

Oh shit. Now there's a picture of Ambrogio. (Oh man, he's hot. I almost forgot. An Italian version of Chris Hemsworth. A slightly more tanned, slimmer Thor.) Did they find a hair inside the trunk? Do they know he was in there? They zoom in on the passenger seat. Beth went for a drive in Salvo's car, the night I murdered her. I remember. It was just last week. She was sitting right there. Did they find her nail? A bit of skin? A fake eyelash? A drop of blood? Could her DNA frame me for Ambrogio's murder?

There's another picture of Salvatore looking rough and tough and mean. His name is in big bold capital letters: 'SALVATORE BOTTARO'. Ha. Do they think he murdered me? Do they think he killed Ambrogio? I bet they do. That's awesome. Salvatore's a wanted man (it's just a shame he's dead). Now there's a photo of me on the screen. It's the same one of me at Beth's wedding: silver fishnets, body-con minidress, just-got-out-of-bed hair. I let my hair cover my face and shrink down in my comfy chair. I bite my thumbnail down to the quick. It bleeds a little bit.

I search for the news on my burner. I call up BBC World. I scroll through the European stories. Perhaps they've published something new? I search for 'Elizabeth Caruso'. The number-one hit is breaking news. I shift to the edge of my seat and chew my bottom lip.

'Police in Taormina, Italy, are looking for Salvatore Bottaro, thirty-one, in connection with the murdered British national Alvina Knightly. Mr Bottaro has been missing since 28 August and could be armed and dangerous. He is also wanted in connection with the suspected murder of his neighbour Ambrogio Caruso, Miss Knightly's brother-in-law. The public are advised not to approach him if they see him, but to call 112 as a matter of urgency, or to contact local police if he has left the country.'

I can't help it. I laugh out loud. Armed and dangerous? *Salvatore?* You've got to be kidding me. He was an *artist*. A sensitive soul. They haven't got a clue. I study the photo of Salvatore provided by the BBC. Yes, he was fit and totally stacked – and having an affair with my twin – but a murderer? I don't think so.

I turn off the news. I don't need to worry. They're barking up the wrong tree. I'm in the clear, scot-free. If the police still want to talk to Beth, it's more to get her version of events. They want to hear her – *my* – side of the story. I'm more of a witness than a *suspect*.

I check Tinder again, but there's nothing from Nino. I need to think of a new way to track him . . . Think, Alvina. Think.

I'm bored of Tinder so I log on to Bristlr: 'Connecting those with beards with those who want to stroke beards.' I read about it in a magazine and I'm keen to explore a new fetish.

Do you have a beard? YES/NO.
'No.'
Are you looking for: MEN/WOMEN/EVERYONE.
'Men.'
Showing bearded people who are within 200 km.

I scroll through the photos. The men all have beards. I guess that's the point. You can rate the beards between zero and five stars, say 'Not a beard' or just 'Skip beard'. I scroll until my fingers ache and my chewed thumbnail bleeds.

But it's not a fucking beard I want . . .

It's a horseshoe moustache.

'Hello. I want a tattoo.'
'Of course. Please, come this way.'
The woman in the shop is tall and pretty. Her back and

neck are inked with stars. Her dyed blue hair is tied up in a funky skull-print scarf. I follow her through the tattoo parlour. There's a smell of other people's sweat. The walls are lined with photos of clients, pen and ink drawings, new designs. Someone's had an excellent likeness of the face of O.J. Simpson tattooed across their bare midriff. Huh. They must be a big fan. There are snaps of people's penises illustrated with Britney Spears, as well as a more unusual selection: life-size portraits of Princess Anne, Ozzy Osbourne and Donald Trump are inked on people's chests and backs. Ellie Goulding looks out at me from a man's shaved thigh. (What happens when his hair grows back? She'll become a bearded lady. I didn't see any of *those* on Bristlr. Now that would be niche . . .)

'Who's that?' I ask, pointing to a tat inked in colour on someone's back. It's a woman with a wide crimson smile, a straight blonde fringe and turquoise eyes. She's sexy in a lacy bra. She could be someone's girlfriend.

'Oh.' She smiles. 'That's Cicciolina. She's very famous in Italy. Well, her stage name's Cicciolina.'

'Stage name? Who is she? A singer or something?'

'No, no, she's a politician.'

'Oh. Right. I see.'

'She was an MP back in the nineties. But before that she was a porn star.'

'A porn star?'

'Uh-huh. She made loads and loads of pornos.'

I look again at the woman in the picture. 'She has enormous breasts.'

'Do you have any exotic actors in power in your country?'

I think of Michael Gove and Boris Johnson. 'I don't think so, but I guess you never know.' (That's not a film I want to see. I hope I don't find it on YouPorn.)

'So, what would you like to have done?' she asks. She picks up her ink gun and smiles.

'I was thinking "DIE NINO" on my bum. Capital letters. Big black font?'

'OK. Absolutely.'

'Cool.'

'That's an excellent choice.'

'It is?'

'Oh yes, that's a popular one.'

I lie down on my front on the little bed and pull my trousers down.

'Really? "Die Nino"?' I ask.

'Absolutely, we get that a lot. "Die Dory", "Die Marlin", "Die Mr Ray". . . You'd be surprised,' she says. 'Hold still now. The needle won't hurt.'

There's a high-pitched shriek as she fires it up: a sound like a pneumatic drill.

Buzz.

'Ow.'

'You need to stop moving. You've got to keep still.'

'Oh my God, that's fucking painful.'

'I haven't started yet.'

'*Such a pussy,*' says Beth.

'Have you got any vodka or ketamine?'

She turns and rifles through a cupboard. Pulls out a half-full bottle of red.

'You can have some Valpolicella.'

She opens it up. It's a screw top.

I take a swig straight out of the bottle. The wine tastes like medicine and plums. I drink some more and brace myself, screwing my fists up into balls. She starts the needle again.

Buzz.

'Ow. OW.'

'I haven't even done the "D" yet.'

'No. That's fine. You can stop there.'

'You just want a "D" tattooed on your ass?'

'Yeah, that's great. That's just what I like. "D" for "dog". I like dogs.'

I get up off the bed and walk to the mirror. Turn round and check out my bum. The 'D' looks red and raw and incomplete on my left buttock.

'*That looks seriously fucking stupid,*' my sister says inside my head.

'OK. Fine. Give me back the wine. You can do the rest. But *gently.*'

Who are those freaks who like pleasure *and* pain? Bondage lovers. S&M. (I'm no Anastasia Steele. I'd tell Christian where to shove it.) How do those girls get addicted to piercings? Tattoos inked all over their skin? There's no danger of that happening to me. I'd be the world's worst masochist. I prefer to *inflict* pain.

'And be *quick,*' I say. 'Super speedy.'

I grab on to the edge of the bed and dig my nails into

140

the mattress. There's a buzz as the needle starts: a deranged dentist's drill.

Buzz.

'Ow.'

'Do you want me to stop?'

'No, keep going.'

I swig more wine. Some of it comes out of my nose. My eyeballs weep and sting.

Buzz.

'Ow.'

Buzz.

'Ow.'

(This continues for some time.)

It feels like I am being stabbed by Borrowers, elves or Lilliputians. An army of tiny, angry people, each with their own sharp knife. I'd really love to strap Nino down and tattoo 'WANKER' on his face, then I'd ink every inch of his skin with thousands of pointless dots. Yes. Yes, that would be fun. I've invented a new kind of torture. I should call a lawyer, patent it and go on *Dragons' Den*. (Deborah would go nuts for that.) I could work at Guantanamo Bay.

'Finished,' she says, after what feels like *for ever*. 'Look. What do you think?'

I jump off the bed and look in the mirror.

It says 'DIE NEMO'.

'That isn't *quite* how you spell "Nino". Otherwise, it's ace.'

Chapter Twelve

I'm totally buzzing from my new tat. I don't want to go back and sit in my flat. I do my hair and make-up and head out into the town. The club is called Radio Londra. It's in an old underground bunker. The pavements above it hum like a train is passing. I feel the energy inside. A woman with a whip and collar rocks a dominatrix look: PVC pants with a cut-out ass. Six-inch-heeled knee-high boots. I push through the doors and step inside to hot steam and sweat. The air vibrates. The bass is deep and fucked up. The DJ's playing tech house so loud it hurts my ears. It feels like being punched in the face over and over and over. The music beats along my bones and echoes around the inside of my skull. I close my eyes and just feel it, become it. I let the track take over. I don't want any thoughts, no pictures, no Nino, no Beth, no nothing. I want to forget all about it, to become numb and void, to get wasted.

Two guys are snogging by the door. I press my body up against the fine black mesh on the speaker. The hairs on the back of my neck stand on end. I feel the bassline pulsing through each cell inside my body. Shivers run up and down my spine. My clit tingles and aches.

Strobe lights flash and I'm blinded, as if by lightning,

just for a split second. And then I see people dancing, moving in stop-motion, white then black then white again: kissing, shouting, laughing all in shattered bursts of light. A woman standing next to me drops a tab of ecstasy; she's wearing dayglo yellow pants with neon-green legwarmers. A man dressed as a werewolf lifts her up on to his shoulders. Smoke machines blast out dry ice, and I taste chalk and powdered sugar. Warm bodies, sticky skin, Davidoff Hot Water; I push through writhing, pulsing crowds and head over to the bar.

There's a man in a tight fuchsia dress. I think it's made of latex. He's wearing too much make-up and a black choker with studs on. I'm boiling in my double leather. The tiles are tacky with spilled drinks. I find a space at the counter. There are silver taps and rows of spirits: Smirnoff, Bacardi, Jack Daniel's, Baileys, Cointreau and sambuca. The barman's cute, but nothing special. A six and a half out of ten. He winks at me. I don't wink back. I look away at the menu: Sex on the Beach, Porn Star Martini . . . Anyway, I've sworn off men. I've gone three days, or is it four? *Ménage à Trois*, Slippery Nipple. So far I don't miss them to tell you the truth. I've barely noticed at all. Screaming Orgasm, Sloe Comfortable Screw. I don't know what I want to order. I think I'll just get a shot.

There's a commotion at the far side of the bar. People shouting. Yelping. If it's a fight, I want to see. I love a spectacle. I push through the crowds and rush over. A woman and a man are fighting. It looks like the woman is winning. She bends his arm behind his back; he's kind of whimpering. She twists him by the wrist and pushes him down over her knee until his head touches the ground.

A silence falls over the crowd.

We all watch them.

This is ace.

'Lick it,' she says.

The man obeys.

He laps at the dirty floor.

Urgh, that's gross. It looks disgusting. Just think of the bugs from all those shoes. Dog shit. Mud. E. coli. Listeria. It's a dirty floor in a busy club. Not even the three-second-rule applies. I look away. That's nasty. She finally lets the man back up. As soon as he's free, he runs away, clutching his fucked-up shoulder.

The woman smiles. She's pretty.

She walks towards the bar through the crowd, a round of applause erupting. Wow. That was cool. It was short and sweet, but she totally showed him. I wonder what that guy did wrong. It must have been pretty awful. I wish I knew how to fight like that. I need to practise more.

I head over to the bar too and squeeze back into my old spot. I pick up the drinks menu and get back to browsing. That's when I see she's appeared next to me and – I can't help it – I stare.

'Hey,' says the woman.

Oh my God, she's *amazing*.

She is unbelievably hot. Up close like this, she looks like Rihanna. I gaze at her face. She's standing right in front of me, pressing her knee into my thigh. (It's really very crowded in here. There isn't that much space.)

She's wearing round black aviators with silver frames and attitude. The logo on the side reads 'Bulgari'. I can see myself in the lenses. The next thing I notice are her lips. I don't know why but I'm drawn to them. They're mesmerizing. Hypnotizing. Round and full with a hint of gloss, in a rosebud shape. She pushes a straw against her lip, drinking something like sparkling water or maybe a vodka and tonic. Whatever it is, I want one too. I want to look like that.

She squeezes her body against me to get nearer the bar. Unisex eau de cologne: a hint of Calvin Klein One. Her hair is long, reaching down to her waist. It falls in one black satin sheet, which shines like the screen on an iPhone. The woman places her hands on the counter and fingers a thin silver ring. It's on her thumb – not a wedding band, so I don't think she's married. She has short, clean nails without any polish. She has twenty earrings in her left ear. Zero earrings in the right.

'Hi, I'm Rain,' she says.

'*Rain?*' I say.

'That's right. Don't you like it?'

I close my eyes and sigh. I remember the rain that fell on my face when I killed that man in Romania. It felt cool and so refreshing against my burning skin. I remember that feeling the last time I came, when I floated as free as the rain.

'No, I like rain. Your name is ace. Is it short for something?'

'Like what?'

'I don't know.' I frown. 'Like *Rainbow*?'

OMG. Alvie, just stop.

'No. It's just Rain as in *rain*.'

'That's a great name,' I say.

'Your accent is adorable. Are you *British*?' she says.

'Yes. No. Maybe,' I say.

I think she has an American accent, but it could be Canadian. We have to shout over the music. We're basically lip-reading. Or perhaps I'm staring at her mouth? I really want to kiss her.

What?

There's something magnetic about her . . .

'My name is Beyoncé,' I say.

'Can I buy you a drink?'

She pushes her shades back into her hair and reveals the palest blue eyes. I swallow hard. She has no make-up on. She doesn't need it. I want to touch her face.

'I'll have what you're having,' I say.

A girl's never bought me a drink before.

'Two vodka tonics,' she says to the barman. '*Grazie*, Marco.'

'*Prego*.' He looks at me and winks. *Again*. Maybe it's just a tic?

I'm jealous. *How does she know that guy? Does she sleep with the barman?*

'So . . .'

Rain takes off her denim jacket and folds it on top of the bar. She's wearing a simple V-neck T-shirt. Nipple rings press up against the thin white cotton fabric.

I take my jacket off as well. It's suddenly way too hot.

She smiles at me so I smile back. A gap between her two front teeth makes her look kind of French. Damn, that's cute. She's crazy sexy. If she were a guy, you know I'd be all over that like a rash.

'I liked your moves, before, in the fight,' I say. 'That was badass.'

'Oh yeah? I could show you, if you like.'

I nod. 'That would be awesome. I'm training to be a martial arts guru . . . What did that guy do to you?'

'He pinched my ass,' she says. 'Do you come here often?'

I look at Rain. Why does she care? She blinks at me slowly.

'I . . . well . . .' I can't find the words. She has pretty lips. Did I mention that?

The man sets down our matching drinks. I take a long drag on the straw. It's bitter. Acidic. At least two shots of vodka. I wish it had three or four.

'What did you ask me again?'

'Do you come here often?'

Oh, that one's easy.

'This is my first time, actually. I'm here on holiday.' *Kind of.*

'So, what do you do when you're not in bars?' She strokes the sides of her glass up and down, wiping away the condensation. Why does she care? Is she chatting me up? Or is she just being friendly?

'My job is actually top secret. I'm not allowed to discuss it.'

I'd better not give too much away. I am undercover.

'Interesting,' she says. 'You're not one of those Mafia

147

lowlifes? There are way too many of those crawling around in here. This place is where they hang out.'

I don't say anything.

Rain puts her hand on top of mine and leaves it there. WTF? She strokes my finger with her finger; it's long and slim, just like a pianist's (that sounds a little bit like 'penis'). I swallow hard. Reach for the nuts. Shove them in my face.

Rain takes a sip through her black straw. She clinks the ice around in her glass. It sounds incredibly sexy. She looks up at me through her lashes. Her gaze is deep. Intense.

'Cuckoo,' says my clock.

'What's that?'

'Oh, nothing. It's just my clock.' I show her inside my bag.

'Aww, that's cute. I like it.'

'So what do you do?' I ask her back, just for something to say.

'I'm in sales.'

'That's *awesome*. What kind of sales?'

'Oh, that's top secret.'

Fair enough, I guess.

She touches her taut, flat stomach. Perhaps she has an itch? The fabric on her top pulls up to reveal a navel ring. A thin silver bar with two balls on it. I wonder what else she has pierced.

I reach for the peanuts and bite down hard, imagining they're Nino's nuts.

She applies a slick of shimmery gloss; her lips look super shiny.

I lick the salt off my fingertips.

'So where are you from, Beyoncé?'

It's safer to remain anonymous. I don't know anything about her. For all I know, she could be police. Could be an undercover cop.

'Um, Archway,' I say.

Shit.

'I don't know where that is.'

That's lucky.

'Where are you from?'

'Chicago.'

'Oh. I know where that is.'

I crunch more nuts. I sip my drink. The ice has melted now. The straw makes a slurp-slurp-slurping sound at the bottom of my tumbler. I could do with another one. Rain lets her hand rest on my waist. Her cobalt eyes twinkle like fire. (The flame on my Zippo is blue.)

'I really like what they've done with these peanuts; they're roasted with just a hint of wasabi . . .'

Rain leans in and bites her lip. I feel her warm breath on my cheek. She puts her hand behind my neck and pulls me in towards her.

'Would you like to come back to my place?' she says. 'I could teach you some of those moves.'

It's just one night . . . I'll find Nino tomorrow . . .

'OK. Yeah sure. Let's go.'

Chapter Thirteen

We're sitting in the back of a cab. It's a silver Prius. The driver's checking us out in the rear-view. Dirty bastard, he's going to crash. He's not looking where he's going.

'Hey. Watch the road, motherfucker.'

I know that's the kind of thing *I* would say, but that was Rain shouting.

The radio's playing Italian rap. I recognize a few of the words: '*fica*', '*cazzo*', '*vaffanculo*'. I feel like singing along, but Rain is sitting on my lap, her hand down the front of my leather top and her tongue deep in my mouth.

There's a tongue ring I hadn't noticed. *Oh my God, that's hot.* This chick is beyond awesome. My tongue explores the silver piercing: backwards and forwards and round and round. It's smooth and round and tiny and perfect. She tastes like vodka and lemons. I think I'm falling in love. I take a deep breath and pull back. That's the first time I've kissed a girl, but it's like that Katy Perry song. You know what, I liked it.

Rain looks into my eyes and smiles. Her pupils are dilated. She chucks her chewing gum out the window then leans back in to kiss me. Her lips feel soft against my lips. She slips her tongue inside. I stroke her hair; it's cool and silky. I love her taste. I love her smell. She is *so* different from Nino . . . a better kisser, a better person (but that's not hard: he's a knob).

Then Rain pulls away. She moves her face towards my breasts. I take a sharp breath. My body's tense. She undoes the buttons on my top.

I talk into her hair. 'So do we need some kind of strap-on?'

Shut up, Alvie, stop blabbering.

'No. We don't. You'll see.'

She pulls my bra down off my breasts and takes my nipple in her mouth. Her mouth feels warm against my skin. I close my eyes and sigh. My head leans back into the headrest. She runs her hand along my thigh and slips it down inside my trousers. *Oh my fucking God*. I smooth her back. Her skin is soft. I feel her tiny waist.

'You have an amazing body,' I say.

'So do you,' she says.

I'm wet. My clit is hot and throbbing. I feel my pussy aching. Her fingers slide inside my pants.

'We arrive,' says the taxi driver.

I watch as Rain pours a couple of inches of bright green liqueur. The label on the bottle reads La Fée Absinthe Parisienne. She takes a silver absinthe spoon and a lump of dark brown sugar, pours the drink over the cube and lights it with a match. There's a scent of burning sulphur. Of sweet aniseed. The sugar caramelizes as the golden flame flickers yellow. The melted sugar drip, drip, drips down through the spoon to the glass below. She adds a splash of water. A few ice cubes. I watch as she stirs. Her slim wrist. Her slender fingers. She hands me my drink and we clink.

I take a sip. It's strong. Delicious. I look around the room. The lights are dim and soft and low. Rain has lit a couple of candles and they cast a warm and amber glow. The room smells of Rain and exotic spices. Intoxicating, heady. There's a framed poster of Brigitte Bardot posing naked on the wall. Pink and white orchids in vases. The flowers all look like vaginas.

Rain turns on her stereo. She's playing an Italian song. It's a female artist singing. Her voice is powerful.

'Wow. Who's that?' I say. 'I don't know her.'

'Elisa,' says Rain. ' "Eppure Sentire". It's my favourite song.'

I down the rest of my absinthe.

'It's my favourite song too.'

'Come here,' says Rain, leaning towards me.

The mattress creaks as we lie down. She looks deep into my eyes, giving me a jolt like an electric shock. She takes a sip of absinthe and kisses me beneath my jaw. She runs an ice cube all the way from my throat to the back of my neck. The ice cube's melting on my skin. I can't tell if it is hot or cold; I just know it feels amazing. Icy water trickles down. My nipples go hard. I pull her body into mine. I want us to go all the way. I want to taste her come.

I move to kiss her on the mouth. The ice has disappeared. Her tongue is freezing, alien, strange. My heart is racing. Breathing shallow. This is all so new.

'I want to hear you scream, Beyoncé.'

'Fuck yeah,' I say. 'You too.'

I tease the stretchy cotton fabric of her thin white cotton shirt. I want to see her body naked. I'm so fucking turned on. Rain takes off her top. *Oh wow.* I was right about the piercings. Her boobs are small and perfectly formed with bars across the nipples. Her areolas are dark. Her skin the colour of chocolate. I lean in and kiss her breasts, feeling a bar inside my mouth. I swirl my tongue around and suck. She pulls my head towards her. Moans. I can't believe I'm doing this, but you know what? It's ace. Fuck you, Nino. In your face. I'm not going to eat my heart out.

Rain strokes my skin with fingertips as light as summer showers. She pulls off my leather top and throws it on the floor. We lie next to one another. I can hear her breathe. It's fast and shallow. I'm alert. Wide awake. Like I've done too much cocaine. I kiss her on her naked shoulder. Then I lick her neck. She tastes likes Swizzels Love Hearts.

Her hands reach down towards my ass. I can't wait any longer. I reach for the flies of her ripped-up jeans. Try to find the buttons. I wonder if she has a Brazilian. Or a Hawaiian wax? I rip open her blue jeans and pull them – kick them – down her legs. There's a tattoo of an orchid on her bikini line. It's small and pink and fucking perfect. It's nicer than mine. I reach out and touch it lightly – stroke the pretty petals – then slide my hand towards her cunt.

'Mmm,' says Rain.

Her head pushes into the pillow. I watch her back arch up.

Dark hair. Something silver. Another piercing in her clit? I take a closer look.

'Oh my God. *That's epic.*'

I touch it with my fingertip. It's tiny. Glinting. Shiny. I kiss her on her pussy; she tastes different. Acidic. I lick and lick and lick. I think of the oysters that I ate on Ambrogio's yacht. Her body curves and undulates across the bed like waves.

'Mmmm,' she says.

I push my fingers deep inside, reach up for her G spot. She moans and then her body shudders. I watch her as she comes.

Rain sits up and looks at me, but I can only stare. She unzips my leather trousers and peels them slowly down my legs. Holy fuck. This sex is on fire.

'Wait,' she says. 'Don't move.'

She gets up off the bed and walks towards a chest of drawers.

'Where are you going? Come back,' I say. Now what is she doing?

Rain pulls out a pair of gloves. They're shiny black and glossy. She pulls them on. They're elbow-length. PVC.

'No glove, no love,' she says.

'I thought that was a metaphor?'

She climbs back on to the bed. Naked apart from the gloves.

Her eyes lock on mine.

She reaches out and caresses me on my cheek. The glove feels cold against my skin, just like drops of rain. My face feels like it's burning. I close my eyes. I'm dizzy. High. Every nerve ending alive. Rain moves down between my legs.

'You like this?' she says.

She smooths her hands across my stomach. Soft lips push against my cunt. I look down and see her long black hair flowing over her naked shoulders. I'm moaning, moaning. Floating. Groaning. Something hard – her tongue ring? – presses down on my clit.

'Oh God. Oh yeah,' I say.

She tickles me with just the tips then pushes her fingers deep inside me.

'You like that, baby?' she says.

'Don't stop. Don't fucking stop.'

She licks my pussy up and down, sucking, kissing, swirling around. She slips another finger inside. Or what the fuck? A *thumb*? And, oh my God, my fucking G spot. I'm moaning. Moaning. Brain exploding. I'm in fucking ecstasy. I can't think or breathe or see. I feel her fingers deep inside and push my body down, down, down. The bed sheets ride up underneath me. I grab hold of her hair.

'Nino. Nino. Fuck me,' I say.

I come again and again and again.

'Nino. Nino. Nino.'

Rain sparks up a cherry vape and blows the steam out in my face. I pull the duvet up over my sticky, naked body.

'Who the fuck is Nino?' she says.

'But you said you'd teach me some killer moves?'

'Oh yeah? Watch this,' she says.

She throws me – hard – down the corridor and I crash into the front door.

'Yeah, not bad,' I say. 'Can I have my clothes?'

I get dressed and burst out of the flat, slamming the door behind me.

BANG.

Oh my God, *Americans*. They're so fucking tetchy.

Chapter Fourteen

The Roman Forum, Rome, Italy

I wrap my arms round myself, shivering despite my clothes. Why did she have to throw me out? Who cares if I forgot her name? It's 3 a.m. Where am I supposed to go? How am I supposed to get home? I scan the dark and empty street. No cabs. No trams. No buses. Great. I am going to have to *walk*. How far is it to my flat? I look around for familiar landmarks, but there aren't any.

What a stupid name anyway. I mean, who the hell is called *Rain*? What is she, a New Age hippy? The personification of precipitation? It makes no fucking sense. I pick a direction at random. Is that south or is that west? I swerve down the deserted street, rummaging around in my bag for my phone. I call up Google Maps. I have to type the address ten times (I've had quite a lot of absinthe), but finally the route pops up. It's going to take me an *hour*. I bet she'll go out tomorrow night and pick up some other British girl . . . *Frailty thy name is woman*. Nino. Rain. Rain. Nino. It was just a slip of the tongue. They're both four-letter words.

I feel a raindrop on my head and then the heavens open. SPLAT. SPLAT. SPLAT. SPLAT. Oh for fuck's sake. Seriously? Now it's tipping down. Yeah, thanks for that,

God. How very apt. Like She's making a point. I run for cover under a tree. I don't have an umbrella. I stand here in the cold damp air. Rain. Of course, what else?

> *Rain, Rain, go away,*
> *Come again another day . . .*
> Or not. *I don't care.*

I really need to pee. I should have gone before in Rain's flat. But it's too late now. I'm not going back. I don't know where it is anyway. Everything's dark and unfamiliar and now it's turning green.

I like absinthe. It's the first time I've tried it. I feel like Mr Soft. The pavement turns into marshmallow and I moonwalk along. There's a sign up on the wall. I float closer, but I can't read. I close one eye and turn my head round ninety degrees: 'VIOLINS AND VIRGINS' or 'VIADUCT VIRGINIA' or 'VIA DELLE VERGINI'. Another sign says 'VIETRI ALLERGY' or 'TREVOR GALLAGHER' or 'TREVI GALLERY'. Another sign says 'FORMICA' or 'FARMYARD' or 'FARMACIA'. Maybe.

The street is lined with closed shop windows, the plastic shutters pulled across. It stretches out to infinity. I really, *really* need to pee. I can't run. My bladder's too full. I'm feeling hot and dizzy. You're only supposed to drink three shots, but I think I had twenty.

I float up and up, round a corner, into something big and white. I gasp. Oh wow. What's that? Towering lanterns with little glass lamps illuminate an oasis. I rub my eyes. Am I dreaming? A marble fountain. Winged horses.

And a god. Who is it? Neptune? Or Triton? A mermaid king. A merman. His robes seem to ripple in the wind. Majestic rocks. A bountiful beard. A seashell chariot. He stands over a shimmering, magic turquoise sea.

Behind him, a grand marble building. Endless tiers of balconies. Corinthian columns stretching up as far as the eye can see. The sun glides over the horizon: the first rays of dawn pierce silver night. The facade comes alive with dancing nymphs, beautiful in the golden light.

I set my bag down on the edge and step into the fountain. The water is cool and blue as I sink into the shining sea. I feel the liquid swirl across and all around my body. I dive down and taste sweet water. It mixes with the liquorice, the weird and bitter green. There are hundreds of coins all over the floor, gold and silver and glistening. I pick up three and shove them in my pocket. I come up for air and rise out of the water. Suddenly the fountains turn on. Water gushing and crashing and blasting in torrents and frothing streams. (I really fucking need to pee. I'm just going to go in the water.) I stand beneath a waterfall and let my hair flow down my back. I am a goddess. A movie star. Anita Eckberg in *La Dolce Vita*. I give myself up to the god.

I feel better now I've had a pee.

'*FUORI DALLA FONTANA.*'

I hear a voice. A man's voice. Is that *God* shouting? Shouting at me?

'Hey you. Get out of the water.'

I wipe my eyes and look around.

'Is a five hundred euro fine.'

A policeman is waving at me. I jump up and out of the fountain and run down the street soaking wet.

Help. Help. That cop's going to kill me. He's after me. He knows what I did. I've got to get out of here. Run away. It's over. The *murders*. I'm *done*.

I turn one corner then another. Run till I can run no more, my heart exploding. I can't breathe. Now I'm lost.

Where am I?

It's some kind of temple. I look around, but that cop has gone. Phew, I must have lost him. It's dark and my sense of hearing heightens: the yelps of fighting animals and the long, low groan of a cat. It's just gone four o'clock in the morning according to my cuckoo clock. I can't walk another step. My feet are killing me. Why didn't I just call a cab when Rain threw me out? I'm not myself. I'm not thinking straight. It must have been all that absinthe.

I'm tired and drenched and shivering. My clothes drip, drip on the ground. Where am I going? What is that column? What is that massive arch? My feet smash sand and broken rock. I check Google Maps again, but I don't know which way round the screen's meant to be. Am I that little blue dot? I squint into the sudden blinding light and try to work out where I am. Rocks. Ruins. Blocks of marble. Mosaics. Floodlights. Shadows.

Urgh.

What's that swooping? Are they *bats*?

I trip over my feet into some kind of column. It wobbles a bit and then falls over.

CRASH.

BANG.

SHIT.

It cracks in two when it hits the ground, then rolls around a bit. Fuck it. It looked really old. Not *irreplaceable*. I run away up crumbling stairs. I try to check my phone again, but the battery dies and I can't use it. Google Maps can't help me now. I am on my own.

I find a wall and then sit down and dangle my legs off the edge. I hold my head in my hands. Why am I even bothering? What do I hope to achieve?

Dad left me and Nino left me. And now Rain has thrown me out. My own twin sister was plotting to kill me. My mother seemed happy I was dead. Tell me, God, if you are listening, did I do something wrong? All my life, all I ever wanted was something like acceptance. Love? Love was always beyond reach, something reserved for other people. For Beth or for the cool kids in school. For characters in storybooks. For 'normal' people who looked good. For my grandma's dog.

'Why not me?' I shout into the sky.

Nobody replies.

No one knows that I am missing. No one cares that I am gone. The only reason my mum and the cops want to find me is because they think I'm someone else. I peer down between my feet. It's a really long way down . . . Would anyone notice if I jumped? Would anyone give a shit?

When sorrows come, they come not single spies but in battalions.

I can't think of one reason to live.

DAY FOUR:
The Nun

LAST WEEK

Friday, 28 August 2015
Taormina, Sicily

The lampshade on Beth's bedside table casts a warm and crimson glow. Nino's face is half in light, half obscured by shadow. I lean in and kiss him on the mouth. I taste his tongue and his lips. We sink into one another. I lie down next to him on the bed, my body melting into his. I feel the heat rise from his skin, like he is made of flame. There is something so erotic about being in my sister's bed. The bed she shared with Ambrogio. They were sleeping here last week, but now they are both dead. I close my eyes and breathe Nino's scent, as his fingers run through my hair.

An owl calls in the garden. Is that a good omen or bad? Huh. I can't remember.

'You know,' says Nino, sitting up and looking me dead in the eye. 'I don't usually like Brits.' He lights a Marlboro Red, then passes it to me.

'Why not?' I say. I take a drag. 'What's wrong with Brits? You like *me*.'

'My papa was killed by an Englishman.'

'Oh. Right. Shit.'

'Enzo, his name was.'

Here we go. Where's the violin? It's time for a sob story.

I pass the Marlboro back again and place it in between his lips.

'I was fourteen when he died.'

'I think my dad might be dead too,' I say, 'but I don't know . . .'

He shakes his head and looks at me. '*I* know,' he says. 'I *saw* it.'

His eyes are wide. He looks spooked. Freaked out. I'll tell him about *my* dad later.

'Papa was fucked by an English guy. He had risked everything for this deal. An art deal. Fucking massive. It was going to change our lives for ever. It was better than winning the Lotto.'

He takes an angry drag on his fag, then turns and studies the floor.

'It was our chance to leave this island, to start a new life in America. Me, my mother, my three young sisters. I remember my papa coming home one night and kissing my mum.' His eyes lock on mine. They spark like fire. 'I'd never seen them kiss like that. It stuck in my mind . . .'

I wonder if he'll go down on me again. That was beyond impressive.

'He had found a buyer for a stolen picture: a painting of the Crucifixion by Antonello da Messina.'

He looks at me. I look back, blank. 'I don't know who that is,' I say. 'I just know the British ones.'

'Da Messina was a Sicilian artist of the Renaissance. He introduced oil painting to Italy. He was very influential.'

I nod. 'He sounds like the real deal. It must have been expensive.'

Nino crushes the life out of his fag as if it were that English guy.

'The buyer took the painting and ran. Left papa with a bullet in his shoulder. No painting, no money, no *niente* . . .'

I liked it when he fucked my ass; that was a revelation.

'The next day, I found him . . .'

'Found who where?'

'. . . hanging from the lemon tree at the bottom of our garden.'

'Oh my God. That sucks,' I say.

'His leather belt was round his neck. He had a fucking erection.'

'*What?*'

'He had only just died,' Nino says. 'Had only just killed himself. If I had been a few minutes quicker, I could have saved him. I could –'

'It's not your fault,' I say.

I massage his neck. It's rigid.

'I had to look after my young sisters. My mother's heart was broken. So I joined La Cosa Nostra, the family business.'

I gasp. 'You were *fourteen* when you started killing?' I feel a stab of jealousy. At that age I was just killing squirrels. Squirrels and Tamagotchis.

He looks at me, the whole world on his shoulders. '*Sì.*
Fourteen,' he says. 'It was me and Domenico. He was only
eleven.'

I wrap my arms round his neck and press my head into
his chest. 'I am so, so sorry, Nino.'

'It isn't your fault, Betta.' Nino reaches for my face. He
cups my chin in his hands. I feel warm fingers stroke my
cheek. 'I never told anyone that . . .'

I breathe his skin. I close my eyes. I can hear his heart
beating. This is the closest I've ever felt to any human
being ever. I want to tell him things that hurt. I want to
share this moment. I want to tell him everything. About
my dad and how he left. The fucked-up things that you
keep hidden. I want to tell him my real name . . . but I
don't want to lose him.

Chapter Fifteen

Thursday, 3 September, 2015
Trastevere, Rome, Italy

Sunrise. Pink sky. The birds have all just woken up. Above my head a big, black cloud of starlings swirl and spiral in a massive murmuration. The birds are fucking everywhere. In my face and in my hair. I'm stuck in the middle of a Hitchcock movie.

SQUAWK. SQUAWK. SQUAWK. SQUAWK. SQUAWK.

A sound like my mother's voice – terrible and witch-like – fills the chilly morning air. It's far worse than anything I have heard in my whole life. It's loud, high-pitched and ominous.

'Fuck off. Go on. Go away.'

What a way to wake up. *Really.* This is beyond a joke. I groan and swing my legs off the wall. Sit up and stretch it out. I am aching everywhere. That was the worst night's sleep of my life. My arm's gone dead from lying funny. It tingles with pins and needles. Who sleeps on *walls*? I mean, what was I thinking? This is worse than that time I passed out in the middle of a roundabout.

'You've reached a whole new level of crap decisions. Well done, Alvie. Bravo.'

OK, this time, Beth has a point. Not my finest moment. But why didn't someone rescue me? Like Princess Ann in *Roman Holiday*? Fine. Whatever. Who needs a hero? I'll just rescue myself. 'A woman needs a man like a fish needs a bicycle.' Gloria Steinem said that.

I peer over the other side of the wall. There's a sheer drop of twenty metres. Oh! That must be the Roman Forum down there. Rocks and columns and bits of marble are strewn across the sandy floor. It's bloody lucky I didn't roll off. I would have fallen to my death. A splat of Alvie/strawberry jelly. I know I fancied death last night, but that would have been a mess.

I ask someone the way to Trastevere. Eventually I find my flat. I climb the stairs and head for my bedroom. Put my phone on charge. There's a missed call from an unknown number. No new messages. No texts. I can't use Tinder to find Nino. I can't use that tracking app. For all I know, he's left the city. This is fucking hopeless.

'*So you're just going to give up?*' says Beth.

'I'm not giving up. No chance. Not ever.'

There has to be another way. This is 2015. I take a calculated risk and turn on my sister's phone.

Ping.

There's one new email from my mum, but I can't be bothered to read it.

I scroll through my sister's contacts. I don't know why, but maybe someone can help me? Anna, Bianca, Carla, Domenico . . .

Domenico? Why does that name ring a bell? I'm sure I've

heard it before. Perhaps he's someone from Taormina? Domenico? Domenico? Oh, now I remember: I met him last week. He was Nino's friend. Another one of Ambrogio's hitmen. But why did Beth have Domenico's number? Was she sleeping with him as well? Urgh, I hope not. He was rough as fuck. More Neanderthal than man. I can picture him now in that creepy wood. He was the one with the cement mixer and the beat-up pick-up truck. He poured cement on my twin sister. A nice guy. A delight. He's probably not mates with Nino any more, since Nino escaped Taormina. I doubt they parted on very good terms. I'm pretty sure he's livid. Nino left a trail of destruction behind him, a murdered priest and a burnt-down villa. He destroyed a painting worth thirty million dollars (if anyone asks, that was Nino, not me). I bet Domenico had a stake in the painting. They were all in on Ambrogio's deal. He royally screwed the lot of us over. I'll bet Domenico's mad like me.

Then I get a crazy idea.

I am going to call him. Yes. It's brilliant. Two heads are better than one. He's tough. He's rough. He's mean. He's perfect. We'll hunt Nino down together. We'll be BFFs.

I click on Domenico's number and call.

'Yeah,' says Beth, 'call Domenico. He's a sweetheart. Really nice. He'll be thrilled to hear from you. I bet he's missed your voice.'

I hang up. Swear under my breath. Sarcastic bitch. But what if she's right? Is Domenico after my blood too? Does he know I was Nino's accomplice? If I call him up and tell him where I am, will I have two mobsters on my ass? Things could go from bad to worse. The shit would hit the fan.

But what else can I do? I'm running on empty here. It was lucky that none of those birds shat on me, but honestly that's the extent of my luck. It's hardly an auspicious day. But you know what? I'll take a chance. I *am* going to call him.

Brrring, brrring, brrring.

'*Pronto*,' says Domenico.

Who does Domenico think I am? Am I Alvie or Beth? Am I *Nino*?

'*Pronto*,' Domenico says *again*. His voice is deep and gravelly. As rough as tonsillitis.

Shit. I don't know what to say.

He hangs up so I call him back. My hands are shaking, sweating . . .

Brrring, brrring, brrring, brrring.

Domenico helped us bury 'Alvina', so I've got to pretend to be Beth. The cops think they've found Alvie's body, so it makes sense. Though what if he's angry with me as well? Mad at *Beth*, I mean?

'*Sì. PRONTO*,' Domenico says. I think he's getting tense.

I swallow. Hard. OK. Here goes . . .

'It's me, Ambrogio's wife . . .'

'Elizabeth? WHERE IS NINO?'

Slabs of marble cast long shadows on the unmown grass. The sun is low in the red sky. I study the tombstone.

'This grave contains all that was mortal of a YOUNG ENGLISH POET,' it says. 'Here lies one whose name was writ in water. Feb 24th 1821'.

I sigh and shove the tiny spoon inside my tub of pistachio gelato.

If I were dead, it could be me. I'm an English poet.

He was only twenty-five when he died. That's the same age that I am now. And look at everything he achieved: 'Ode to a Grecian Urn', 'Endymion', 'When I have fears . . .', 'To Autumn', 'Bright star . . .' I know, I'm under no illusions. Keats was a better poet than me. My haikus show potential, it's true. I'm impressed I make the effort at all. The height of art for my generation is taking a shit and then taking a photo and posting it on Instagram. Some of my haikus verge on genius; there is no denying that. But I shouldn't compare myself to Keats. He was a master. One of a kind. A *little* bit better than me.

The graveyard's filled with statues of angels and sculptures of women draped with robes. Some of the graves are a hundred years old. It's beautiful. And creepy. Death is fucking *everywhere*. It's under the surface, so you can't see it. But dig down a couple of feet and it's coffins and maggots and bones.

I've neglected my poetry of late. I've been so caught up with all this killing. That's really where my talents lie. I suppose I should focus on that. I'll give it my best shot. Keats may have been the better poet, but I am way better at death. 'Alvie Knightly: Murderess'. Man, that sounds romantic. That's what I want on my tombstone. That and some TayTay lyrics.

I finish off the ice cream and then lick out the tub. I throw the plastic spoon on the grave. I don't have any flowers. The pink spoon is kind of pretty. A pop of neon in the sun. The only colour among the greens and browns and greys and blacks.

I'm going to focus on the killing. I'll make a career of that. I google 'Dark Web' on my phone, but it's not that easy. I have to download something called Tor. It takes a couple of minutes. When I get on I have a browse. I search 'Hitman to hire'. There are hundreds, no *thousands*, of contract killers offering their services. All you need is a website and some software so people can pay. I don't need a 'boss'. Don't need a *partner*. I can work freelance for myself. I'll have to get paid in something called bitcoins, but I'm all right with that. I click into a couple of hitman websites. One them offers to 'neutralize' your ex, but where's the fun in that? No, I'm going to do it myself. That's far more satisfying. I channel my inner Emmeline Pankhurst or Mary Wollstonecraft. I am an independent woman. Hear that, Nino? Just watch.

The going rate for a single hit is about $10,000. Not bad, I guess. (I'd do it for free. I'd do it for the rush.) One site boasts that they always make the victims' deaths look like suicides. Ha ha. No way. Not me. No chance. I'm going to have some kind of symbol. A calling card, like a spray-paint tag. I want the world to recognize me. I don't want to be *anonymous*. What's the fucking point in that? They'll never catch me – I'll make sure of that – but I'll go down in history. I'll be fucking infamous. I'll star in real-life crime documentaries. Be the subject of non-fiction books. Now what would be an awesome tag? Something to get me noticed? Perhaps a smiley face drawn in lipstick on the victims' chests? Or maybe I'll paint their nails lime green. No one else would think of that . . .

I click on a few more sites (they're all 'hitmen', there are no 'hitwomen'). They all seem to feature a blacked-out model posing with a gun. Some of them have rules, I see: 'No kids', 'No politicians'. Otherwise, anyone's game. Oh my God. I can't wait to get started. It's going to be SO MUCH FUN. I'll create a super-fancy website on Wordpress or something. Then I'll type up my CV and upload it, then wait for the phone to ring.

Curriculum Vitae
~~Name: Miss. Alvina Knightly~~
~~Name: Mrs Elizabeth Knightly Caruso~~
Name: TBC
Email: Just tweet me @AlvinaKnightly69

I am a highly motivated and talented killer, looking for a breakthrough role as a professional hitwoman (a bit like Angelina Jolie in *Mr. & Mrs. Smith*).

Qualifications:

• None

Experience:

• Murdering my twin sister
• Bludgeoning her husband to death (in self-defence)

- Killing a really old and annoying priest in cold blood
- Chopping up fish at a discount Japanese sushi restaurant
- Shooting ~~two~~ ~~three~~ several Mafia hitmen
- Classified advertising sales representative
- Massacring a mugger
- I did three days' work experience with an experienced assassin from the Cosa Nostra this summer
  ~~He didn't think I was very good, though.~~
  He thought I was a natural-born killer

Hobbies:

- Tweeting Channing, Taylor and Miley
- Mr Dick (eleven-inch vibrating dildo)
- Coke, speed, weed, hash, ketamine, ecstasy, MDMA
- Martini, Pinot Grigio, grappa, WKD Blue, Bloody Marys, Malibu, gin (either straight up or with tonic. I don't care which kind of tonic, but definitely not slimline), Absolut vodka, Smirnoff vodka, Grey Goose vodka (if it's on offer in Tesco's)
- Watching a wide variety of international porn
- Writing haikus

Skills:

- I can speak English ~~quite well~~ ~~really well~~ fucking exceptionally
- Basic Italian (swear words ~~from watching the afore-mentioned foreign porn~~ from absorbing the rich language and culture while living in Sicily)

- Killing
- I know 326 different sexual positions

References:

- Giannino Maria Brusca (Nino). Address: no idea
  (If you find him, tell him I'm coming for him)

Ping.
It's my burner phone.
I click into the message.
Ooh, it's from Domenico.
'DOWNSTAIRS', it says.

Chapter Sixteen

The River Tiber, Rome, Italy

An angry ape or pissed-off grizzly? A rabid, hungry man-eating zombie? Domenico looks like all your worst nightmares featuring a killer. *Baddie* is written all over his face. Broken, snouty nose. He is two hundred pounds of mean standing right outside my flat. And he is not alone. He's brought two rough-looking heavies with him. I wasn't expecting *that*. It suddenly occurs to me that Nino might be here as well . . . I take a step back.

'Elizabeth?' Domenico says. 'You look . . . different.'

He holds me in a tight embrace and cracks a couple of my ribs. Now remember, Alvie, you are *Beth*. He thinks you're his dead boss's wife. I'd better dial up the blonde and dial down the bloodlust . . .

'As soon as I heard that *stronzo* was here, I came straight away,' he says. 'Do you know the shit I've had to deal with ever since he left town? I've got Don Russo's guys on my ass. Nino killed Franco Motisi.'

'Oh no, that's awful,' I say. 'Bad day at the office.'

Domenico shakes his hog-like head.

'This is Riccardo and Giuseppe.' He gestures to the men.

Like Rosencrantz and Guildenstern, except that they are dead.

Riccardo is tall and very thin with shaved-off hair and weird crossed eyes. Giuseppe is short and very fat. He's either nine months pregnant with twins or has a beer belly; he's as wide tall as he is tall. There's a bullet-shaped scar on his left temple (someone obviously just missed). He smells of something like beef jerky. He's missing a couple of teeth. I stare at them, then notice the bags. They aren't exactly travelling light. There are three bulging suitcases. A violin case. A hatbox. What's all this? A travelling circus? Are they planning on staying the night?

I let them through and they dump the cases just inside the entrance hall.

Then Domenico grabs my arm.

'Hey, what're you doing?'

'You disappeared. You and that *stronzo*. And Ambrogio is dead. I want to know what the hell's going on. Come with me,' he says.

'Where are we going?'

'We're taking a walk.'

'Hey. Get off. Let me go.'

He pushes me out on to the street and slams the door behind him. Riccardo takes my other arm and I freak the fuck out. I struggle and strain, but there's no point. There are *three* of them and *one* of me. That carving knife is out of reach inside my Prada bag. Fuck, this was a bad idea. I should have listened to Beth. Riccardo and Domenico frogmarch me across the street and down some stairs to the river. We walk along the Tiber till we get to an old bridge.

'Now will you let me go?'

Nobody replies.

We're standing underneath the bridge. It's dark and grimy. Dirty. The water is black and apparently deep. A damp smell. Something rotten. My guess is corpses and dead fish. I gag. It's all I can do not to vomit. He is going to throw me in. This is it. The end.

Domenico reaches into his jacket to reveal a gargantuan gun. His hand slides past it, further along. My eyes stay on the gun. The handle's engraved with golden initials: 'D. O. M'. That's him. Oh man, that's one mean-looking weapon. Just the kind of thing I need. I wish I could steal that one, but it's not looking promising. Domenico pulls out a tin cigar box. He offers one to me. What's all this? *The last cigar?* Fuck it. I'll take one. I pick a smoke and stroke its smooth and crisp tobacco shell. I breathe its loamy scent: rain-soaked earth. I can't wait to burn it. Domenico sparks up a long match. I lean in and light it up. I roll the smoke around my mouth. I might as well enjoy it.

'So, you saw him?' Domenico says.

He's asking about Nino. That's good. Must mean that he's not *here*.

'Yeah.' I nod. 'I did.'

'Why are *you* chasing him?' he asks.

'The money . . . he stole the money,' I say. 'For the Caravaggio.'

Domenico shakes his head. 'That fucking painting. That fucking guy. You let him get away?'

'He was at the Piazza di Spagna yesterday. I lost him on the underground.'

'*Minchia*,' growls Domenico. He glares at me.

Hopefully he just wants to *chat*. I can do that. No one gets hurt. But it's an odd place for a catch-up. And there's no way to escape. The other two guys stand and stare without saying a single word. They don't give the impression there's much going on beyond those vacant rolling eyeballs. But I could be wrong. I shouldn't judge. They could be quantum physicists with part-time jobs in the mob.

Domenico looks up at Giuseppe then nods towards my handbag. Giuseppe snatches my Prada bag and empties it out on the ground.

'Be careful with that. It's new,' I say.

The bag falls in the mud. Bits of shit and grit on the leather. Everything spills and rolls around. Riccardo eyes my cuckoo clock. (He doesn't know there's money inside.) Giuseppe bends over and picks up my knife. Hands it to Domenico.

'What is this?' Domenico says.

He turns the knife around in his hands, inspecting the serrated blade. He runs his thumb along the edge, then hurls it in the river. It disappears with a splash. There goes another weapon . . .

Domenico spots Nino's phone. He bends down and picks it up.

He recognizes it.

'I . . . I can explain.'

He brushes some dirt off the cover.

'I was tracking him with an app.' I wait for that genius move to sink in. 'But then he sent his phone to Romania with some skanky tramp. I managed to retrieve the phone . . . but Nino wasn't there.'

The mobsters look at one another and then burst out in violent laughter.

'He sent his phone . . . ?' Domenico says. 'He sent his phone to *Romania*?'

'It isn't fucking funny.'

Riccardo and Giuseppe are both bent double, creased with laughter.

'Shut the fuck up. It's not fucking funny.'

I suck on my cigar. Cough. Cough. (Oh, now I remember. Just like Bill Clinton smoking pot, you're not supposed to inhale.)

The heavies wipe the tears from their eyes and try to resume straight faces.

'I'm not laughing. We lost him,' I say.

I'm glad they're entertained.

'I don't believe you,' Domenico says.

'Well, it's true,' I say. 'Can I fix my bag?'

Nobody replies. I repack all my dirty stuff. Urgh, my bag is filthy. This is getting ridiculous. Now I've only got one left. Oh, why did I buy them in cream?

Domenico turns his attention back to Nino's mobile phone. He taps the screen.

'You won't be able to see anything. He's locked it with a PIN.' Domenico types in a four-digit code.

'How did you know that?'

'Twenty years we've been working together. You don't think I know his birthday?' he says.

'Oh, when is it? Just out of interest.'

'The fifth of September.'

'Ace.'

Ooh, I think that's Saturday, isn't it? (Not that I care. I'm not buying him a present.)

Domenico scrolls through Nino's phone. 'He deleted his call history and all his messages . . . But not his contact list,' he says. '*Si. Si.* I know this person. They are here in Rome.'

Domenico turns the phone round to show me the details of someone.

'Dynamite,' he says.

'Cool name.' I wish I'd thought of it first. I think I might steal it.

'They're a contact of ours in Trastevere.'

'So . . .' I say. 'Nino could be with them?'

Domenico looks over and nods at his heavies. They grab my arms *again*.

'Hey, not the river,' I say.

They march me out from under the bridge towards a rusty fence.

'What the . . . ? Where are you taking me?'

My cigar falls to the ground.

Domenico follows close behind. He hisses something in my ear.

'If I discover you are working with him, you are dead. You got that?'

The mobsters grab the back of my head and shove it through the iron bars.

'Ow. What? Why? Fuck. No. No. No. I'm not. I swear. Let me go. LET ME OUT.'

I grip the railings in my hands. My face is wedged right through the gap. I try to pull my head back out, but my ears are stuck and it's totally jammed. I've got my head trapped in the railings.

SHIT FUCK SHIT FUCK SHIT.

I hear the mobsters' footsteps slowly fade, fade, fade away.

'Come back. Come back. I can help you,' I call.

I hear them laugh.

It's worth a shot.

'Nino, he likes me. He's got a crush . . .'

Silence. Nothing. They've gone.

Chapter Seventeen

I try to pull my head out again but the cartilage in my ears goes *crack*.

'OW.'

What the hell? This is so unfair. I'm going to get cauliflower ears like a beat-up rugby player. I don't believe it. I can't move. What am I going to do? Breathe, Alvina, breathe, breathe. If you got *in*, then you can get *out* again. It's basic physics. A universal law. Come on, Alvie. GIRL, YOU GOT THIS. I pull again: IT HURTS. This is never going to work. I rest my chin on the wall at the bottom and whimper a little bit.

Beth's laughing hysterically in my head. She's having a fucking field day.

I try to yank my skull back through, but somehow it seems wider this way. It's still wedged in good and proper. I hyperventilate. What if Nino sees me here? I'm an easy target. A sitting duck. I've got to get out. No time to lose. What I need is some kind of lube. If only I had some K-Y Jelly . . . But then I remember. In my bag. There's that emergency bottle of Durex Play that I bought at the chemist's. If I can just reach . . . I hook my toes through the straps and pick it up with my right foot. I lift it towards my hand. Reach inside and grab the tube. Yes. Yes. This has to work. It's one of my brilliant ideas. I squeeze a big blob in my palm and rub it all over my ears. It's wet and slippery. It's *perfect*. I take a deep breath – *one, two, three* – and pull my head back through the bars.

Yes. I'm free. At last.

I crash down on the ground and catch my breath. Then something strange happens. A hot sensation. Holy fuck, my ears are burning. Why the hell are my ears on fire?

Hot. Hot. Hot. Hot. What is going on? I flap at the sides of my face with my hands. I need some ice. I need water. I rush over to the river, kneel down and splash water on to my burning ears. I spot the lube on the floor: it's Durex Play Warming. Oh. Right. I forgot. It isn't *hot*, just a *warming* sensation. I'm going to be all right.

I lie down on the ground and scrunch up my eyes. But I'm not *Beth*; I'm not going to *cry*. I might be drenched in stinking water . . . But I'm free and I'm Alvina Knightly. I'm getting back on the fucking horse. I don't need anyone helping me out, especially not those Cro-Magnons. I'll find Dynamite by myself. But first I need some wheels.

I climb the stairs up to the street then scan the road. A cab? A bus? A helicopter? Nothing. I need to get a car of my own. But not a Rent-a-Car. I'm not giving Enterprise my details. I don't have a licence anyway. There's no way that they'd loan me a car. I need to go off the grid before those guys come back. I don't think my ears could take any more.

I turn the corner into a quiet street. An obese man stands by his car. The door of his Fiat Cinquecento hangs open. It's a pretty duck-egg blue. It's the tiniest car I've ever seen. It looks like an old paint can. It was probably made in the fifties or sixties with a curving bonnet and silver bumper and goggly bug-eyes. I can hear the little engine humming. I want it. It is *mine*. The man bends over to pull a newspaper from a dispenser on the street. Then he turns back to the car.

'I'll take that,' I say, sprinting over.

I grab the paper from his hands. Then shove the man out of the way and jump inside his car. I throw the paper on the back seat. Make sure the doors are locked.

'No. *Aspetta. Aspetta*,' he says.

His face appears at the bottom of the window. He grabs on to the handle and pulls on the door.

'Sorry, I need it. *Mi dispiace*.'

Oh my God, it's a sardine tin. Even smaller than it looks. My head's pressed up against the ceiling. Was it built for a child? For an elf? How the hell did *he* fit in here? The man's stomach is at eye level. I spot a hefty roll of flab flap over his waistband. The air inside smells stale and musty. The stench of several decades of driving fills my nose and makes me gag. The seat is lumpy and broken. Hard. A metal spring sticks up my ass. The man's red face is now pressed up against the side window. I try to drive, but stall the car.

He bangs hard on the roof.

'*Esci dalla mia macchina*.'

'Go away. Get another one.'

I turn the key in the ignition. It coughs and splutters,

but doesn't start. You have got to be kidding me. What a joke. Why of all the millions of vehicles . . . ? This is the worst ever getaway car. I try again to floor the gas. The Cinquecento groans and wheezes. Chokes but doesn't start. Oh man, it's ancient. Broken down. I'll try just one more time. I slam my foot down on the pedal. Twist the stupid key. Eventually it comes to life. Fucking *finally*. I swerve out from the kerb and hit the gas. The man's still holding on to the door. I'm dragging him along the road, like that lady with the dachshund. Oh God, just let it go.

'I'll bring it back when I'm done,' I say.

I stick it in second gear. The engine growls an angry growl, but the car doesn't seem to go any faster. It's like trying to ride a clockwork mouse. I'm doing 15 mph. It would have been quicker to *walk*. My heartbeat's faster than this car. At last the man goes 'ARGH,' and lets go of the door. He stumbles after me for a while, waving his arms and shouting, '*TORNA INDIETRO*'. I watch his figure fade away in the rear-view mirror. He's huffing and puffing and waving his fist. It's amazing he tried to run at all; he doesn't look very fit.

Where am I going? Maybe back to that club? Rain said Mafia types hang around there. I'll go back and ask around. Surely someone will know Dynamite?

I grab the newspaper from the back seat as I chug down a dusty back street, and start leafing through the pages. I check the news for any developments on my sister's case. I'm looking for 'Alvina Knightly' or 'Elizabeth Caruso'. I check the headlines, but there's nothing. Scan the pics, but they're not of me. I chuck the paper in the back. Glance up through the windscreen.

Ooh, look, what's that?

There's a gladiator on a Segway. He's wheeling along the street at about three miles an hour. Holy fuck. This guy is *fit*. Is it Russell Crowe? No, it's not. Naked torso, sculpted pecs, a deep, dark tan from the summer sun. He's wearing a silver helmet with a bright red feather. A glinting shield and shiny sword. Serious six-pack. Leather skirt. Awesome flowing cape. Old-fashioned sandals lace up his legs and over his bronzed and bulging calves. Oh God, I love Italian men, especially ancient Romans. I watch his bum glide by. I know, I know. I've sworn off men. But I'd make an exception for this guy. I want to take him home with me and keep him as a sex slave. I'd chain him to the bed and . . . No, no, no. I can't do that. Just look at the size of him; he'd be too expensive to feed. The gladiator turns the corner. I crane my neck and watch his perfect ass go by. His little skirt barely covers his bits; it waves and flaps in the wind. I could at least follow him?

No. *Dynamite.*

I look up to see a nun. Where the hell did *she* come from? God, it's like Piccadilly Circus. She's trying to cross the road. I honk the horn, but she's still in my path. She's in the middle of the street, walking slowly and unsteadily. Her back is bent and all hunched up. She leans on a walking stick. She looks a bit like Mother Teresa, but dressed all in black, just like Darth Vader, Marilyn Manson or Simon Cowell. It's cool. I like her look.

I wind the window down and shout, 'Move. Get out of the way.'

I'm not slowing down. Not now. I can't. It took me this long to speed up. I'm doing twenty-six miles an hour; any second now . . . I'll be able to get it in third.

'Move. Move.'

I honk the horn and try to swerve the car.

BANG. WHACK.

'Damn.'

Chapter Eighteen

It's not my fault. She came out of nowhere. It's like she had a death wish.

My eyes flick up to the rear-view mirror. I see her lying on the ground. There she is, like a hit-and-run bird, sprawled out in the middle of the road. Fuck, fuck. This wasn't the plan. I can't just leave her there. What if she's hurt? She's *definitely* hurt. Oh shit, what if I've killed her? I know I want to be an assassin. But not like *this*. Not *now*.

I should go, but she might have seen me. What if she has a photographic memory and remembers my face or the licence plate? Oh man, this is the last thing I need. At least this isn't my car.

I scan the street. There's no one else here. I slam on the brakes.

I leave the Cinquecento running; the engine chug, chug, chugs. The door swings open and I jump out and run over to the nun. I watch as her chest rises and falls. Good. She is still alive. I bend down and study her face. She's old; I'd guess eighty-five? The skin on her cheek looks wrinkled and soft. It's fine like crêpe de Chine. She smells clean, just like fresh laundry. But now her wimple's creased and dirty, soiled from the fall. She's bleeding from the side of her head and blood snakes down in a line to her neck. Shit,

I didn't mean to hit her. What am I going to do? She opens her eyes and looks up at me. They're pale blue, like Rain's. I cup her chin. Her eyelids flicker and she peers into my face. We share some kind of intimate moment . . .

'Oh man, I'm sorry,' I say.

She groans – her moan almost inaudible – and says something in quiet Italian. I look again, both ways down the street. It's clear, but for how long? I am going to have to hurry. I don't want anyone to spot me. It's just a matter of time before those psychos track me down again. Or Nino. Or the fucking police.

I study her prostrate figure. Her long black habit has track marks on it. Now I see her eyes are closed. She seems kind of *flat*. I reach for her wrist to feel her pulse; her arm is frail and light. She looks so peaceful lying there . . .

Suddenly – she gasps. Her whole body spasms and she sits up.

'ARGH,' I scream. 'WHAT THE ACTUAL FUCK?'

I jump up, trip over her legs and fall down to the ground.

Definitely not dead then.

'Come on, get up,' I say to the nun. 'You can't stay here. Come with me.'

She reaches her hands towards my throat like some evil Catholic zombie. Her fingers are cold; they grip my neck.

'*Demone*,' she says. '*Demone.*'

Her grip is weak and I shake myself free.

'URGH. Get off. Get off me.'

I hook my hands under her arms and try to pick her up.

'Come on, stand up. Get in the car.'

I haul her over to the Fiat, huffing and puffing and sweating and swearing. A trickle of blood trails red on the road. It looks just like wet paint. There's nothing I can do about that. Perhaps it will rain and wash it away? It will be all right. I'll be OK. Chop-chop. Get on with it, Alvie. There's no time for fucking around. Someone could come at any minute. I open the door and push her inside.

'*Ospedale*,' she says.

'*Ospedale?* What's that? Hospital?'

I slam the passenger door.

I need a fucking cigarette. Or something strong to calm my nerves. I swallow the last of the painkillers I got for my new nose. I jump inside the Cinquecento and spark up a Marlboro Light. I take a deep breath. OK. That's better. The fag hangs out of the corner of my mouth as I crank the gear into first. The motor groans, just like the nun now sitting slumped in the passenger seat. The ancient Fiat bumps and lurches and the top of my head rams into the ceiling. The wheels skid and scream. Bump. Bump. Bump. Bump. Over the cobblestones. I wish this bra had more support. It's not made for this rough terrain.

I do nought to ten in twenty seconds. This is ridiculous. If I had a *proper* car, I wouldn't have to deal with this. A Maserati or Ferrari. None of this dicking around. I try for third. The cogs catch and grind. I floor the clutch and just shove it. Why didn't I steal an automatic? Oh man, this is hard work.

I grip the steering wheel tight and sweat drips down my brow. I'm panting.

The nun is moaning. There's blood on her habit and in her hair. She's bleeding all over the passenger seat. It looks like an abattoir. There's no way I can return the car now. Sorry not sorry, mate.

I speed off along the street at 22 mph. I look around for witnesses . . . But that gladiator's gone. That's when I see her coming out of a gate. Oh my God. Am I dreaming? *Another* nun is standing there, right on the fucking corner. Bloody hell. It's *rife* out here. How many nuns are there? A sign on the walls says '*Convento*'. Oh. A convent. I guess that makes sense.

' "Get thee to a nunnery . . . To a nunnery, go",' I say.

Hopefully she didn't see anything. I'm sure she wasn't there before. I'm going to have to just leave it now. I can't kidnap her as well.

'*Ospedale,*' she says again.

'I can't take you to hospital. They'll see my face. They'll see the car. They'll know *I* did this to you.'

Shit. What am I going to do?

She groans.

'Just let me think.'

'*Bravo, Alvie,*' says my twin. '*First a priest and now a nun. You've reached a whole new low.*'

Goddamnit, she's right. I don't want to kill her. I don't want her to die. She was just an accident. Wrong place. Wrong girl. Wrong time.

'OK. OK. *Ospedale,*' I say.

The nun doesn't reply.

This is a massive pain in my ass. She's wasting my time. I'm a woman on a mission. She's *really* crossed the line.

I spot a sign by the side of the road: '*Ospedale San Giovanni*'.

'See that? That's lucky. It's your lucky day.'

Again with the silent treatment.

I'll just . . . drop her off. And then I'll leg it. As fast as I can in this bag of rust. I swerve to the right and follow the signs. Pull over by the kerb. If I just roll her out of the car and leave her somewhere near the main entrance, then someone will find her in no time at all. She'll be right as rain.

I reach into my handbag for Nino's hat. Pull the fedora down over my face. It's not ideal, but it's better than nothing. OK, here we go.

I look over at the nun. She is very pale. Her head's flopped back against the rest and her mouth hangs open.

Oh.

Her eyes have rolled back in their sockets.

I watch her chest.

It isn't moving.

Oh God.

Not now.

Not *this*.

I slap her. Hard.

'Come on. Wake up.'

I listen for her breath.

Fuck.

Why *me*?

Now she's *really* dead.

My stomach sinks. There's a lump in my throat. What have I done? How did this happen?

Shut up, Alvie. Deal with it. Don't you want to be a mobster? A fucking *hitwoman*?

I feel sick. I don't think I can do it. Beth was right, I am pathetic. I'm going to need therapy for this one. I'm going to have to call Lorraine, that counsellor from school.

She'll be back to torment me. Every nun will have her face. I'll see her in my dreams.

I floor the gas and skid the Fiat out into the busy road. The nun's head bob-bob-bobs beside me, like one of those nodding dogs. Now what am I going to do with her? All this shit is slowing me down. Giving me grief. Cramping my style. I'm running out of time. I need to find Radio Londra. I want to get to Dynamite before Domenico does. But now I've got to lose this body. Everything's going wrong.

I drive until I leave the city far, far behind me. The sun is setting on the horizon. The sky is the colour of blood. The adrenaline rush is wearing off. I drive and drive and drive. I must not fall asleep, even though I'm tired, so tired of all this shit. I stare at the road and blink, blink, blink. I stifle a sleepy yawn. The moon comes out. The stars. My eyelids are heavy and weak. I consider propping them open with toothpicks or matches or knitting needles, anything to stop them from closing. But I don't have any of those things and they're closing all by themselves. The road is long and straight and endless. I can see the black of the sea up ahead. I won't stop till I get to the shore. Perhaps Nino will emerge from the water, like one of those guys in *Ex on the Beach*. We'll have a screaming blazing row, and then we'll make it up. This crazy feud will all be over. He will give me back my cash. 'Alvie,' he'll say (he'll know my name), 'I missed you. I'm so sorry . . .' We'll make love right then and there on the sand. On a towel so it doesn't get gritty. My eyes close again and my head flops down on to the steering wheel.

Ping.

A new message. I check my phone. It's Nino. Now what does he want?

'WANT TO HAVE PHONE SEX?'

I kind of do.

'NO, I'M NOT TALKING TO YOU.' I hit send.

Huh. That's funny. It's like he knew I was thinking about him. Dreaming about make-up sex. Perhaps we have a psychic bond? Perhaps *his* ears were burning?

I yawn. I need to stop the car. I rub my eyes and look around for somewhere to park. The road is surrounded by towering pine trees. I'm deep in a forest. Great. I'm lost. How the hell did I end up here? It looks haunted. Deathly quiet. It's perfect for me, actually. It looks like a good place to hide a corpse.

I turn the steering wheel slowly and drive into the trunk of a tree. The car goes THUD – and the windscreen cracks. Then I fall asleep.

DAY FIVE:

The Hooker

SEVENTEEN YEARS AGO

Friday, 19 June 1998
St Basil's Junior School,
Lower Slaughter, Gloucestershire

'Answer the question please, Alvina.'
I fidget in the lumpy chair. The material's all sharp and scratchy on my thighs under my skirt. The 'counsellor' is studying me from behind her plastic clipboard. I don't like her and she doesn't like me. She wants me to call her 'Lorraine'. The window is open, but it's still hot. The higher up you go in this building the hotter it gets. That's 'physics'. It's summer now and this is a 'heatwave'. But we're only on the ground floor. I can see some kids messing around in the playground. I wish I was out there too. Kicking the football into the teachers. Beating them all at kiss-chase. I look at my shoes, at the scuffed black leather, at the mud that's caked to the sides from the field. There's a blade of grass still stuck to the inside of one of the mucky soles. I swing my legs. There's a cut on my knee. It's started to scab and it's pink at the edges. I didn't want a stupid plaster. I'm not a *wuss*, like Beth.

'I don't want to talk to you,' I say, hissing like I'm spitting out feathers. 'I want to go home.'

'You've only just got here,' the counsellor says. 'Let's try another question.' She bites the top of her chewed-up pen. 'Do you know why you're here?'

I shoot her a look. It's my *best* look. A look designed to scare. I narrow my eyes. Glare through my fringe.

'The car,' I snap. It's got to be that. Grown-ups always go nuts about fire. 'It wasn't me. I didn't do it. I didn't burn it down.' I know that's not *true*, but it's worth a shot. Sometimes it's OK to lie. Sometimes, like every day. 'Little white lies' they're called. They're ace. They get you out of trouble.

'Alvina, the head said he *saw* you do it.'

'It wasn't me, it was Beth.' She raises an eyebrow. That's not going to cut it. Beth is a suck-up teacher's pet. She is Little Miss Perfect. 'OK. Fine. So what if I did? That was last week anyway.'

I'd almost forgotten about it.

I don't see why it's such a big deal. It was a horrible rusty old car with peeling paint and an ugly shape. It looked like a four-year-old had built it. Nobody is going to miss it. Now he can buy a nice new one.

The counsellor sighs. She smells like soup, that gloopy stuff they serve in the canteen. I don't trust *that* and I don't trust *her* and I don't eat anything green.

'Let's start from the beginning,' she says.

I let out a growl like an angry cat. We're going to be here all day. I'll miss *Round the Twist* on TV. I need to plan my escape. I want to get up and run away, leave the school and never come back. Perhaps I could go and live in the playground in the village park?

'The headmaster told me what you asked him . . .'

'I didn't ask him *anything*.'

'He said you asked him to marry your mum. Is that why you set fire to his car?'

I hear a high-pitched humming noise: louder and louder and louder and LOUDER. It's like a plane's taking off in my head. I screw up my eyes and cover my ears. But the noise is still there . . .

'Alvina?'

I can still hear her voice. It's smaller. Softer. It sounds like shouting underwater. Sometimes I like to hold my breath and sit down for as long as I can on the bottom of the swimming pool. The water is cold and you feel so alone. It's like outer space. I open my eyes and shake my head. The sound's still ringing in my ears.

'Were you cross with the headmaster because he wouldn't marry your mum?'

'Mum didn't want to marry *him* either.'

Urgh. He's such a demon headmaster, just like that show on CBBC. I thought he was nice, but he's not. I was wrong. He's just like all the others. The caretaker. The gardener. Jenny Anthony's step-dad . . .

'Is everything all right at home? Do you miss your dad?'

I pick at the crusty bits that have formed round the edge of my new scab. I pull some off and feel the sting. A shiny blob of blood.

'Let's go back to sports day,' she says.

'I don't want to talk about *that*.'

I jump up. My hands ball into fists. I feel my heartbeat in my ears. I'm too hot in my wool cardigan. I tie it round my waist. Pull the arms in a tight knot.

'Sit down, please. Have a biscuit,' she says.

She pulls the lid off a metal tin that's sitting on the coffee table. She offers me a digestive. Finally. I'm starving. I had been wondering what was in there. I thought it *might* be biscuits. I take three and then sit down. She puts the lid back on the tin so I can't take any more. She pushes her glasses back up her nose and then she tries again.

'Can you tell me what happened at the parents' race?'

The rule was one kid, one adult, and Mum and Beth ran together. I look at the clock on the wall by the door. The slow hand drags like it's stuck in Pritt Stick.

'OK, let's talk about something else . . .' She shuffles the papers on her clipboard. 'We had a complaint. From Mandy Simms. She said that you attacked her dad? Do you remember giving her father a nosebleed?'

'HE WAS DRESSED AS A CLOWN.' (And he wouldn't marry my mother either.)

She writes something down.

'Can I go yet? I'm bored,' I say. The hands on the clock still haven't moved.

'What happened in art class today?'

I stare at a poster on the wall. It's an advert for something called 'Childline'. The girl in the photograph looks sad. But she can't be sadder than I am. There's a number you have to call: 0800 something. If I called it, what would happen?

Would somebody rescue me? But I can't call it anyway. I'm not allowed to use the phone and I don't have twenty p.

The counsellor is talking at me. 'You were supposed to be making Father's Day cards . . .'

I leap up and push over the coffee table. The biscuit tin and her mug go flying. There's a massive BANG and the counsellor says, 'What the fuck?' She's covered in tea.

I run and make a leap for the window; I fly through it and I'm free.

'Fuck'? What's that? A new swear word? I like it. I'm going to keep it.

I fall to the ground and I'm face down on concrete. The cut on my knee opens up again. A line of blood flows down to my sock; the cotton turns bright red. I wipe the grit off my palms on to my skirt then sprint over to the gate. I push through it and I'm gone. I run and run as fast as I can, past the kids holding hands with their dads as they go out for ice creams or to kick footballs in the park. Perhaps they're going to watch a movie? It's Friday night. That's a dad night.

I slow to a stop. I don't know where I'm going. Don't want to go home and see Beth or Mum. I stand in the middle of the road, my heart BU-BUMP BU-BUMPS. Now where do I go? I take a street to the park. I run to the tallest tree and climb up. I hide out beneath the leaves. I'll stay here until it gets dark.

I scrape 'ALVIE' in the bark with my nail. Then I carve out 'FUK'. I lean my head against the trunk and close my eyes. That night, I sleep in the tree and I dream about finding my dad.

Chapter Nineteen

Friday, 4 September 2015
Ostia, Rome, Italy

I wake up in the car on the edge of a wood, my forehead stuck to the steering wheel. I try to sit up, but blast the horn.

BEEEEEEEEEEEEEEEEEEEEEEP.

What am I doing in a forest? I remember that time I slept in a tree. I was only eight or nine years old. I'd almost forgotten that. I'd woken up stiff and freezing cold, with leaves in my hair and ants in my pants. I was balanced on the upmost branch. It's amazing I didn't fall out. My mum went nuts at me the next day. I've never seen her so mad. She wasn't cross because I'd stayed out. She was angry because I came back.

The nun's flopped in the passenger seat. Her face is flat against the dash. I prod her, but she doesn't move. She's cold. Not breathing. Still dead. I really didn't mean to kill her. Now what am I going to do with her corpse? She was an accident. A mistake. I feel kind of bad. Almost *guilty*. It's just like that time I ate ten chocolate Pop-Tarts all in one go back in Archway. I shouldn't have done that. I lean her back in the passenger seat, close her eyes and stroke her face.

'I really am sorry,' I say. 'This was never part of the plan. If it makes you feel any better, you won't have to hang with my sister in heaven.'

She doesn't reply.

My mouth is dry and my throat is sore. My shoulders and the back of my neck are sizzling, scorching, hot. The sun is high up in the sky, its laser rays piercing through the glass: magnifying, intensifying. Oh my God, it's crazy hot. It feels like my skin is about to ignite. It's that Durex Play all over again . . . I must have slept for too long in the sun. What time is it? Twelve o'clock? I check my (still wrong) cuckoo clock. I do a quick scan – head to toe – of my body. Nothing's broken. Nothing hurts (except for my nose, which is still a bit tender. I check it out in the rear-view: hot). I study the crack in the broken windscreen. A spidery cobweb spreads through the glass. I can't have been going fast enough to do any real damage. It was more of a nudge than a crash. But the car is wedged at a funny angle, tipping over at forty-five degrees. It's making me feel kind of seasick, off balance. I need to get out of here.

What is this shit? A nun? A forest? What the hell am I doing here anyway? I'm surrounded by branches and foliage. Trees and hedges. Wild flowers. An earthy smell and dirt. Decay. This isn't central Rome. How long was I driving for? Did I drive to Umbria? *Tuscany?* I turn the key in the ignition and try to reverse the car . . .

But it doesn't start. Ace. Fucking fantastico. I've only had this car five minutes and I've already written it off. I check the gas, but the tank's not empty. Perhaps the engine overheated. The metal melted in the sun. No great loss. It was antique, on its last legs anyway. By the looks of its faded and dated interior – cream plastic steering wheel, beige leather seats, silver dials, a tiny mirror, small round retro speedometer – this thing is fifty years old. I try to open the driver's-side door, but it's stuck firm against a tree. I lean over the dead nun and try the passenger side. That door won't budge either. Oh my God, I'm trapped inside. I'm captive, like a hamster or a goldfish. I sit and scowl in the boiling car; it's heating up like a Hanoi whorehouse.

What fresh hell is this?

I crawl over the seats till I'm in the trunk. There's some kind of metal can. I pick it up, shake it a bit and give it a sniff. It's petrol. Or possibly diesel. I chuck it back into the boot. The liquid swishes and sloshes around. I look around for some kind of handle, but I can't open the trunk from inside. I pant and sweat and swear until suddenly I look up. There's a sunroof. Huh, that's lucky. A bead of sweat slides down my neck. I crank it open. Fresh air. I need a drink, some vodka or something. I'm wilting like a pot plant. I wriggle up and out through the gap. A cool breeze flows through my damp hair. Yes. Yes. I'm finally free. Now I know how Mandela felt in 1990.

I wobble on my hands and knees on the hot tin roof, thinking about cats and Tennessee Williams. Then I jump down to the forest floor and take a look at the car. There's a streak of blood on the bumper. Oops. I try to wipe it off.

I hear a man's deep voice and jump.

'*Ciao, come stai?*'

For a second I think it's Nino. But it's not his voice. It's just some guy.

'Oh. Chow,' I say.

I turn round. But it's not a man; it's a woman. I think. I'm confused.

'*Tutto bene?*' she says.

I study the woman: big hands, big jaw, Adam's apple, stubble, tall. She has broad, manly shoulders. She's wearing a bra and a short pink skirt. High heels (inappropriate for a forest.) Too much make-up on. Ooh, I like her sparkly earrings. I wonder where she got those from. She's made quite an effort for a woodland stroll. Perhaps she's lost, like I am?

'Um, oh. I don't speak Italian,' I say to the woman. What's *she* doing here?

'No problem, sugar,' she replies. 'Are you looking for something, sweetheart?'

'No. Not really. No,' I say. Apart from vodka. And Nino . . . 'Actually, my car won't start. Do you know anything about mechanics?'

'You're asking the wrong girl.'

She holds my gaze a little longer, then shrugs. '*Ciao.* Have a nice day.'

She turns her back and walks away, her buttocks wiggling in the tight pink skirt, her heels sinking into mud.

'Hey, no wait. Come back,' I say.

The woman walks along the road. Then she stands and stares at nothing, at the place where the pavement should be. Why is she waiting there by the road? It's not a bus stop or anything. What an odd place to hang out. Unless she's trying to hitch a ride? I glance at the fucked-up Cinquecento. You know what? I'll hitch-hike too.

Oh no, I get it. She's a hooker.

I'm about to walk over and join the woman when I stop.

Oh shit. The nun.

I don't want the cops to find her body. My fingerprints are all over the paintwork. Her blood is smeared all over the bumper. I don't want that death coming back to haunt me (I've had enough of that with my twin). Perhaps the car's owner got a good look at me and gave the cops a detailed description? What if that other nun saw my face and has done an unflattering sketch? No, there's only one thing for it. I need to torch that tin-can car. I need to lose that nun in a furnace of ash and smoke and flame. I reach inside my Prada bag and rummage around for my purple Zippo: condoms, lipstick, Nino's phone, cuckoo clock, cock ring, my lighter . . . I turn back towards the car. I spring back up on to the roof – the skin on my kneecaps sizzling, burning – then dangle down through the sunroof. I grab the can from the boot and winch myself up. I pull all my stomach muscles.

I remember the last time I torched a car, the headmaster's car at my old school. I can still feel the warmth of the blaze on my face. I can still smell the toxic fumes. In hindsight, he made the right decision when he wouldn't marry my mum. But I still enjoyed destroying his ride. And that was excellent practice. I open the can and sniff.

My eyes sting. Perfect, that ought to do it. I glance at the woman, but she isn't looking. She's a good hundred metres away.

I pour some petrol through the sunroof and into the Cinquecento. GLUG, GLUG, GLUG, GLUG. This stuff really stinks. I pour some over the nun, her wimple, her hair and her long, black habit.

'I am so, so sorry,' I say.

I wonder if she'll ever forgive me. Of course she will; she's a Christian. Forgiveness is what Christianity is all about.

I shake out the last few drops, then chuck the can inside the car. I reach down for a broken branch and set fire to a leaf with my Zippo. Another leaf. Another twig. A few more leaves and twigs. They're bone dry. The flames flare up, hot and red and orange. It's a familiar smell. My eyebrows are singeing. I throw the branch inside the car, then jump down and jog away. There's a WHOOSH as the petrol ignites and the fire spreads through the rusty Fiat. I crouch down low and peer in through the glass. The seats are burning nicely. The flames spread up across their backs, consuming the cracked leather. The fire flickers to the ceiling, engulfs the interior. Goodbye, Fiat. So long, sister. Another sister. *Great.* Now I *really* need that drink. A chocolate milkshake with Baileys, Kahlúa or a strong Long Island Iced Tea.

There's a toxic stink of burning rubber from the thick, black, ugly smoke. A crackling sound, a pop, a hiss. I breathe it in and choke.

I walk over to the woman.

'Hey, hey you,' I say.

She looks over. Clocks the Fiat.

'Your car's on fire.'

'I know.'

She gazes out towards the road. Gold eyeshadow. Too much rouge. I like her diamanté lashes; they look really cool. In a clearing in the woods I spot a little two-man tent, the modern kind with a low roof. Guy ropes. A purple door. We're standing right next to a dual carriage-way. What an odd place to camp.

'Do you know where I can get a drink?'

'Cuckoo,' says my clock.

The woman shakes her head. 'Uh-uh.'

'Some vodka or a bar or something?'

'There's nothing around here.'

There's a hum as a car approaches. A Lancia parks up on the road. I watch a middle-aged man step out. He's average build, an average height. Pretty nondescript. I watch as the woman approaches the man, wiggling her tight derrière. The two of them head to the tent.

I smell the smoke from the burning Fiat. I can hear it snap and roar. It tastes like a crematorium. Tiny flakes of ash float by and settle like snow on the scorching tarmac. The flames are spreading to the trees. I could watch for hours. But I can't just stand around all day (even though that fire looks awesome). I've got shit to do. I've got people to kill. I need to get back to Rome. I have to look for Dynamite. *Now.* Before Domenico does. I'll get to Nino first.

I check my phone. No internet. And no fucking signal. I can't call myself a cab. I can't walk from here. Perhaps that guy could give me a lift when they are – you know – finished?

I turn and watch the forest fire; the Cinquecento's disappeared behind an incandescent glow. Ten or twenty trees are burning. That nun will be barbecued. I watch the tent rock to and fro. I'm guessing they could be a while. I stick out my thumb and scan the road. A Maserati. A Prius. A SEAT. Another Fiat. I feel the warmth of the spreading fire. It stings my sunburnt skin.

I walk further up the road away from the blazing furnace. I hallucinate a rum mojito: a slice of lime, some mint, brown sugar, paper parasol . . . I wave my thumb, but no one's stopping. They all race past, ignoring me. There's a THUMP as a branch crashes down to the ground, the leaves orange with flame. I glance towards the little tent. It's still rocking, swaying. The fire is just a few metres away. I wiggle my thumb.

At last, an azure Mazda approaches. It's a young man driving the car. He stops and winds his window down.

'*Quanto?*' he says.

'Oh. English?'

'How much for a suck and fuck?' he says.

'Fuck you. I'm not a hooker. Although I am impressed by your English. Can I get a lift? To Trastevere?'

He winds his window up again. Then he speeds away.

'Hey. Where are you going?' I shout.

This could take some time.

An Alfa Romeo approaches. This time, I'll get it. I stick out my thumb. I wave my arm around like a windmill (I would never pick me up). The vehicle slows and stops. I run over to the car. The driver is a middle-aged woman. Her frightened eyes are open wide.

She points at the raging fire. '*Mamma mia. Un fuoco?*' she says.

I glance at the tent.

'Oh God. Wait a minute.'

Flames are inching up the guy ropes.

Why do I have to do *everything*? Those two will be burnt alive.

I sprint through the forest to the tent. Hot flames lick at my heels. I cough, cough, cough in the blaze.

'Hey. Get out. Get out,' I say.

I unzip the tent and rip open the door. I burn my little finger.

'You've got to get out of here.'

The pair are naked and, clearly, fucking. They jump out through the open flap. We run away from the wild fire and out on to the road.

The woman in the Alfa Romeo stares at us in disbelief. Her mouth drops open: Oh. (I guess we must look quite a sight. I'm the only one who isn't naked, which is unusual for me.) She revs her engine and swerves away. Great. *There goes my ride.*

That's the very last time I do something nice for anyone ever again. Nino was right: *it doesn't suit me.* I don't know what came over me really. I must still be in shock.

I study the pair. They're stark bollock naked: two hard cocks and a pair of tits.

'Can I get a lift to Rome?'

The one without tits says, 'Yes.'

He limps over to his Lancia parked a little way up the road. I watch his bum as he opens the boot; it's soft like pizza dough. He takes out a bag then slams it shut. He holds the bag over his bits.

He says, 'You can wait in the car.'

I open the door and get in. The Lancia is spacious, nice. It's a brand-new model. I watch the prostitute walk off butt naked along the road. I wonder where she's going now. Perhaps she's got a mate down there who can lend her some clothes? The other guy walks into the woods and disappears between some trees. I watch him through the passenger window. Has he gone in there to get changed? I check the ignition: damn, no keys. I guess I'll have to wait.

The flames are spreading quickly now. I watch the fire for a couple more minutes, then a priest emerges from a burning bush. For a moment I think I'm tripping. Is that . . . is that *Moses*? He's wearing a cassock and a clerical collar; his long black cape falls to his feet. He walks through flames towards the car, opens the door and gets in.

'You're a priest?'

'Yes, I am.'

I don't believe it. *Another* priest. I already had to kill one last week . . .

'What? What's the matter?' he says.

'It's just that. Oh . . . forget it.'

He starts the engine and pulls out on to the carriage-way. 'Come on,' he says. 'Don't be naive. You don't think priests like transsexual hookers? This is 2015.'

'Oh. Right. Of course, I suppose . . .'

'Priests are their number-one clients.'

We speed along a pine-lined road and into central Rome. I must have driven all this way sometime last night, but I don't remember. I must have been half asleep.

'Thanks,' he says, 'for saving my life.'

'Yeah, yeah, whatever.'

He doesn't know I started the fire. I guess it's better this way.

I stare out of the window at ancient ruins: old brown bricks and Roman villas. A sign on the road says '*Ostia Antica*'. I thought all the roads lead to Rome?

'So,' says the priest, 'are you visiting for business or pleasure?'

'Both,' I say. 'Actually, neither.'

I can't be bothered to explain. It's way too complicated.

'Are you enjoying your trip so far?'

'No. Not really,' I say.

'Have you been to Italy before?'

I sigh. Ace. He wants to talk. He wants to make friends. Let's be pen pals.

'I've been to Pompeii, Milan, Taormina.'

Probably shouldn't mention Taormina . . .

'How wonderful. I love Sicily. And where have you been in Rome?'

I stifle a yawn. I wish he'd shut up. I want to catch up on some sleep.

'The Trevi Fountain, the Spanish Steps, the River Tiber . . .'

'You *must* visit the Vatican City. It's the most beautiful place in Rome.'

'It's not *in* Rome,' I say. 'It's a city state surrounded *by* Rome.' You'd think a Catholic priest would know that.

'I'm going there now; I'll take you,' he says. 'I just got changed for work.'

We drive through the dusty streets. I try my best to fall asleep, but the priest carries on talking. After a really, really long time we arrive at the Vatican City.

'This is me,' says the priest. 'That's St Peter's Basilica. It's going to be busy today. We're just in time for mass.'

I sigh and get out of the car. I didn't want to come here at all, I wanted to go to Trastevere. Hundreds of people file into a piazza. There's an obelisk in the centre. I recognize it from *Angels & Demons*; that's where the helicopter was. I liked it when the sky exploded. That was an awesome scene.

He bleeps his key and the lights flash once to show that the Lancia's locked.

'And you won't tell anyone about this?' He fixes his eyes on mine and bites his bottom lip.

'Who am I gonna tell? *The pope?*'

I don't even know his name.

He nods. He seems relieved. Convinced. He lets out a sigh.

'Since you saved my life,' he says. 'I'm going to do you a favour.'

'Oh yeah?' I say. 'What's that then? *Save me?*' I don't want to be baptized . . .

'I'll sneak you inside past the queue. You need to see St Peter's.'

'No. It's fine. Really. I'm Jewish.'

'I absolutely insist.'

Chapter Twenty

St Peter's Basilica, Vatican City

We wander on to something called the Piazza di San Pietro. I take an obligatory selfie, but my heart's not really in it. The square is round and circular. I guess it's not really a square (it's a circle). Long, straight, geometric lines dissect the tiled floor. Standing at one end of the square is a massive show-off church. It's the biggest I've ever seen. It's a 'basilica'. The dome is tall and wide and round and towers over everything. Along the top of the facade are dozens of life-like statues. Perhaps they're saints or favourite popes? I can't tell from down here. I follow the priest across the piazza and towards St Peter's.

I'm knackered from a crap night's sleep in that Oompa-Loompa car. My sunburn stings. I'm dehydrated. I accidentally killed *a nun*. I'm no closer to finding Nino. This whole thing's a fucking mess. I look around at all the people. Tourists everywhere. What am I even doing here? I feel like lying on the ground and bawling my eyes out. I want to crawl into a corner and die. But there aren't any corners in this square, because it's a fucking circle.

A friendly-looking nun passes by. It's not the same one as before (not the dead one, obviously, or the other one from the convent). She smiles at me for no reason. What is her problem? What does she want? Why is she so *happy*?

One may smile, and smile, and be a villain.

I learnt that the hard way from Nino.

I follow the priest up a flight of steps and through an enormous bronze door.

'You're going to love it,' he says.

Inside, St Peter's is filling up. It smells of incense and tourists, and thousands of tiny candles burn in rows on metal tables. The air is cool and damp and I shiver. I wish I had a cape like that priest. Capes are *big* this season in Rome. It must be a hot new trend. I look up at the man standing at the altar. Who is that? *The pope*? He is also wearing a cape and long flowing robes like Gandalf. I should have got a leather cape the other day in Prada. I'll have to go back and buy one soon. I need a new bag anyway.

'So, what do you think? Magnificent?'

'Yeah. *Shalom. Mazel tov.*'

I crane my neck and stare up at the ceiling. Dazzling shafts of light shine down in columns of pure bright white. Everything's covered in glittering gold. There are sculptures of cherubs and Jesus. I'm blinded by something behind the altar: a majestic, golden sun. The enormous church is crowded and bustling with hundreds, no thousands, of people. The pope (?) is saying mass in Italian. Or possibly Latin. I don't know.

'Now remember our little secret,' the priest says. 'God be with you. *Ciao.*'

He gives me a cheery wave then heads off down the aisle.

I flop down on the nearest pew. I hold my head in my hands. Oh my God, this is beyond shit. Where did it all go so wrong? Just last week, it had all looked so promising. I was on the run with my sexy new boyfriend, a fucking Brad Pitt lookalike, and as far as I knew we were soulmates (so what if he didn't know my name). We were on top of the world. I'd found my true calling. My dream job. We'd managed to escape the mob and hide out at the Ritz Hotel. We had diamonds and a Lamborghini, a suitcase filled with fuck-you money. But now it's all gone and what have I got?

'*You've got me,*' says Beth.

Alvie, seriously, sort yourself out. Pull yourself together.

Enough of this shit. Absinthe? Hookers? Fucking forest fires? *It is but foolery.* Girl, you've got work to do. Vengeance. Nino. Come on, focus. A little *discipline.* I'll go and find this *Dynamite.* That's my sure-fire route to Nino. But how? It's not a real name. It's not like I can look him up in a directory or a phone book. And Radio Londra will be closed right now, so there's no point going there. I'll have to go and steal Nino's phone from Domenico. If I can get my hands on the phone, then I can find Dynamite's number and set up a meeting. That's going to be easier said than done. But I'll do it. I have to. I do. Perhaps I could steal Domenico's gun? While I'm nicking the mobile phone. And then I'll go and catch that *stronzo.* Yes, yes. That's what I'll do. I'll get my shit together.

But what if Dynamite's a red herring? A false lead? A lame duck? How am I going to find Nino then? And how am I going to steal from a mobster with two fucking body-guards? No, this is ridiculous. I'm beginning to give up. *I have of late . . . lost all my mirth.* It's so unfair. *Why me?* I feel like I am on a wild-goose chase. I am running on a tread-mill, but never getting there.

I scan the crowd. People are praying, hands together, eyes closed. They're kneeling on red-leather cushions, their heads all bowed down low. They're whispering something. You know what? I'll give it a go. There's a first time for everything. And I'm *desperate*. I need God on my side pronto. I think I can officially say that I have hit rock fucking bottom. What have I got to lose?

I grab the little leather pillow hanging from a hook on the bench. I kneel down, close my eyes and press my palms together:

> *Dear God, please help me:*
> *I need to find Nino. Right*
> *Now would be quite nice.*

I wait a bit for the prayer to sink in, then open one eye and look around.

NINO? WHAT THE ACTUAL FUCK?

It's him. Did my haiku prayer work?

Nino is praying two rows in front. I recognize the back of his head. He turns his face to the side and – yes – that's him. (I think. *Perhaps.*) What the hell is he doing here? Oh yeah, he's really religious. He has that tattoo of the

Madonna inked all over his back. A picture of Jesus was taped to his dashboard. The guy's a devoted Catholic. Of course he's here when he's in town. It's bloody obvious.

I push past the people praying on my pew and sprint down the aisle towards Nino. *Cheers, God, you absolute boss.* I promise to be good from now on. I mean it. Pinkie promise. I reach the end of Nino's row, but . . . he seems to have vanished. I scan the crowds for his slick black hair, his chiselled chin, his handsome face, the long, pink scar on his right cheek . . .

'NINO. WHERE ARE YOU?'

I spot a worn black leather jacket making its way towards the door. The man turns and looks over his shoulder. Is that a horseshoe moustache? People are staring, tut-tutting at me. You're not supposed to shout in church. Or run. Or swear.

'Fucking hell.'

I sprint back down the crowded aisle, my body hot with perspiration, sweat beads prickling my brow. There are shocked expressions on everyone's faces. The pope (?) stops talking and stares at me.

I swirl like a whirling dervish. 'RAAAAAAAAAAA AAAAAAGGGGHHHH.'

I push through the door. Is this some kind of *miracle*? I'm sure he wasn't here before. He appeared as if by magic. I swear I'm converting. *This shit is real.* It's a revelation. I scan the circle/square below. There. Over by that fountain? I sprint across the busy piazza, zigzagging like an autumn wasp. I can't believe God answered my prayers. I should *never* have doubted Her.

A guy in a black leather jacket . . .

I hurry over.

It's not him.

But . . . Oh man, where has he gone?

'Nino?' I say.

I stand in the middle of the piazza, but I can't see him. He's disappeared. Was he real? Or an apparition brought on by stress and sleep-deprivation? Was that my ex? Am I going nuts?

I let out a blood-curdling scream. 'I HAVE HAD ENOUGH.'

Next time, I'll get him. I'll get him. I will . . .

I slump down on the tiles, my head flops in my hands.

Why, what an ass am I!

Cuckoo. Cuckoo.

'Are you all right, my dear?' I look up and see a nun. 'Did you have a religious experience?'

'Yes, yes. I'm in ecstasy.'

'It happens all the time.'

Chapter Twenty-one

Trastevere, Rome, Italy

'How the fuck did *you* get in here?'

The mobsters are in my apartment. They're sitting in my lounge playing cards and drinking Italian beer.

'Elizabeth, the door was open.'

'No, it wasn't.'

Domenico shrugs.

'Whatever,' I say. '*I'm not working with Nino.*'

He looks up at me and glares.

'Look,' I say. 'I want him dead. Same as you do. See?'

I show him the tattoo on my bum.

'Die Nemo?' Domenico says.

'Yeah. Well. That's just a typo. I swear, we're on the same team.'

I glance around my living room. Empty cans of Nastro Azzurro. An ashtray filled with cigar butts. It looks like they've been here a while. I guess they were waiting for me.

'I saw Nino at the Vatican.'

Domenico frowns. 'You sure it was him?'

'Yes, I think so. But, actually, no. I'm not sure. Might have been.'

Domenico gets back to the card game. '*Scopa*,' he says. He wins.

'I want to meet this Dynamite.' Fuck it, perhaps we can visit together.

Domenico nods. '*Sì*.'

I spot a vase of tall red roses standing on the coffee table. They definitely weren't there before. Oh God. What does this mean?

'Domenico, did you buy me flowers?'

Domenico looks at the bouquet of roses. 'No, why would I do that?'

'I have no idea.'

I glance at Riccardo and Giuseppe. Blank faces. It wasn't them.

'Shit . . . I think Nino's been here. Domenico, was the door really open?'

'That is what I said.'

I check the vase for a note or a card, but there's nothing. Roses. *Red* roses again, just like at the Ritz.

'The flowers, I know it. They're from him.'

Aww, bless. That's really sweet . . .

No, Alvie, don't fall for it. It's only because he's feeling guilty.

And so he should. The twat.

Or – more likely knowing him – are they intended as a threat? I study the crimson blooms. The thorns on those stems look sharp.

Domenico shakes his ugly head. 'Why would Nino buy you flowers?'

'I told you already. He's got a crush . . . Shit, that means he knows where I live.' Was he following me? Did he track *my* phone? But that's impossible. 'What if he's still here?'

Domenico downs the rest of his beer and slams the bottle on the table. Riccardo and Giuseppe exchange glances.

I say, 'We gotta search the flat.'

Domenico pulls out his gun and I follow just behind. I'm ready with my killer move. I'll knee him in the balls. We burst out of the lounge and into the bedroom. I wish I had Domenico's gun. We check the kitchen, bathroom, study. He isn't in the guest bedroom or any of the cupboards. He isn't hiding in the attic or underneath the bed. We search the flat from top to bottom.

'He isn't fucking here.'

'*Minchia*,' says Domenico.

'*Stronzo*,' I say.

Domenico sits down again. I shake my head and sigh. I'm feeling beyond gross. All sticky. Smoky from that forest fire and I've still got Durex Play all stuck in my hair.

'I'm going to take a shower,' I say. 'Then let's get out of here.'

I walk into the living room in my double leather. I'm washed. I'm dressed. I'm ready for action. I'm *pumped*. I'm fucking psyched. The mobsters are snoozing on the sofa.

There's a knock at the door.

Oh no. Who's that? The fucking police? Not Nino, he never knocks.

Domenico's hand is on his gun.

'Wait a minute,' I say under my breath. 'That could be anyone.'

His body tenses. His shoulders raise. There's a grim look on his brutish face. Have the cops come to bust me for the murder of my sister? For Ambrogio? That mugger? The nun? I take a deep breath.

'I'm coming,' I say. 'Just give me a sec.'

Domenico dives into the bedroom, out of sight. Good idea.

I smooth my hair down. Bite my lip. Fiddle with the double lock. The key clinks up against the metal. My hands are trembling, fingers fumbling. My palms are slippery with sweat. The door swings open to reveal . . . my mother with Ernie in his carrycot.

My jaw falls open and hits the floor. *How the hell did she get here? Is this some kind of bad joke?* Mum and I have always got on like a house on fire. Oh no, that's not it . . . *I want to set her house on fire.* This is worse than the police. I'd rather go to jail.

'*Alvina?*' says my mother.

She covers her mouth with both her hands. Devastation all over her face. She looks like she's just seen a ghost and, in a way, she has.

Shit, this could get really awkward. My mum's the only one who can tell us apart. She always knew, no matter what. It's almost as if she could *smell* it. Ronnie and Reggie. Jekyll and Hyde. The man in the iron mask . . . Well, I guess that settles it then. I'm going to have to be Alvie

228

from now on. There's no way my mum would keep this a secret. It's written all over her face.

'Actually, Mum, I go by *Beyoncé*. That's my name these days.'

'I thought you were dead,' she says.

My mother has a high-pitched voice. An Australian accent. It jumps between *EastEnders* and *Neighbours* like it can't decide where it belongs. She's spent the last ten years in Oz, where all the poisonous creatures live. I'd hoped she might stay there for good. But, oh no, here she is. She pulls lace gloves off, finger by finger, then folds them up and pops them into her pocket. She's wearing a stiff crimson skirt suit, sun hat and 15-denier tights. The kind of thing Theresa May might wear while saying something really annoying.

'Mum? What? But how did you find me?'

'It wasn't *that* hard. You're not a yeti.'

No, I'm the Loch Ness Monster.

'I thought . . . I thought.' She stifles a sob. 'I thought *Beth* was alive.'

A single tear streams down her face. She wipes it away with a finger.

I look at Ernie in his cot; he's mine. I don't want *her* to have him. I pick him up and give him a hug.

'Ma ma ma,' he says.

'Hello, piglet,' I say and stroke his soft, pink, chubby cheek. Now that I've finally got him back, I'm not letting him go again. I look into his big blue eyes. 'So, baby, did you miss me?'

My mum pushes past me, letting herself in. There's a bitter stench of Elnett. She always uses too much hairspray; her head is highly flammable (useful). Coriander. Tuberose. Lashings of opoponax. A chemical bomb/Dior Poison, her signature insect repellent. She puts the carrycot on the ground and examines the mess in my new flat. She eyes the thugs sprawled on the sofa. Then she seems to see my nose for the very first time.

'Oh,' she says, raising an eyebrow. 'You look . . . odd. Have you put on weight?'

'It's great to see you too.'

She spins me round and checks out my bum.

'What on earth have you been eating?' She shakes her head and tuts. 'How many times do I have to tell you? Pringles are not a staple diet.'

Ernie does a little burp and then spits up on me. I wipe it off with my shirt.

Riccardo and Giuseppe yawn and stretch out on the leather sofa. Muddy boots and messed-up slacks, dirty, grimy faces. My mother crinkles up her nose, then crosses her arms and waits.

For what?

We stare each other out.

Domenico reappears from out of the bedroom. He blinks and studies my mother as though she were an exotic bird. A bird of paradise, perhaps? A glossy-mantled manucode or ribbon-tailed astrapia? Only I know she's an *albatross*. A bad omen. An evil curse. You're not supposed to kill them.

'Well, aren't you going to introduce me?' my mother says, removing her hat and handing it to me (the *help*?). It's a straw hat with an unreasonably large brim and a fussy pink scarf tied round it.

Why didn't I kill her in Taormina? I should have waited until she arrived and popped a bullet between her eyes. Now she'll ruin everything. Now she'll want to *talk* . . .

'*Signora*, allow me to present myself. My name is Domenico Osvaldo Mauro. I am a dear friend of your daughter's. It is an unexpected pleasure to meet such an enchanting young lady.' He reaches for my mother's hand and brings it lightly to his lips. 'Please, excuse my slovenly appearance; I have not had a chance to dress.'

Wait a minute, young? *Really?*

It looks like my mother is blushing, but it's hard to tell under the make-up. She's really plastered it on today; it's like some kind of death mask.

'Domenico, meet my mother, Mavis. Mavis, meet Domenico,' I say.

'Mavis? But what a beautiful name,' Domenico says in shocked surprise.

You've got to be kidding me.

My mother reclaims her hand. 'Oh? Thank you. It's French for *song thrush* . . .'

Erm, no. It isn't.

'Mum. So. It's nice to see you. You didn't tell me how you found me?'

'No. I didn't, did I? I must say this is most unusual. I want to know what's going on.'

She looks around for somewhere to sit and finds a moss-green armchair. She brushes off dust before sitting down and rearranging her skirt. She crosses her legs and looks up at me.

'Aren't you going to offer me a cup of tea? Or a glass of Champagne?'

Her crested head is cocked to one side like an insolent cockatiel.

'I don't have any tea. Or Champagne. I've only just moved in,' I say.

'Well, what a way to treat a guest. Anyone would think you were raised in a barn.'

My mother picks invisible fluff off the sleeve of her red jacket. 'And I don't suppose you have anything to eat. Never mind that I'm half starved.'

'Like I said, I've just —'

'And *no*, I don't mean strawberry *Pop-Tarts*. You don't know the hellish journey I've had, travelling up here from Taormina. All on my own with your orphaned nephew and no one to carry my bags. And now . . . and now . . .' She gestures to me, then buries her face in her hands. 'And now *this*.'

I presume she means that I'm alive. She's clearly disappointed.

'Well, nobody *asked* you to come,' I say. I look at Ernie dozing in my arms. 'So . . . Mum, how did you find me?'

'The police tracked your sister's phone, of course,' she says. (Shit, I should never have turned it on. I knew that was risky.) 'Though why you have Elizabeth's mobile is a mystery to me . . . The police will be here any minute.

They're just parking the car.' She fixes me with a piercing stare. 'You know your sister's dead?'

I stare back at my mum in silence.

Domenico clears his throat. 'We'll . . . we're going out,' he says.

Domenico walks towards the sofa. His thugs are man-spreading all over it. Giuseppe's mouth is open wide and drool dangles down from an unshaved chin. Riccardo's half sprawled on the armchair, half on the living-room floor. Domenico kicks Riccardo in the shin. 'Oi. *Stronzo. Sveglia.*'

He smacks Giuseppe around the face. Golden rings and jagged knuckles.

The men wake up and leap to their feet.

'*Che cazzo? Che cazzo?*' they say. They stand there rubbing their eyes and yawning.

'*Polizia,*' he says.

Domenico turns towards my mother. 'The pleasure, Mavis, was all mine. I hope we meet again sometime.'

He actually fucking bows.

I knew the cops would find me eventually. Shit, I've got to run. But I'll look guilty if I leave. If they caught me, I'd be screwed. Perhaps they just want to ask me some questions? They think I can help them with the case. Those halfwits think Salvatore did it. I'm going to be OK. I'll have to be Alvie now my mum's here. I'll play the part of the loyal twin. It would help if Domenico fucked off . . . One wrong word. A hint. A clue. He could blow everything up.

There's a sharp rap on the front door. Domenico goes

pale. I roll my eyes and open it. Whatever. It's too late. Two policemen stand in the hall. It's Commissario Savastano and Commissario Grasso, the same two jokers I met in Taormina. They came to the house when Ambrogio died. I recognize them straight away.

'*Buongiorno, signora,*' say the cops.

'*Buongiorno,*' says Domenico.

'*Buongiorno,*' says Riccardo.

'*Buongiorno,*' says Giuseppe.

'Chow, Chow, Chow,' I say.

'We were just leaving,' Domenico says. He turns to the mobsters. '*Andiamo.*'

The three of them squeeze past the policemen.

'*Arrivederci,*' says Domenico.

I watch them disappear down the hall.

The two policemen look at me.

'Signora Elizabeth Caruso?'

'No, it's the other one,' says my mum. She chokes on strangled tears. 'Officers, this is Miss Alvina Knightly.'

They look at me and frown.

'And the body in Taormina?' Savastano asks.

'*That* was Elizabeth Caruso.'

My mother sobs a noisy sob.

Oh God, I wish I was dead.

'I was in Taormina for one night only. My sister annoyed the hell out of me.' (That bit's true, at least.) 'So I told her I had to go back to London. Something to do with work. I know, I know, I shouldn't have lied, but I needed an excuse to leave. She was really, *really* doing my head in. My sister was a pain in the ass. Now I feel guilty, of course. I do.' (*I don't*. She was a cow.) 'I told her I had to return to England, but instead I travelled around the island visiting all the famous sights. I even climbed to the top of Mount Etna; the views were sublime.'

'Where did you sleep? In which hotels?' asks Commissario Savastano. His pencil is poised to capture my answer on his spiral-bound pad.

'I slept beneath the stars. The weather was warm and dry, so I didn't mind.'

My mother tuts. She totally buys it. She remembers the time I slept in that tree . . .

'And then what did you do?'

'I caught the ferry to the mainland on 30 August then took the train up here to Rome. I wanted to do some sightseeing before heading back to the UK. The Spanish Steps, the Vatican . . . Excuse me, but I'm very upset.'

I hide my face in my hands. I heavy breathe a little bit. Make my shoulders heave. I peek up through a gap in my fingers. Ernie's fussing in his cot. My mother is glaring at me. The officers sit opposite, scribbling something in their notebooks.

'There's something I don't understand,' says my mother, narrowing her eyes. 'Why do you have Elizabeth's phone?'

I shoot my mother a murderous look. She doesn't seem to notice. If I didn't know any better, I'd think she and the cops were colluding to get me convicted for murder. Oh, no. Wait. They probably are.

'*Sì, sì*. We'll take the phone,' says Grasso, reaching out his hand. 'If you don't mind, Signorina Knightly.'

I reach into my Prada bag and retrieve my sister's iPhone. I place it in his outstretched hand. I rack my brains. What's on that phone? Is there anything incriminating? I think I covered my tracks pretty well. I used my new phone for texting Nino and all of those selfies in Prada.

Commissario Savastano takes the phone and seals it in a see-through plastic bag.

'My mobile broke, so Beth gave me hers. I guess she was nice *sometimes* . . .'

The policemen nod. My mother frowns. She still can't believe Beth's the one they found.

'But why did Beth call me when I was in Australia to tell me *you* were dead?'

The policemen exchange puzzled glances. Shit. She's right. Why did I do that? I didn't want to leave loose ends and it seemed like a good idea at the time. I called my mum, pretending to be Beth, and told her that Alvie had popped her clogs. I said she'd died in the swimming pool. That bit is true, at least.

Three pairs of eyes are fixed on me. Suddenly it's way too hot.

'Mum, I think you've misremembered.' I place my hand on my mother's hand. I make my voice go quiet. 'Sometimes your brain plays tricks like that. It tells you what you *want* to believe when the truth is too . . . fucked up.'

My mother retrieves her hand. She's sobbing, howling

now. I guess reality's just sunk in. She's fucking hysterical. That's good. She looks proper mental. My story will stick.

I hear Mr Bubbles's laugh echo around inside my head.

Commissario Savastano strokes his greying stubble.

'So you were at the Carusos' villa on the night of 26 August?'

'Yes, that's right. You can ask Emilia. She's their nanny,' I say.

The policemen nod. They've already quizzed her.

'Just one night?'

'That's right,' I say.

'And while you were staying there, did you see or hear anything suspicious? Anything that might have alerted you to the fact that your sister was in danger?'

'Um, well now, let me see . . .' I furrow my brow. Pretend to think. Search the recesses of my brain. 'I know she was fucking her next-door neighbour – Salvatore, I think he was called. Do you think that might have had something to do with it?'

Nailed it.

That was awesome.

My mother lets out a high-pitched squawk, like a strangled parrot.

'Ah yes, Salvatore Bottare.'

'That's him. That's your guy,' I say.

'And you suspect this neighbour, Signor Bottare, might be guilty of the heinous crime?'

'Oh yes. That's him. I bet he did it.'

He sighs. 'Very well.'

'Now all you have to do is find him.' I try a winning smile.

Savastano clears his throat. He takes a sip of water. 'Signore Bottaro's body was discovered last night. He was found in a wood outside Taormina, not far from Elizabeth.'

I stare at the cop.

'I'm sorry, *what*?'

'Salvatore is dead.'

All the blood drains from my face. I'd wondered where Nino and Domenico had buried him. This is *not* going well.

'You found Salvatore's body?'

'That's right.'

'Dead in a wood?'

Beth's hysterical in my head.

'Shut it, bitch.'

'I'm sorry?'

'Oh, I wasn't talking to you.'

My mother frowns. I sweat.

'We have reason to believe that the person or persons that murdered your sister also murdered Ambrogio Caruso and Salvatore Bottaro.'

'Oh. Do you really think so?'

I squirm in my seat.

'And tell me, Signorina Knightly, did you hear anything about a painting? A Caravaggio?' asks Grasso.

I stare at the fraying carpet. My mother kicks my shin.

'Alvina, the officer asked you a question.'

'*You're losing it*,' says Beth.

238

Shut up shut up shut up shut up.

'Come again?' I say.

'Did you hear anything about a Caravaggio while you were staying at the villa?'

'No. Absolutely not. I don't know what that is.'

My mother rolls her eyes at me. 'A *Car-a-vag-gi-o*,' she says. She looks over at the cops. 'She failed art.'

The policemen look at one another. Click their pens and close their books. 'Thank you, you have been very helpful.'

I look up and nod. A broad smile spreads on my face.

'Anything I can do to aid your investigation. Really, anything at all . . .'

They get up. We shake hands. They leave.

Whoop! Whoop! That was *easy*. I'm taking it all in my fucking stride. I'm a true *professional*. It's almost like I've got nothing to hide. I kept it cool. I stayed on track. That was worthy of an Oscar. Even when they dropped that bombshell about finding Salvo's body, I handled it with great aplomb. I barely even flinched.

My mother walks over to me and narrows her eyes. 'Wherever you go, disaster follows.'

'Hey, Mum, don't blame me. Wrong time, wrong place. That's all.'

'There's more to this than you let on.'

I reach down to pick up Ernie and tickle him beneath the chin.

'No, there isn't. Don't be so dramatic. Don't get your knickers in a knot.'

★

After the police have left and Mum has made herself at home, Domenico and his heavies come back.

'*All good,*' I mouth. '*They've gone.*'

'What did the pigs want?' asks Domenico.

'Nothing,' I say. 'It's cool.'

'*Nothing*?' Domenico shakes his head.

I double lock the door.

He clears his throat. 'Ahem.' I jump. It's an explosive sound: an AK47. 'It would be my greatest honour, ladies, to take you out for dinner this evening.'

Oh God. Please no. I roll my eyes. 'Domenico, *really*. It's fine.'

Domenico's looking at my mother. My mother is looking right back.

'I know a charming little place on the Piazza Navona. It is, how you say, *romantic*. The view of Bernini's magnificent fountain, La Fontana dei Quattro Fiumi, is simply incomparable.'

'No. No, *thank you,*' I say. I widen my eyes. I give him a *look*, but he doesn't get it. Or he doesn't care. He's gazing at Mum like she's Marilyn Monroe or Helen of fucking Troy. Urgh. My mum is gazing back. What is going on? Domenico gets down on one knee like he's going to propose.

'When the moonlight kisses the marble skins of the gods of the four rivers you will feel the presence of the Almighty Himself. It is – *come si dice?* – divine.' He kisses his fingers then makes a star. The star explodes into the air.

'No. Just no. *Just no,*' I say.

My mother tucks an imaginary curl behind a pearl-encrusted ear, looks down at her feet – Ferragamo sandals – and bites her bottom lip.

Domenico leans in a little closer and lowers his voice to an intimate tone. 'I will personally ensure your taste buds are delighted by Rome's most sumptuous delicacies: *baccalà* and *zucchini* flowers in the lightest batter, *saltimbocca di vitello* wrapped in sweet *prosciutto*, and *rigatoni carbonara* so exquisite you will weep.'

'No way. Seriously. *We're not going.*'

Oh sweet Jesus, I think he's *flirting*. That is beyond gross.

'*Maritozzi* with whipped cream and candied orange peel. *Tiramisu* steeped in the finest *Marsala* . . .'

'Well, I want to go, Alvina,' my mother says, smoothing her skirt and shifting in her chair. 'I'm really quite peckish. So that's that.' She picks up her handbag ready to leave. 'Thank you, Domenico. That would be very nice.'

Domenico shoots me a puzzled look. I can read his mind: *Alvina? That's not your name, is it? That's the girl we buried.*

I clear my throat. 'What about Ernie? He's sleeping. He can't go.'

Phew. That has distracted them. But for how long? I'm screwed.

Ernie's asleep in the carrycot. He is snoring softly in and out. I watch his eyelids flutter. He's content with dreams of milky breasts (or whatever it is that babies dream of; he's a boy, so probably breasts).

My mother leans over and pulls up his cover, tucking it

underneath his chin. 'What kind of restaurant is it, Domenico? Will it be all right if we take the baby?'

Domenico looks down at Ernesto then over at Riccardo and Giuseppe. They're passed out on the couch again. They're more like animals than humans. Like lions, they sleep a lot.

'*Non si preoccupi, signora,*' Domenico says with an almost imperceptible bow. 'My men will be delighted to care for your grandson. You can enjoy a relaxing evening, unburdened by these responsibilities.'

'*Stronzi,*' growls Domenico. The mobsters wake up. 'Watch the kid.'

These guys? No. He's got to be kidding.

'Oh,' says my mother. 'Are you sure?'

'Yeah,' I say, '*are you sure?*'

Riccardo gets up and looks at the baby like he's not even sure what it is. Giuseppe gets up and scratches his arse, then frowns at Domenico.

'But of course,' says Domenico. 'Mavis, you have nothing to fear. Now please excuse me while I get dressed . . .'

I follow him towards the bedroom. 'What about Dynamite?' I say.

'*Domani.* Tomorrow. *Un po di pazienza.*'

He closes the door in my face.

Domenico emerges from the bedroom. I do a double take. Is this the same guy? The cold-blooded killer? The thick-as-pig-shit mobster? I try to remember the first time I saw him in that wood in Sicily: sitting on the back of a pick-up, smoking a Cuban cigar. Torn overalls. Beat-up face. Dirt under his fingernails. The wrong side of overweight. He poured cement all over my sister. He said his brother had been 'disembowelled', which seriously grossed me out. And now here he is in a three-piece suit, looking as fly as a white Chris Eubank or Daniel Craig in *Casino Royal*. As slick as fucking Drake. Purple paisley necktie with a matching silk kerchief. Shoes so shiny he can see up your skirt. Where the hell did he get that bowler? Oh, that's what was in the hatbox. (What is it with mobsters and millinery?)

The apparel oft proclaims the man, but I guess in this case it's lying.

My mum gawks at Domenico. She looks like she's about to come.

'*Andiamo*, ladies. Let's go,' he says and opens the front door.

Chapter Twenty-two

Piazza Navona, Rome, Italy

We're sitting out on the terrace of an old-fashioned restaurant right in the heart of Piazza Navona. This place is unbelievable. Textbook romantic. It's me, Domenico and my mum; we're like the fucking Brady Bunch. Next thing you know, I'll be calling this merciless mobster 'Dad'.

I study the menu. The rich aromas of *lasagne al forno* and *spaghetti alla puttanesca* fill the soft night air. Flickering candles cast warm shadows over the ancient square. The tables are covered with red-and-white-checked cloths. There are olives the colour of emeralds; I pop one in my mouth and crunch its salty, meaty flesh. Bernini's famous masterpiece is only a few metres away. A towering Egyptian obelisk penetrates the starry sky. Bountiful fountains ejaculate torrents of crashing and splashing white water. I light a smoke and close my eyes. Try to pretend that I'm not here, that I am somewhere else: *driving with Nino through Tuscany, in a hot tub with Nino at the Ritz, in bed with Nino in my apartment* . . .

'Filthy habit,' says my mother, coughing at my cigarette smoke.

Domenico stubs out his cigar.

I spark another fag.

Ping.

A text. It's him. Of course.

'DID YOU LIKE THE FLOWERS?'

I'm about to delete it, but then . . . I don't.

'WERE THEY A GIFT OR A THREAT?'

A man playing a violin approaches our little table. He's playing that song about the moon hitting the sky like a big pizza pie.

'*That's amore . . .*' sings Domenico, tapping his foot to the rhythm. He gives the man a €500 bill.

'*Grazie. Grazie,*' says the man. He waves his bow in the air with a flourish and turns towards my mother. '*Signora,* perhaps you have a request?'

My mother sits up in her chair. She dabs her mouth with her serviette. 'Oh yes, thank you. What's that one they always play, you know in films set in Italy?'

' "Tu Vuò Fà L'Americano"?' I say.

'You know, the one that Jude Law sings in *The Talented Mr Ripley*?'

'It's "Tu Vuò Fà L'Americano",' I say.

'It goes something like this,' she says. 'Mericano, mericano, mericano . . . de, de, de, de, de, de, de.'

'Ah,' says Domenico. '*Sì. Sì.* I know it. "Tu Vuò Fà L'Americano".'

'Yes. That's it,' says my mother.

Goddamnit, I just got hepeated.

'*Può suonare questa canzone?*' Domenico says to the musician.

The violinist starts to play; he's standing right beside my ear.

'*Mericano, mericano, mericano,*' my mother sings at the top of her lungs.

I think I'm getting a migraine. I rub my temples and then pick up my knife. I run my thumb along the blade. Who shall I kill first? The fiddler or my tone-deaf mother? Decisions, decisions, decisions . . .

'Mavis,' says Domenico, leaning in across the table. 'Tell me, please, be so kind. What did the police want today? I'm so sorry we had to leave.'

I pick up my wine glass, but it's already empty. I grab my mother's glass instead and take a swig of hers.

'They wanted to ask my daughter some questions. She was in Taormina around the time that her twin sister was murdered. Tell me, Domenico. How long have you known my daughter?'

Domenico frowns and looks at me.

'Since she first arrived in Taormina.'

'So not very long then.'

'No.'

'And she hasn't tried to sleep with you yet?'

'*Mum,*' I say. How could she?

Domenico looks at me. 'No, not yet,' he says.

'You're one of the lucky ones,' she says. 'You're the one that got away . . .'

I grit my teeth. If I smash this glass, I could use a shard to slit her throat.

'More wine?' asks Domenico, pouring the red into my mother's already half-full glass.

Urgh, he's trying to get her drunk. She's starting to slur; it's working.

'Oh, I'll have some more too,' I say, as he empties the bottle.

'Thank you,' my mother says, taking a sip. '*Delizioso.*'

Domenico and my mum clink glasses for the sixth or seventh time. I stare at the empty seat opposite. It's like I'm not even here.

'I trust you're enjoying your linguine, Mavis? Tell me, is it to your taste?'

'Oh yes,' my mother says. 'And tell me, Domenico, your English is *fantastic*. May I ask you where you learnt it?'

I've been wondering that myself . . . It's all very *Regency*.

'I learnt English at school, like all the kids in Sicily. But I was fortunate enough to own a copy of Jane Austen's *Persuasion* in the original English. It is my favourite book,' he says. He turns to my mother and reaches over to grab her hand across the table. ' "You pierce my soul. I am half agony, half hope. Tell me not that I am too late, that such precious feelings are gone for ever. I offer myself to you again with a heart even more your own than when you almost broke it, eight years and a half ago." '

'Oh, Domenico.' My mother fans herself with the wine list.

' "Dare not say that man forgets sooner than woman, that his love has an earlier death. I have loved none but you." '

'Oh my.'

I stab and stab at my pasta. I push the last of the ravioli around on my plate and mop up the sauce. We sit for a while in painful silence.

'Alvina,' says my mother.

Domenico frowns. 'Elizabeth?'

'Beyoncé,' I say.

'Alvina?'

'Betta?'

'Cough. Cough. Cough,' I say.

'Can't you get a glass of water?' asks my mother.

'Let's go to the bathroom,' I say.

'Well, *he* seems like a nice young man,' my mother says to the cubicle door. Is she talking about *Domenico*?

'Yeah, sure. He's a delight.' I flush the loo and meet her by the sinks.

'What line of business is he in?' she asks, fluffing her hair. She looks in the mirror and pouts. Then she reapplies her lipstick even though it's still there.

'Pest extermination,' I say. *A bit like you with your perfume . . .*

I reach for the soap and run the tap. It scalds and burns my hands.

'Ah. Well, that *is* useful. Is there a lot of demand for that kind of work? You know, down there in Taormina?'

'You'd be surprised . . . It's seasonal.'

She opens her powder and dusts her face with a poufy puffy thing.

'It certainly seems to pay very well. Did you see how much money he gave that musician? A €500 bill.'

'Oh yeah, it does. I mean, no, it doesn't.'

'I'll be honest with you, Alvina.' She sighs. 'It is *not* going well with Rupert.'

Urgh. Rupert Vaughan Willoughby, my mother's second husband, the biggest loser in history. (Oh no, that's Nino. *Second* biggest then.)

'No? And tell me, why is that?'

Has he finally twigged you're a succubus? Did he see your serpent tails and birdlike claws? Discover you're the Queen of the Demons?

'It's been a number of years that he hasn't been up to it *in the bedroom department*. And I am a woman. I have needs.'

Oh God, I shouldn't have asked. I am not here. I am not having this conversation. *Nino in a Lambo. Nino in speedos. Nino covered in Nutella . . .*

I head towards the bathroom door, but my mum's still talking to herself in the mirror, transfixed like the Wicked Witch watching Snow White.

'I mean, it was never much more than a *mushroom*, but at least in the past —'

'I'm going, Mum. Byeeeeeee.'

'Ernie and I are moving in. We'll take the guest room,' she says.

I push through the doors and back into the restaurant, a little bit of sick rising up in my throat. She isn't serious. She's not going to stay. I'll delete that from my brain.

Domenico is waiting for me just round the corner. He pushes me into an alcove and up against a wall.

'*Che cazzo?*' he hisses into my ear.

I roll my eyes. 'What is it now?'

'You are . . . the *other twin*?'

Oh my God, not this *again*. I am *so* over it . . .

'Yeah, fucking bite me.'

He reaches into his jacket pocket. I feel the metal of his gun. He shoves it underneath my ribs into my diaphragm.

'OK. OK. I can explain.'

'I'm waiting,' he says.

Now what?

Beth says, '*It's over, Alvie.*'

'*Ambrogio* killed Elizabeth because he wanted to be with *me* . . .'

Nice one. Go me.

Domenico raises his eyebrows. I think he buys it.

'*Minchia.*'

'We were having an affair. We needed my sister out of the way . . .'

Brilliant, Alvie. This is *great*. You're fucking on *fire*. Top marks for thinking on your feet. He's going for it, sucker.

'So *Ambrogio* killed Elizabeth? *He* murdered her?'

'Yes, he did. Last week,' I say. 'He always preferred *me*, you see . . .'

I was the sexier twin. I could elaborate for hours about how Beth was shit in bed. I could list all my qualities and drag her name into the mud.

'And your sister was fucking Salvatore?'

'She was, but how did you know that?'

'Nino told me,' Domenico says.

Right. Makes sense, I guess. Nino and Domenico are like brothers. They go way, way back. 'So then when *Salvatore* found out about Beth . . .'

'*He* killed Ambrogio.'

'Exactly,' I say. 'Domenico. Please . . . just . . . let me go. I'm sorry I lied.'

I flutter my eyelashes. Stick out my chest. Do my best 'damsel in distress'.

He pushes the gun further into my organs. He's going to puncture my fucking lungs.

'Don't do it again,' he says.

I shake my head. 'I won't.'

He lets me go and walks away. I lean back against the wall. When I finally catch my breath I follow him down the hall.

We meet my mother back at the table. Domenico glowers at me.

'Ahthereyouare,' my mother slurs. 'Shallwegetthebill?'

We're walking back towards the flat, Domenico and my mum in front. I am trailing just behind. The breeze is as soft as a Gucci cashmere and merino jumper. The tinkle of a water fountain sounds just like Vivaldi. Giant sycamores wave in the wind as we stroll beneath their branches. We turn a corner on to a bridge that leads us over the River Tiber. The water snakes and sparkles in the light of the silver moon.

'Oh, Domenico, it's *beautiful*,' my mother says, gazing out at the view.

'*E bella come te*, Mavis. *Beautiful like you.*'

We turn into my winding side street of cobblestones and balconies. Ancient wooden doors are adorned with the roaring heads of lions. I look around – just in case – for Nino, but there's no sign. At least, not yet. Domenico and my mum hold hands. I feel like a gooseberry.

'Well, thank you, Domenico, for a wonderful evening. You really didn't need to spoil us like that. It was really very chivalrous. Say, thank you, Alvina.'

'Yeah. Cheers. Thanks,' I say. She thinks I'm five years old.

'The pleasure, *signora*, was all mine. You are as young and as beautiful as your daughter, if not more so. I trust you enjoyed your supper?'

'Oh yes. Very much. I especially liked the red wine. What was it called again?'

'*Regina di Renieri.*'

'Ah yes. *Regina*,' she says with a hiccough.

'*Regina* means *queen*,' says Domenico.

But really, who gives a shit?

'And I loved those chocolates they served with dessert. *Baci* or something?' she says.

'*Sì, Baci. Baci* means *kisses*.'

'They were too sweet for me,' I say. 'Kind of saccharine.'

We climb the endless flights of stairs that lead to my apartment. We stand at the top, huffing and puffing, as I look for my keys. Domenico and his two heavies seem to have made themselves at home. I don't know where my mum's going to sleep. It's a two-bedroom flat. She'll have to go out and find a hotel . . . at this time of night. With the baby. We push through the door and into the lounge. Riccardo and Giuseppe look up. They're playing with a laughing baby Ernesto, tickling his tummy and ruffling his hair as he crawls around on the living-room floor. Baby toys are strewn all around them. They look like they've had a ball.

'I wish you goodnight,' Domenico says, kissing my mother's outstretched hand.

My mother giggles like a teenage girl.

I roll my eyes. 'Goodnight,' I say. 'I'm going to bed.'

I can't take any more of this. This evening has been hellish. It couldn't *possibly* get any worse. I slam my door and flop down on the bed. I stare at the ceiling. There's a water mark over there in the corner. Upstairs must have a leak. I turn off the light and I'm just drifting off when I hear something bang against one of the walls.

BANG.

BANG.

BANG.

BANG.

'*Domenico. You Italian stallion.*'

'*Make love to me, Mavis. My queen.*'

Oh my God, *I bloody knew it.*

'*That is beyond gross,*' says Beth.

For once she's said something I agree with.

I pull the pillow over my head. It does nothing to block the noise.

BANG.

BANG.

BANG.

BANG.

There's a CRASH as my bedroom door smashes open. I sit up in bed and turn on the light.

What is it now?

Domenico's standing there, fully aroused and naked from the waist down. *Someone kill me. Kill me now.*

'Your mother says, "Do you have a condom?"'

I open my mouth and close it again. I've lost the power of speech.

My fucking mother. This fucking guy. She's sixty-one. Nearly sixty-two. He is half her age.

'No, I don't,' I say.

(Yes, I do. But he's not having it. There's a packet of ribbed raspberry-ripple rubbers somewhere in my Prada bag, but I'm saving those for a special occasion. I want them for when I find Nino.)

'Don't worry,' I say, 'she's too old to get pregnant.'

'I know, but I have Hepatitis A, B and C.'

He closes the door and leaves.

There are muffled voices in the lounge. I hear him asking the two mobsters. I guess one of them must have a johnny because two or three minutes later:

BANG.

BANG.

BANG.

DAY SIX:

The Cop

LAST WEEK

Saturday, 29 August 2015
Taormina, Sicily

My sister's dead. I'm fucking rich. It's time to celebrate. I do a line off Nino's chest then lick the residue. Hot, salty sweat. Acidic cocaine. My brain ignites again. I slide my tongue along his skin. My mouth feels numb. Tastes bitter. I run my fingers through the soft black hair on Nino's pecs.

'You want another line?' I say, passing him the rolled-up fifty. 'Go on, have another one. This shit is really bomb.'

Nino racks up on my body. He does a line between my breasts. He licks me from my pubis all the way up to my neck.

'Hey. Stop that. It tickles,' I say, wriggling out of the way.

He licks me some more on my face then bites me on the ear.

'Stop it. Stop. I'll kill you,' I say. His tongue is hot and wet.

I whack him over the head with the pillow. He pretends he's dead. A tiny white feather escapes and floats down on to the bed. I watch it settle on the sheets, then lie down next to him. There is something so erotic about fucking in my dead twin's bed. The sheets still smell of Ambrogio, of Armani Code Black. That's my sister's lingerie all over the floor. I'm even wearing Beth's lipstick: Rouge Allure by Chanel. There's some on Nino's dick.

We listen to the silence pulsing, to the quiet, empty night. There's nothing there beyond these walls. We are everything. There is no dead Salvatore lying on the kitchen floor. No Domenico cleaning him up. No sister buried in the wood or Ambrogio cold in a morgue. Nino and I are all that matters. We make the world go around.

'Betta,' he whispers in my ear. Warm breath – goosebumps – on my neck. I smell his musky, manly scent. 'Come with me. I have an idea.'

He grabs my hand and pulls me up. Leaps off the king-size bed.

'What? Why? Where are we going?'

'It's gonna be great. You will love it.' He finds his clothes on the bedroom floor. 'I've done it lots of times before. It's crazy. Fucking fun.'

He's speaking fast. His eyes are glassy.

'Done what? What's great?' I say.

I want us to stay right here and do some more cocaine.

Nino is already leaving. I watch him pull on his blue jeans. He has a body like Brad Pitt, like Tyler Durden in *Fight Club*. That scene where he's topless in the basement. That scene where he's naked in the bath . . . Brad's perfect, like an action man, but he's not a patch on *him*.

I find my clothes. My pants. My bra. I can't see my dress, but fuck it. There's no one around to see us now. Most of them are dead. He disappears through the bedroom door. I follow him, half naked. I run down the hall in Beth's lingerie, the lacy red La Perla, then all through the villa and out the front door. We're outside in Beth's garden. There's the pool like molten silver. I half expect to see my twin. But no, she's gone: don't be an idiot. It's just us. Relax.

The night is almost pitch-black, but there's a waning gibbous moon shining bright over Mount Etna.

Nino turns and flashes a smile. He looks youthful, almost boy-like.

The sweet night air and frangipani: sugary as candy.

The sound of crickets chirruping.

A sultry summer's night.

'Nino.' I laugh. My head is fucked up. A wide grin spreads across my face. I sing 'Nino. Nino. Nino' to the tune of a fire engine.

'Hurry up, Betta. Come on.'

I've got the church giggles. I bite my lip to try to stop. It's all I can do to stop myself shouting *my name is Alvina*.

We push past leaves. Some lemon trees. Some olive groves. Some houses. A warm breeze blows across my face. We come on to a quiet clearing. That's when I catch up with him. Oh fuck man, I'm so high. I lean over to put my hands on my knees; I'm dizzy. I look up to see where I am. Nino walks over to me. He takes my arm and I follow him. We look out over the edge of a cliff and stand in the breeze holding hands. He leads me to the very edge. It's a fucking long way down. It looks dangerous. Deadly. The moonlight casts an eerie glow, rippling on the silent water. Everything's in black and white, just like an old movie. My heart is beating faster now. What are we doing here? This looks like the cliff where we dumped Ambrogio. My whole body freezes.

'Nino, what was your idea?'

'We are going to jump.'

'Are you out of your fucking mind?'

'Do you trust me?' he says.

I pause. That's a very good question. Is he going to lose me like he lost my twin? He made her disappear.

Nino grips my hand even tighter. His palm feels slippery in mine.

'*Uno, due . . .*'

'Nino, wait.'

'*Uno, due, tre.*'

First he fucked me, and now he's killing me. It's a tale as old as time. But why? Oh God, does he know I'm not Beth? Does he know I murdered his boss? If he knew I killed Ambrogio, that I had smashed his head in with a rock, he'd get revenge and murder me, just like he did with Salvo.

He pulls me and – I can't help it – I jump.

The ground gives away to nothing . . .

Nothing . . .

and we're falling,

falling,

screaming.

'AAAAAAAHHHHHHHH.'

A wall of cold sea air slams into me.

The starlight blurs.

My stomach flips.

The rush is nuts, like nothing ever.

I'm completely off my tits.

I leave my mind and watch us fall from way up high. I see our bodies tumbling. The curve of the world as it turns. The Earth's a shrinking blue-green ball.

Then we crash into the water.

There's a deafening noise. A thunderous ROAR and I'm back. Wide awake. I'm buzzing. My senses way too sensitive. I feel crazy alive. And now we're deep down under water. There's a tug on my right hand as Nino pulls me up. Cold, black, heavy, freezing water. Bubbles streaming from my mouth. I swim as fast as I can to the surface, kicking my legs. Thrashing my arms. Nino's still holding my hand. He never even let go. We burst up through the icy water, out into the midnight air. I'm gasping. Splashing. Swearing. Rushing.

'FUCK. FUCK. FUCK.'

Nino kisses me. He squeezes my body against his wet skin, slippery and sliding. Our hearts pound as one. We're treading water in the waves under the vast and starry sky. We rise and fall and rise and fall and rise and fall and rise . . .

This kiss. The salty sea. His icy lips. I'm shaking. Shivering in the water. And I can hardly breathe.

Nino pulls me closer again.

'Betta,' he says. 'You like it?'

Urgh. There's that name again. I'm just going to tell him.

I close my eyes and let him hold me. Feel his naked chest on mine.

'Nino, there's something I have to tell you.'

I stop.

I don't think I can do it.

I picture Beth's face in my head.

I look up at him, afraid.

His eyes are shining black in the moonlight.

'What is it, Betta? Come on.'

'This is the best night of my life.'

This time, I kiss him.

Chapter Twenty-three

Saturday, 5 September 2015
Trastevere, Rome, Italy

I find my clothes on the bedroom floor. I pick them up
and pull them on. Prada knickers. Leather trousers.
Leather pumps. Black leather jacket. I check myself
out in the full-length mirror. Run my fingers through my
hair. That pink dye is washing out. I'll have to do it again.
Not *now*. There's something far more urgent, more important than my hair. I wipe yesterday's mascara away with a
licked fingertip and apply some concealer to cover the
bruises – blue and green – on my new nose. Purple lipstick. More mascara. I add the mirror shades. I pull out
Nino's old fedora. Tilt it at a jaunty angle. Try it on the
other way around. It looks fab with my pale fuchsia hair.

Right.

I'm ready for Dynamite.

I'm ready to find my man.

Nino will wish he hadn't messed with me. He'll be sorry
that we ever met. I'll find him and I'll bed him. (A quickie.
Just one more hit. I deserve that.) And then, when he thinks
he is safe, when he thinks he is in the clear, I'll kill him,
slowly and painfully. And then he'll disappear.

I double-check my cuckoo clock. The money's still inside, that's good. But I need to travel light today. I can't lug all this stuff around. I might need to leave here in a hurry. I may never come back.

I grab the banknotes from the clock and shove them down my push-up bra. What else? What else am I going to need? I look around the room. I can't take all these clothes with me, the lube, the electric toothbrush . . . All these things are heavy, bulky. They would slow me down. I'll have to be selective, discerning. I wish I had a carving knife, but there aren't any more sharp knives in the kitchen. I've already looked. I take the cock ring and the condoms, my cigarettes and my passport. I don't need my sister's any more; everyone knows she's toast. I zip up my bag. Let's do this thing. I light myself a fag.

I tiptoe into Domenico's room and check he's still asleep. He is in bed with my mother with Ernie passed out in between them. The baby cuddles Domenico's face and sucks his tiny thumb. They're the picture of a happy family. I still can't believe he fancies my *mum*. Perhaps he's into necrophilia? Each to their own, I suppose.

Poor Ernie, I'm leaving him *again*. This is the second time now. I can't help feeling bad about it. Abandoning him with my mad-whack mum and that fucking psychopath. Poor kid's going to need some serious therapy. Probably even more than me. You know what? I'll take him too. I don't want my mother to have him. I'll adopt him. That's an awesome plan. I'll steal the kid, find Nino's phone and Dynamite's number. Then I'll take the gun.

The floorboards creak as I creep in and look around for Domenico's weapon. I rifle through his jacket pockets, but it's not here. Goddamn. I can't find Nino's mobile either. Can't see it on the bedside table or charging somewhere by a wall. What the hell has he done with it? I need it for my plan.

I bet Domenico sleeps with his gun underneath his pillow. I know I would if I were him. Perhaps the phone and the gun are both there? It's got to be worth a look. I sneak over to the bed and peer into his brutish face. He's snoring loud and snarly snores, as I imagine an ogre would. He seems to be in a deep sleep. Fuck it, I'm going to try it. I slide my hand under his pillow, slowly, slowly, inch by inch. He rolls over and traps my arm. His nose an inch from my tits. If I move now, he's sure to wake up . . . Well, *that* didn't work.

'Shit,' I say under my breath.

My mother wakes up.

'Alvina?' she says, rubbing her eyes and sitting up.

Her voice pierces my eardrums like needles. It's way too early for this shit. She's wearing a lacy scarlet slip. Her make-up is smeared and her hair's a mess. *Oh God.* My mum and Domenico. That's something I can never un-see. I close my eyes, but all I see is Domenico's massive erect penis. It's burnt on to my retinas for all eternity. It's like some kind of phallic screen saver I don't know how to delete. I open my eyes again quickly.

'Hello, Mum,' I say.

Domenico rolls over and I reclaim my arm.

'Did you have a nice time last night?' I ask. Of course she did; I heard EVERYTHING.

'Oh *yes*. Thank you,' she says.

Urgh. Post-coital bliss.

I check Domenico's hog-like face, but he is sound asleep and snoring.

Ha. Have you eyes? You cannot call it love.

Even I wouldn't shag him.

I hear my cuckoo clock chime in the next room.

I get an idea.

'Hang on, Mum, I got you a present.'

I run back into my bedroom and grab the stupid clock. She follows me out into the hall. I give my mother the clock. She eyes the gift suspiciously, as though it were a home-made bomb.

'Did you steal this from Grandma's house?'

'No, I bought it in London.'

She winds the clock forward an hour, then gives it back to me.

'Domenico doesn't know a *thing* about pest extermination. I asked him the best way to get rid of a cockroach and he suggested that I shoot it. Have you been lying again, Alvina?'

'That is actually very effective. Cockroaches are hard to kill.'

'Why are you up so early?' she says. 'This isn't like you.'

'I'm just popping out to get some milk.'

My mother raises an eyebrow. 'Well, there's a first time for everything.'

I look into my mother's beady eyes: a pterodactyl from the Cretaceous period. I'm just going to ask.

'Can I take Ernie out with me? I'll give you a break. You look like you could use some help. You're too old to look after a baby.'

My mother frowns. She's not convinced.

'If Celine Dion can have a child at the ripe old age of forty-two, then I can look after my grandson,' she says.

'But you're in your sixties, not your forties.'

'Nonsense,' she says. 'My dermatologist says I have the skin of a thirty-year-old.' She definitely doesn't. She's probably fucking him. 'You're as old as the person you feel.'

I picture my mother feeling Domenico. It is way too graphic.

'Well, I think you should give Ernesto to me. I look a little bit like Beth, so he might think I'm his mum.'

'Ha. You and your sister are nothing alike. Now, that's the end of the subject.'

'But I gave you a cuckoo clock . . .'

Ernie starts crying inside the bedroom. My mum goes back into the room.

I sigh. For once, at least, she's right. It was hard enough dragging that puppy around, never mind a *baby*. I have a vision of Ernesto strapped to my chest in his papoose, screaming all the way through a shoot-out. Guns blazing. Bullets flying. No, no, no, I can't be arsed. It's tough to 'have it all'. It's hard work juggling kids *and* a career. What the hell were those feminists thinking? I guess I'm just not that maternal.

'All right. Fine. Whatever.'

Domenico emerges from the bedroom. He stretches out and yawns. The inside of his mouth looks just like a hippo's. A hippo with lots of fillings.

'I need to talk to you,' I say.

He closes the door behind him.

'Dynamite?' I say. 'Come on, let's go. Right now.'

'*Sì*. We can go today. But she might not talk,' he says. 'She might be loyal to Nino.'

'Dynamite's a *she*?' I say.

'*Sì, sì*, she's a she.'

I don't know why, but I'd assumed that she would be a guy.

'Don't you have ways to make people talk?'

'I don't torture women.'

I follow him into the lounge. I scoff. 'You tortured *me*.'

'We did not,' Domenico says. 'We left you in a fence.' He sits down in the living room and turns on the TV. 'You still have all your fingernails. You still have all your toes . . .'

'All right. OK, I get it.'

He skips the channels on the TV to get to the news.

'I don't care. I want to see her. I'll make her talk,' I say.

This place looks familiar. I don't know why. I've never been here before. All of these cobbled streets look the same. All of these wooden doors . . .

Domenico's fist pounds the front door:

I hear a voice call from inside.

'Hold your horses,' it says.

The door swings open to reveal . . . *Rain*? It takes me a second to place her. She's drinking some kind of protein shake from a blender cup, standing before us in skin-tight leggings, Nike trainers and an exercise bra that's turned see-through with sweat.

'Rain?' I say. 'What are *you* doing here?' He must have got the wrong door.

'Beyoncé? I tried to call you . . .'

She grabs me and throws me into the hall. Pins me up against the wall. 'You *fuck me* then you don't answer my calls?'

She lifts me off the ground.

'The police. They took . . . they took my phone.'

Now that is *true*, if not relevant.

Damn, my killer move won't work. She doesn't have any balls.

I struggle and strain, but her grip is firm. My feet kick out at nothing.

She drops me and I crash to the floor. I rub my shoulder. That hurt.

Fucking crazy violent bitch.

I think it's dislocated.

Rain pulls me back up to standing. I grab my Prada bag. Domenico steps inside the flat and closes the front door.

'Oh, hey, Domenico,' says Rain.

'*Ciao*, Dynamite.'

'Wait a minute. What the fuck? *You* are Dynamite?'

'I am. Well, that's my nickname really . . . like Beyoncé, I guess?'

Rain lets us through into the hall and checks the door behind us. She bolts it three times and hooks a chain, then peers out through the spyhole. She's more paranoid than I am. I don't think there's anyone there. She turns and looks into my eyes, then gives me a quick kiss on the lips. 'I was hoping I'd see you again . . .'

'You two know each other then?' Domenico says, scratching his head.

'Yes we do,' says Rain. 'She's a bad, bad bitch.'

I could say the same.

She rubs sweat from her brow with a purple towel.

I shake my head. Who *is* this woman? What is going on?

'Come and sit down,' says Rain.

She gestures inside her flat. There's a Fitbit on her wrist. Her nails are bright turquoise. She's painted them since I last saw her. It's a cool colour; I like it.

We follow Rain into the lounge. The air is hot and stuffy. I haven't been in *here* before. I would remember *this* . . .

There's a treadmill spinning in the middle of the room. 'Drag Me Down' by One Direction blares from a wide-screen TV. The boys are dressed as astronauts. Orange spacesuits. Floppy hair. Dancing around on a shiny space-ship. She must have been working out. Rain grabs the remote control and then mutes Harry Styles. The walls are lined with shelves and stacked up high with plastic cases. There are hundreds and hundreds of them piled on top of one another. I spot an open cardboard box on the floor just by the door; I take a look inside. It's full of small round silver objects roughly the size of pears. I frown. They look like hand grenades. Oh, no, wait. They probably are.

'When you said you worked *in sales* . . .' I say.

Rain takes off her translucent bra and peels her leggings down. She steps out of a barely there black lace G-string and stands naked in front of us. We make eye contact for a second, then she turns and leaves. I watch her toned and muscular back.

'Won't be a sec,' she says.

Domenico and I sit down and watch some MTV.

'That's one hot piece of ass,' he says. 'You tapping that?'

'I am. What happened to the Jane Austen?'

'Oh, that was for your mum.'

After six or seven minutes, Rain comes back into the room in a spandex minidress. Her hair is wet. She's taken a shower. She looks like an Adidas model. She sees me checking her out and smiles.

'I like your trainers,' I say.

'So what will it be?' asks Rain. She gestures around the cluttered room. 'I presume you are here for a weapon?'

Domenico and I exchange glances.

'I have some gorgeous sawn-offs at the moment, fresh from the USA. Or if you're after something old-school, I have a 1972 Lupara. It's really pretty, good as new.'

She shoots a wink at me.

I look around the living room. These cases must be full of guns. It's like we're in some kind of warehouse/living room/gym.

'No, no. I don't need a weapon,' Domenico says, opening his jacket. The handle of his gun sticks out. You can't really miss it.

'Nice, is that a Colt?' she says.

'*Sì*, a 10mm,' he says. 'It used to be my father's.'

'Oh, I need a weapon,' I say.

Domenico shakes his head.

Rain smiles a radiant smile. She's stunning. More beautiful than I remember. Everything's fuzzy from that night. She is a vision. A goddess.

'And what would you like, sexy?'

Ordinarily I would say *the bigger the better*. But I'm on the move. I'm stealthy. Sneaky. A killer undercover.

'Something small I can fit in my pocket?' I show her the pocket of my jacket.

'Hmm. Now let me see.'

She takes a clipboard from a shelf and leafs through a couple of pages. '*Dum-di-dum-di-dum*. Oh, yes, I have a Diamondback 9mm, a Karh Arms CW380, a Kel-Tec P-32, a FN Baby Browning .25, or a NAA-22S Short. All great weapons. Top of the range. What would you like to see?'

She looks at me expectantly. Legs like a racehorse. Washboard stomach. Man, I wish I had her figure. But without the treadmill thing.

'The first one you said, with the diamonds?'

She nods, then turns away. I watch as she walks to a row of cases, then climbs to the top of a folding ladder. She takes a small black plastic case from the top and brings it to me.

'Ta-da. This is the DB9.'

She flips open the case to reveal a tiny matt-black hand-gun. The handle has a diamond pattern: a cute design with raised plastic shapes, but there aren't any actual jewels. Shame. I guess I could buy some diamanté and jazz it up a little?

'Don't you just love it?' she says.

Domenico frowns at me. 'This isn't really why we're here . . .'

'Oh? It isn't?' says Rain, looking up.

'No, it isn't,' I agree. 'But as we are all here . . .'

I take the pistol from the case. It's light, so light it doesn't feel real. It seems more like a children's toy, but I know it's lethal. It can stick a slug inside your brain. It can shatter your patella.

'So why *are* you here?' says Rain.

She stands with her hands on her hips. She's as toned as a synchronized swimmer.

I try to hide the gun in my pocket. It fits perfectly.

'I wanted to take you out tonight. You know . . . out for dinner.'

'Like a date?' she says.

'Like a date.'

She leans in and kisses me. Her lips are soft and warm and sweet from the protein shake.

'Nino,' says Domenico. 'Have you seen him recently?'

'Who's asking?' asks Rain.

'I am, actually.'

'Ohhh . . . *that* Nino,' she says, turning to me. 'So that's who you were talking about. How weird we both know the same guy.'

Domenico shakes his head and lights himself a cigar.

Ha, see that, Domenico? No *torture* required.

'I have seen him. *How much?*' she says.

She looks at Domenico then me.

Domenico sighs. 'Alvina, are you going to buy that lame-ass gun?'

I pull the pistol from my pocket. Weigh it in between my hands. I feel the tiny raised diamonds and stroke the pistol like a cat. 'You know what, I think I will.'

'How much for the info and that gun?'

I glance at the cardboard box by the door. 'Ooh and a hand grenade. I want one of those as well.' Might come in handy. You never know. They look really fun.

Domenico rolls his eyes. 'Are you sure you know how to use them? They're very dangerous.'

'Yes, I know, that's why I want one.'

'They can cause a lot of damage. They're more power-ful than a gun.'

'Jesus, stop with the mansplaining. I understand. *I want one.*'

Domenico shrugs and turns to Rain. 'How much for the info, the gun and a hand grenade?' Rain downs the rest of her protein shake. 'Tastes like shit. Don't know why I drink them. Can I get you people something? A bourbon perhaps or a mint julep?'

'*Niente*,' says Domenico.

'I'll take a bourbon,' I say.

I need a drink. I'm freaking out. Was Nino right here in this room? Standing here where I am standing? What did he want? Did they have *sex*? *O most pernicious woman!* Did she fuck my guy? She opens up a drinks cabinet and pours out our drinks. One for her and one for me. She hands me a couple of inches of bourbon; it's dark and gold like honey.

'Ice?' she asks.

'No, neat,' I reply.

'What's your favourite kind of restaurant?'

I say, 'I don't know. Italian?'

'So how much?' interrupts Domenico.

Whatever it is, I'll pay it. I can't take any more of this. It isn't good for my mental health. I need to find that asshole *yesterday*. I'm getting all stressed out. I can't remember the last time I wrote a haiku. My mind's a messy blur. I down the drink in one. The bourbon burns the back of my throat.

'Ten thousand euros,' says Rain. 'And I'll throw in some ammo for free.'

She puts some bullets in the case with the gun.

Domenico whistles through his teeth.

'Fine,' I say. 'Where is he?'

She raises a thin, perfect eyebrow. She's looking right at me. 'First I want the money, baby.'

'Do not *baby* me.'

I grab a thick handful of banknotes from inside my bra.

'One, two, three, four . . .' I count out €10,000.

'Nino came here a few days ago.'

I knew it. I could smell him.

'He wanted a new identity. I got him a passport, a driving licence . . .'

'Ooh, can I get one of those?'

'He's changed his name to "Luca Mancini".'

'Luca? What the fuck?'

'And he bought a gun. A new Glock 40 –'

BANG. BANG. BANG.

Someone's knocking on the door.

I hear a voice call from outside. '*SIGNORINA. POLIZIA.*'

Chapter Twenty-four

Piazza della Republica, Rome, Italy

'POLIZIA. POLIZIA.'
It's a kid's voice: high-pitched and whiney.
'Shit. It's my lookout,' says Rain. 'Let's go.'
She stuffs the money in a handbag lying on the sofa. It's a Marc Jacobs satchel in sapphire like her eyes.

Domenico growls. '*Che palle.*'

Rain says, 'Follow me.'

She sprints out of the back of the flat and through the kitchen door. It's lucky we're on the ground floor.

I grab my gun out of its case and a handful of bullets and the hand grenade. I follow Rain and Domenico out and through the garden.

I stuff the weapons in my pockets as we sprint out through the gate.

Rain turns and glares at Domenico. 'Why are the cops here?'

'I don't know. *I* didn't call them.'

'Beyoncé?'

'No idea.'

I bet it's those Sicilian cops after me again. Oh man, why won't they leave me alone? Will I always be on the run?

Rain, Domenico and I race along a cobbled street into a crowded square. It's called La Piazza della Rotunda. Oh look, there's the Pantheon. How cool is that? It's splendid. Majestic. Fucking sublime. It's nearly a mile high with towering columns and an enormous dome. The facade's engraved with Roman letters. I have no idea what they say. I look around for the police, but I can't see them. Yet.

'I'll take you to where Nino is staying,' Rain says. 'Come on, this way.'

We follow her across the square. 'Hey, slow down.' I'm out of breath. She's so much fitter than me.

We run past a trattoria; it's bursting with city life. This place would be great for people watching. I could sit here all day long, eating ready-salted crisps and drinking cold white wine. But not right now, I guess; we're busy. We're going to find him.

Holy fuck.

THIS IS IT.

Any second now.

We turn a corner on to a street. Rain stops and points to a building.

Peach shutters. Cream walls. Pretty flowers in boxes.

'Are you kidding? He's in there?'

'Shh,' says Domenico.

He pulls out his foot-long Colt. I grab the Diamondback.

I stop.

There's a chill in the air.

Then a sudden, deafening noise:

KA-POW. KA-POW.

I turn round.

Rain is down on the floor.

Two black holes have appeared in the middle of her forehead. Shit. What was that? Was that *me*? I study the gun. Look down the barrel. But it's cold. I didn't shoot. It isn't even fucking loaded. It wasn't me. So who? The cops? Domenico? I look up and see Domenico sprinting across the square. But it can't have been him; he was up ahead. I could see what he was doing. People are screaming. Seriously, *what is going on*? I scan the square. No cops. But then . . . Nino. Of course. He must have seen us. We're standing right outside his flat. I look up and see that a window is open. A lacy curtain billows through. He saw us or heard us. He was waiting, the wanker. There's a sick feeling in my stomach. A swirling mess inside my head. I look down at Rain's chest. It's still. She isn't breathing. Fucking Nino. This fucking sucks. Why did he have to kill Dynamite? What am I doing, just *standing here*? I need to run.

I hear a loud siren.

A panda car approaches. It's a sleek black car with thin red lines and '*Carabinieri*' written on it in white. The car swerves right and heads for me, blocking off the end of the street.

A cop jumps out and shouts at me. 'Blah, blah, blah, blah, blah.'

He points *his* gun right at my head. I look down at the Diamondback in my hand. I'm faint. My ears are ringing. I turn and run back through the square. Past a fountain. A side street. A terrace café. Rome whizzes by in a dizzying whirl. I'm panting. Sweaty. Gasping. Heart pounding. Where am I going? I run and run and run. As soon as I start, I realize my error. I am *really crap* at running. What was I thinking? Oh my God, I need to sit down.

I find an alcove and collapse against a cool stone wall. I spark myself a Marlboro Light and take an angry drag. And then, from out of fucking nowhere, someone rugby-tackles me. SMACK. I'm down. I'm on the pavement. I see a dark blue uniform. Someone else's gun. I drop my fag and my Diamondback.

Damn, I just got that gun.

'*Tu sei in arresto*,' the cop shouts in my ear. He's lying – heavy – on my back, crushing me into the ground.

'*English* please. Do I *look* Italian?' When will people learn?

'*You are under arrest*,' he says.

'OK. Yeah, I got that.'

I breathe street dust. Taste dirt. The cop rolls me on to my back and then he pins me down again. Metal hand-cuffs clink round my wrists. Without even checking if I'm OK he hauls me up and pushes me. Really, some people. *No bloody manners.*

'This is an outrage. It wasn't *me*.'

The cuffs are tight. Uncomfortable. He drags me towards his car. Another cop car, then another, speeds on to the piazza.

'Dude, you're making a huge mistake.'

The policeman shoves my head down hard. He slams me into the back of his car, then jumps in the front seat. He floors the gas and sirens blare.

'What the hell do you think you're doing? I told you already, it wasn't me.'

'You were standing by a *corpse* with a *gun* in your hand,' the cop shouts back at me.

'I know. I know. But I didn't *shoot* her. You've got the wrong person. I swear.'

'We'll see about that. We'll do a post-mortem.'

'*Ha ha,*' says Beth. '*They've got you this time.*'

'I want a fucking lawyer.'

Chapter Twenty-five

Piazza Venezia, Rome, Italy

This is all just *typical*. The *one time* I didn't kill them is the time that I get caught. It's ironic, like that song by Alanis (I don't need a spoon; I need a gun). But they'll let me go. They have to. They've got to. They'll see it's a different kind of bullet. They'll spot it was a long-range shot. At least, I hope so. This whole thing's a joke. I AM SO PISSED OFF.

'It's Nino. He's the one you're after. He's the fucking *serial killer*.'

I glare at the cop in the rear-view mirror. Oh, he's actually quite fit. It's the first time I've had a proper look. He looks just like a Disney prince. An Italian version of Aladdin: floppy hair, good eyebrows, nice eyes. He's even handsome when he scowls (he's scowling at me right now). I have a thing for uniforms, and, I have to say, *Italian cops*. It's almost worth getting arrested. I'm already wet.

We speed along the busy streets, swerving in and out of traffic. Sirens blaring. Blue lights flashing. The handcuffs dig into my wrists. Lucky they're fastened on top of my lap. Ha, this guy's an amateur. They're supposed to be behind your back. There's still no way to get them off. I lean my head on the window and sigh a long, deep sigh. This is *shit*. I've got to get out of here. Need to find Nino. That fucking guy. I can't believe he just shot Rain. What did she do wrong? Was it because she took us to his place? Or because she knew his new ID? She was the one who got him the passport. Perhaps he was tying up loose ends. He was covering his tracks. I bet it was Nino who called the cops. The bastard sent them to Rain's flat.

The glass is cool against my hot cheek. I need to escape. But how? This is ridiculous. Why me? That *stronzo*'s out there running free. He just murdered that girl in broad daylight. She was *three feet* away from me. And you know what, I was starting to like her. She was really growing on me. I liked her trainers. Her nail polish. I really liked that Marc Jacobs bag. I wish she hadn't beaten me up, but other than that she was cool.

The Disney prince has got my gun, but I've still got that hand grenade. (Man, it's lucky he didn't frisk me. I bet he thought that was my only weapon. Ha ha. Big mistake.) The hand grenade weighs heavily inside my jacket pocket. I can feel it there now, resting on my hip. They're bound to search me at the station. It was just an oversight. When they find it they will take it and I will be in deep, deep shit . . .

I get one of my mad ideas.

I set my jaw.

It's *ace*. You know what? I'm going to do it.

I glance up at the rear-view mirror. The cop is focused on the road. I reach round with my cuffed hands and pull the hand grenade out. I twist my wrists and the cuffs dig in, cutting deep into my skin. It hurts, but I know it's worth it. This is going to be great. I cup the uneven metal shell between my hands. The police car speeds and bumps and sways. I hope I have time. I inch forward as far as I can until I'm literally on the edge of my seat. (It's lucky I'm not wearing a seat belt. Hey, isn't that *illegal*?) I tense my thighs and lift up my bum. I can feel the stretch in my hamstrings burn. I pull down my trousers and pants, just like in that cab with Rain. It's tricky, but the leather's stretchy and my thong is minuscule. I reach down between my legs, my wrists aching, straining. Ow. Ow. Ow. The cuffs are tighter than I thought. The metal digs into the flesh, scraping at the bone. Slowly and *carefully* I push the hand grenade inside. I feel it moving up, up, up my (slightly wet) vagina. The silver shell is cold and hard and – oh – quite knobbly. I stretch my fingers and thrust it all the way with my fingertips. Fucking hell, it feels intense. No scratch that: *fucking awesome*. The metal's flush against my G spot. I'm panting, wriggling, groaning.

'OOOOOOOOHHHHHHHHHH.'

'What the hell are you doing back there?'

'Nothing. *Oh, oh, OH.*'

I pull up my pants and trousers and slouch back heavily. The car bounces over a pothole. The explosive jiggles around inside. It feels just like a massive love egg or a big ribbed Ben Wa ball. He slams on the brakes outside the station. I think I'm going to come.

Now remember, Alvie, this is important. Let's call it an urgent note to self: don't pull on the ring like a tampon string. That wouldn't go down well.

★

They search me *almost* everywhere. They don't find anything. They throw me inside a cell and lock the metal gate. I listen to the guard's footsteps as he walks away. Then it's silent. Nothing. No one. Only me. The cell is small and very dirty. Just like fucking Archway. Grey ceiling, grey walls, grey bed, grey floor. The air smells of piss and despair. The bars are too narrow to stick your head through (that's a plus point, I suppose). The window's too high up to see out of. The mattress is tiny, with a thin blanket. The toilet used to be white. No cover. No seat. I don't want to touch it. I'll just hold it in till they let me out. It can't be that long, surely?

Someone's written their name in blood; it's scrawled across the wall: *Anna, Augusto 2013*. Someone else has tried unsuccessfully to scrub it off. Bloodstains are a bitch to get out; I learnt that in Sicily. I wonder who 'Anna' was. Was she innocent like me?

I grab on to the bars and roar into the corridor. 'NINO. YOU UTTER BASTARD. JUST WAIT TILL I AM FREE.'

Last time he left me at the Ritz with hundreds of thousands of pounds' worth of diamonds. But *this time* he shot my hot new date and left me to rot in a cell. This is a whole new level of nasty. This is a new kind of betrayal. If I was *mad* at him before, this time I'm fucking *mental*. I am getting out of here. Then I'll go A-bomb on his ass. I'll blow up his dick in his face. Alvie will have the last laugh.

I pace up and down the cell. Down and up again. I need a new foolproof plan. I've got to figure this out. The cops will realize their mistake and soon they will be after Nino. They'll want to look for the real killer. They'll work out it wasn't me. They've got manpower, technology. And now that Dynamite is dead I'm fresh out of leads.

What if we all work *together*? The cops can help me find him (and kill him). I need to win the Disney prince over and convince him I can help. But how can I get him on my side? What can I do to persuade him?

I'll worry about that later on.

But first, the murder weapon.

I check the hall outside my cell, but I can't see anyone. I pull down my pants and thong to remove the hand grenade. I bite my lip. My fingers twitch. I've got to get this right . . . Slowly and carefully I reach my fingers up inside . . .

'*You're going to explode,*' says Beth.

And I freak the fuck out.

OH MY GOD.

WHAT THE FUCK WAS I THINKING?

THERE'S A BOMB INSIDE MY MUFF.

Where's the pin?

I'm going to die.

I reach my fingers up, up, up but I can't seem to grab it.

I don't think I can get it out.

It's stuck.

It's stuck.

It's stuck.

'Fucking Nino, fucking FUCK.'

I hyperventilate. In, out, in, out. Air whistles out of me in a high-pitched squeak. I sound like an asthmatic guinea pig. I need a brown paper bag to blow into. Some gas and air or something . . . I need to *not have a bomb wedged up my cunt*. What the hell am I doing?

I lie on my side in the foetal position on the cold, hard, concrete floor.

Come on, Alvie. What the hell? You can't just leave it there.

'*This is the best day of my life.*'

'Fuck you, Beth. You're dead.'

I take a deep breath and reach my hands through my legs. I reach up a bit higher. But I don't know which bit to pull? One wrong move and this thing goes off . . . I can't squeeze my fingers up round the sides. Oh God, I give up. There's no way I can pull it out. This is a fucking mess. I'll have to go to hospital and tell them everything. But how the hell do I explain this? I take a deep breath. *Come on*. It's fine, they've seen it all before. People go to A&E every single day of the week with foreign objects stuck inside various orifices: glass bottles, aerosol canisters, lager cans and hamsters. I once read about a man in China, who got an eel stuck up his bum. The eel was alive and bit his insides to shreds. A hand grenade? That's *nothing*. They won't even bat an eyelid. I'm sure they see it all the time. But once they pull it out, what then? *Aye, there's the rub*. I'll get done for possession of illegal weapons. First the gun and then the bomb. No, no, no, this is suicide. I need another plan.

Chapter Twenty-six

Come on, Alvie, think, think, think. Where is your poetic genius? I've got to think *outside my box*. I'm going about this thing all wrong. It's not *pulling* I need to do. I know, I've got to *push*. I have another look down the corridor, check both ways, left and right, but it's clear. OK. Let's do this. Let's give birth to a baby bomb. I squat down low, as low as I can, and *squeeze, squeeze, squeeze, squeeze, squeeze*. I push the hand grenade down, down, down (it's lucky I have a great pelvic floor). I feel it move down my vagina and pop out in the palm of my hand. Ha ha. That was actually quite easy. (What is the fuss all about?) I didn't need an epidural or caesarean like Beth. I study the hand grenade in my palm. That's better than a ping-pong ball. I could have my own show in Bangkok. I wipe the explosive on the bed sheet then shove it in my jacket pocket. Phew, that was close. Things could have got ugly. But no, it was fine. I'm a pro . . .

A man's voice.

'Signorina Knightly?'

'Yes? What's up? Are you letting me go?'

'The commissario would like to see you. Please, come with me.'

The guard unlocks the metal gate. I can see he has my

handbag. Ah, that's good. They're returning my things. They're probably letting me out. I take it from him and sling it over my shoulder.

'Can I use the toilet?' I say. 'The one in there was filthy.'

'Of course. Please follow me.'

Once I'm locked inside the loo I find the pills tucked away in my wallet and scan the label: double strength. I pop one of the bad boys out of the plastic. Then another. And another. The silver foil crinkles and crackles. They plop into my palm. They're tiny; no bigger than a pin-head, a pretty little diamond shape. But I know that size can be misleading (not when it comes to dicks or dildos, but with other things, like drugs). These pills pack a punch and a half. I lick one of the cobalt tablets; I need to check what it tastes like. I don't want it to be obvious I've doped him. The Disney prince would *not* be pleased. The coating is bitter. Acidic like lemon. Sharp like MDMA. I'll have to mix it with something sweet or he'll notice straight away.

Three pills at *double* strength; am I overdoing it? I want them to be quick. Effective. But two would probably do it. Fuck it, I'll have one myself. Who knows? It could be fun. I pop a tab into my mouth and wash it down with tap water. I wipe my face with a paper towel. I wonder what it will do. I've never taken one before; they're for the guys, obviously. I guess I'll have to wait and see . . . Ooh, this is exciting. I feel like Alice in Wonderland; will I shrink or will I grow? It's like nibbling a magic mushroom. Eat me. Drink me. Fuck me. I slip the other two pills in my pocket and shove my purse back in my bag. I check myself out in the full-length mirror, ruffle up my hair and pout. Spin round to assess my ass. Not *bad*, I guess. But still, not *perfect*. I wish I had some of Beth's magic lingerie. Some crotchless pants or a latex basque by Atsuko Kudo. I walk out of the bathroom and close the door.

The guard leads me down the hall to an office. I have the Viagra in my left pocket, the hand grenade in my right. It's lucky I always carry them with me. You never know when they might come in handy. When it might be an emergency. *Be prepared*. Yes, that's my motto. I learnt that in the Girl Guides.

I peer through the gaps in the narrow blind slats; there he is, the Disney prince. I can see him sitting at his desk. It's lucky it's not an interrogation room; that would have derailed my plans. Cameras and all those two-way mirrors. He's drinking something out of a can. It's blue and yellow. I can't see the label from here. I step back from the glass when he looks up and sees me. The guard knocks on the door.

'*Sì. Chi è?*'

He opens the door and steps through. 'Signorina Knightly, *commissario.*'

'*Grazie,*' says the Disney prince, standing up from his desk.

I step inside the room and then the guard leaves. I close the door behind him softly, turning the key inside the lock so no one will hear. I pocket the key and then pull down the blind so no one can see in.

'Bit bright,' I say with a shrug, turning to face him. 'You look *great* this afternoon. Have you done something different with your hair?' I sit down opposite his chair and put my feet up on the desk.

The Disney prince frowns. 'So, Miss Knightly, are you ready to talk?'

'You never told me your name,' I say.

'I am Commissario D'Amore.'

'That's a lovely surname,' I say. 'You got a pretty *first* name to go with that?'

He sighs. 'My name is Alessandro.'

Alessandro frowns. His dark brown fringe flops over his forehead. His Disney prince eyes look annoyed. The yellow can is Limonata, that sparkling soft drink by San Pellegrino. It's in the middle of his desk, but I can't tell from here how much is left.

'That looks good. Have you got one for me?' I gesture to the can.

He rolls his eyes, but gets up and walks over to a fridge. It's one of those mini ones you buy for chilling beer. He keeps his eyes on me as he opens the door. I smile my sweetest smile. He reaches inside the fridge. As soon as his back is turned, I slip two pills in his can of pop. I pick it up and swirl it around. The liquid fizzes and froths. I put it down as he approaches.

'Mmm, looks nice,' I say. He hands me a can and I lick my lips. 'Oh. Do you have a straw?'

I tug on the ring pull; it makes a 'PHFSSSSSSSSSSSST' noise. The fresh scent of citrus.

He rolls his eyes. Again. Alessandro opens the drawer of his desk and rummages around inside. He pulls out a long paper straw, the kind you get with shakes from McDonald's, and tosses it to me across the desk. I stick it in my can.

'Anything else?' he says.

'No, I'm good. Have you had lunch?'

(In my experience, Viagra takes longer to work if the man has eaten, sometimes as long as *ninety* minutes. I hope he doesn't have a full stomach. That would be catastrophic.)

'No, I haven't. I've been working my ass off.' He raises an eyebrow and looks at me as though it's my fault my ex-boyfriend's a psycho. 'I've got the whole of Rome's press harassing me for an arrest. Not to mention the mayor —'

'Hey, Alessandro. Don't blame *me*. Nino's the one you should be mad at. But I understand, you're stressed out.'

'Stressed? Stressed? Of course I'm stressed. I'm having a nervous breakdown. A sniper shoots a woman dead in one of the city's busiest squares. Outside the fucking *Pantheon*. In the middle of the day. And he's still out there on the run? It's the height of the tourist season.'

'Baby, you need to *relax*.'

He picks up his drink and takes a swig. I'm sure he wishes it were something stronger. I wonder if the Viagra's dissolved. Now I wish I'd given him three . . . I watch his throat move in and out, in and out, as he swallows.

'Ach,' he says, smacking his lips then slamming down the can. The aluminium wobbles on the polished surface and makes a tinny sound.

I bet that was *bitter*. Limonata's already acidic, but with those double-strength pills mixed in it must have been off-the-scale sour.

'So, you worked out that I didn't shoot her. That's an excellent start.'

'Your gun wasn't loaded. Had never been used. That was a long-range shot,' he says.

'Uh-huh. That's what I told you.'

Men, do they ever listen? I'm always repeating myself.

I take a sip of my drink through the straw; it's fizzy, icy cold. I suck it in a suggestive manner. I wonder if he'll get the hint.

'Of course,' he says; he sounds annoyed. 'You are just an innocent witness, who *happened* to be at the scene of the crime holding a fucking gun.'

'That's right,' I say. 'A coincidence.'

'A gun that you don't have a licence to own.'

'I was just about to go and get one. Being crap at personal admin does *not* make me a murderer. I told you, that was Nino.'

Alessandro stands and presses his fists into his shiny desk, his shoulders hunched, his forehead creased. He reminds me a bit of the Beast in *Beauty and the Beast,* but with less facial hair and better teeth. I look up through my lashes and bite my bottom lip. Then I suck a bit more on my straw.

'And you *happen* to be friends with the man you claim is the perpetrator.'

'Nino is an ex-acquaintance. I wouldn't call him a *friend.*'

Alessandro punches his desk. The boom reverberates.

'So . . . what else have you figured out?'

His expression says it: *nothing*.

Ha. I'm really enjoying this.

'Well, I know who did it. Nino Brusca is armed and dangerous. I bought the gun to protect myself. To protect myself from *him*.' Something's tingling down below . . . I think those pills are working. 'I can't believe you arrested *me*.' I do a wounded Barbie face.

'I was just doing my job.'

I hold back crocodile tears. He passes me a tissue.

Alessandro shakes his pretty head. His hair is thick and glossy. I wonder what conditioner he uses. My hair never shimmers like that. He grabs his can and knocks it back, glugging down the rest of the drink.

'Ach,' he says, again.

I watch him wipe his mouth with his hand and throw the can at the bin. (I'm impressed; it actually goes in. That never works for me.) I sip my fizzy drink. I can tell he doesn't know what to think. His handsome face looks confused, like if you'd just asked Ken to choose between Sindy or Barbie. He really is a beautiful creature, as handsome as Justin Trudeau. He hasn't got any dirt on me. Everything's circumstantial. And here I am, offering to help. Offering a lot more too . . .

'Alessandro,' I say, leaning in. I let my voice tremble. 'I'm scared. I think he might have been aiming for *me*, not that other woman . . .'

His Ferrero Rocher eyes look into mine. I think he's coming round.

'If you . . . if you promise to keep me safe, then I can help you find him,' I say. 'You and me, we're on the same team. We're both on the same side.'

There's an odd sensation in my pussy; the blood is really starting to flow. My clit feels suddenly enormous, too alert, too sensitive. My vagina is starting to throb. What is going on down there? I shift a little in my seat. I only took *one* of those things and my vulva has doubled in size.

'Is it just me, or is it hot in here?' I take off my leather jacket and drape it on the back of my seat (being careful not to knock the explosive; I'll need that later on). Alessandro watches me. He lets his eyes linger on my chest for just a nanosecond too long. I play with my hair, cock my head to the side, look at him like I really want him. I uncross then cross my legs. (I wish I wasn't wearing these trousers, a skirt would have been so much better, or maybe a little dress. Ideally I would have no pants on, like Sharon Stone in *Basic Instinct*. Now that would get his attention.)

Alessandro looks down at his messy desk and shuffles some papers. I glance at the clock. Every second counts. Nino could be leaving the city or even on his way out of Italy. I know he's got a fake passport . . . the money . . . the fucking motive. I'll give it a minute, then make my move. But sometimes policemen are too formal. Correct. Aloof. Professional. Reluctant to go to bed with their suspects or have casual sex with their witnesses. I know, I know. This is *Italy*, not the UK. It's not like the same rules apply. EU rules or whatever. Most policemen are corrupt.

They're horny. Insatiable. But still, it's a risk: full sex in his office? There is a *chance* that this won't work.

Alvie. Stop. You can't think like that.

'*There's no way this will work,*' says Beth.

Whether you think you can or think you can't, you're right. Who said that? If you can dream it, you can do it. Some bullshit like that. But it's *true*.

I'm feeling sticky, flustered. Waves of heat wash up and down and up and down my body. My cheeks are flushed. My pussy's wet. I swivel in my chair.

Alessandro takes his jacket off and hangs it on a hook by the door. He loosens his tie, takes that off too. I wish he'd take off more. I can tell his body's ripped beneath that fitted tailored shirt. He walks back towards the desk, but suddenly stops and freezes. A look of panic crosses his face. I check his crotch and – yup – there it is. It's worked. My madcap plot. It looks like a substantial erection, but the proof of the pudding is in the eating and I can't wait to get him undressed.

I spin round in my swivel chair and give him a hungry look. I twizzle a strand of hair in my fingers and channel my inner Megan (Fox). Work it, Alvie. You're a *star*.

'I feel so safe with you, Alessandro. You're such a big, strong, handsome man . . . I know you'd never hurt me, like Nino. You can be my *hero*.'

Alessandro blushes a violent red. I lean towards him in my chair.

'I, erm, I . . .' he stutters. Falters. '*Un momento*. Please.'

He turns and runs towards the door and pulls on the handle, but it's locked. It gives me the split second I need.

I jump up and follow him. This is my chance. He can't leave.

I leap on him like a piggyback and hook my ankles round his waist.

'No. Don't go. I want you so bad. You're driving me wild. Ever since the first moment I saw you . . .' (Earlier this morning when he arrested me.) 'You're all I've thought about.'

'Alvie?' he says. '*Che cazzo* . . . ?'

'Take me now or lose me for ever.'

He staggers backwards into the room and we crash on to his wooden desk. His waist's stuck firm between my legs. I'm not letting go.

Chapter Twenty-seven

I spin him round and kiss him.

'Alvie?'

'Alessandro, *scopami*.'

I pull off my top. My bra. I unzip his flies with one hand. I squeeze his butt cheek with the other. He moans and pushes himself towards me. He's going for it now. I kiss him again to stop him from talking or thinking or running away. I grab him by the dick and pull it up out through his boxer shorts.

'Mmm, Alessandro,' I say. 'You're so sexy.'

It's good I found out his first name. These things work better on first-name terms. Otherwise, it's too formal.

I leave him sitting on the desk and kneel before him on the floor. I take his dick inside my mouth. It's big and hot and throbbing. I lick it up and down the shaft. Taste tea tree shower gel. I push my head down all the way and feel him at the back of my throat. I swirl my tongue round the tip. I stroke his lovely balls.

I pull away and then stand up. I peel my leather trousers down. I step out of my tiny G-string and look him in the eyes.

'This is what we're going to do . . .'

I sit down naked on his desk and spread my legs apart.

'You are going to take me to Nino. I need five minutes alone with him.'

He nods. Puts his fingers in my mouth.

'Pour it into me, fuck boy.'

He just keeps going and going and going, again and again and again. He comes and then about two seconds later he's ready to go again. (*Five* times.) It's like he's possessed or on drugs. (Oh yeah, I suppose I did drug him.) I'm getting tired and really sore. I don't think I can take any more. I lean over the filing cabinet and watch the spinning floor.

'Enough,' I say, dripping with sweat. I can't seem to catch my breath. 'Let's . . . go . . . and . . . find . . . Nino . . .'

I hear indistinct Italian chatter as I follow the Disney prince into the briefing room and then flop down, destroyed. I move my chair a little closer so our thighs touch under the table. I give his knee a little squeeze. Alessandro clears his throat. I look around the meeting room. There's a two and a half, a three and a half, and a six and a quarter. Alessandro's definitely the fittest (he's a nine and a half, at least). I'm glad he's the one I had to seduce. It's fun mixing business with pleasure.

'*Oggi*, we need to speak *Inglese*,' Alessandro says. 'Signorina Knightly does not speak Italian. *Va bene?*'

'*Va bene*,' say the cops.

This is going well.

Alessandro sits at the head of the table in the cramped and over-bright room. A neon light flickers overhead.

The three other cops are seated around us on the cheap office furniture, dressed in super-sleek blue suits. I guess they're standard police uniforms, but they look like they're hot off the runway of Armani's latest show. Alessandro's lapel has the most pins and badges. I guess that means that he's the boss. He looks even hotter all showered and changed after our mega-sesh. He smells clean, like antiperspirant. I kick off my shoe and run my toes up and down his calf.

'Signorina Knightly has kindly agreed to help us with our investigation into the murder of Rain Campbell –'

'Dynamite,' I say.

'Pardon?' He turns to me. All the other cops stare.

'*Dynamite?*'

'What?'

'Forget it. It doesn't matter. That's her mobster name.'

'Miss Knightly is acquainted with the suspect, whom she informs us is named . . .' He checks his pad. 'Signor Giannino Maria Brusca.'

'He's called Nino,' I interject. 'The killer's name is *Nino* . . . He's in love with me.'

Alessandro frowns. I smile at him. 'OK, dear, carry on.'

'The CCTV footage shows the suspect leaving La Piazza della Rotunda and walking to the Hotel Raphaël on Largo Febo. We have been surveying the exits to the building and believe he is currently inside.'

I nod my head. This is all very serious. I do a solemn face . . . but inside I'm bursting with fireworks and sparklers; I think I'm about to ignite. Mwah ha ha. My plan is working. They are going to lead me straight to him. All I need is *one minute* alone; he'll be *chilli con carne, salami, pastrami, carpaccio de boeuf.* It will be different to last time, when he nearly threw me in front of that train. This time I'll have the upper hand. I'm calling the shots in this game.

Alessandro takes something out of a bag and lays it flat on the wooden table. It's a long black wire with a little black box and what looks like a microphone. He finds a roll of sticky tape and places it next to the black thing.

'What is *that*?'

'Miss Knightly,' says the Disney prince, turning to me. 'You will wear this wire under your clothes.' He blushes. It's really cute. 'When you meet with Signor Nino you must act natural, *normal*. Begin a casual conversation. It's imperative he does not suspect. You will have until 21.00 hours to elicit a confession. The suspect must admit that he fired the shots that killed Signorina Campbell. The moment the recording is complete my colleagues and I will apprehend him.'

'No way. I'm not wearing that.'

Alessandro whispers in my ear. 'If you don't wear it, the deal is off. You'll be charged with illegal possession of a firearm . . .'

'It's an excellent plan,' I say, jumping up and punching the table. 'I love it. It's ace.'

'Why would he confess to you?' asks one of the cops.

'Like I said, he's got a crush. He keeps on sending me red roses. Sexy texts. You know, he's obsessed. But he's really not my type.' I wink at the Disney prince.

Beth says, '*Puh-lease*. You're *obsessed*.'

'*È chiaro?*' Alessandro asks, looking around.

The men all nod their heads. '*Sì, commissario.*'

My hand runs up his inner thigh. I massage him under the table. Alessandro swallows and closes his eyes. The Viagra hasn't worn off. I reach up towards his crotch. Ooh, look, yes, here we go . . .

I lean in and whisper in his ear. 'If I do this, can I have my gun back?'

'No.'

I let him go.

Alessandro picks up the wire and fiddles with a little switch. '*Uno, due, uno, due,*' he says, testing the microphone.

I grab the tape and pull up my top. 'Come on, boys. *Let's do this.*'

'You will have ten minutes,' Alessandro says, turning round in the front seat, 'until we apprehend the suspect.'

I nod. I'm sitting in the back seat, fidgeting, wriggling. I can feel the wire and the sticky tape stuck across my chest and stomach. It's not very comfortable. It's tickling, pulling on my skin, catching all the fine blonde hairs. It's going to smart like a bitch when I rip it off.

'It's long enough to get a confession.'

'Hmm, yeah, well. We'll see.'

'He has to admit that it was *him* who shot Signorina Rain Campbell.'

'All right. OK. I get it,' I say. 'It isn't rocket science.'

Anyway, I just need a second to pull the pin in my

grenade. I'll kill Nino and these cops in one fell swoop. Then I'm free. I'm gone. I'll throw it, then run in the other direction. I don't want to blow myself up as well. It's a shame about killing the Disney prince, but you can't make an omelette without breaking eggs.

We're in a convoy of unmarked cars driving fast through central Rome. We turn a corner then pull over on the Largo Febo outside Nino's hotel. I peer out of my tinted window. Wow. The guy has taste. The Hotel Raphaël is covered in ivy; it's a dark and luscious jungle-green with vivid purple flowers. It's the most beautiful building I've ever seen. No wonder he came here.

The cops kill the engine. There's a knot in my stomach. My shoulders tense. I set my jaw and stroke the hand grenade in my pocket.

And now I'll do it.

It is fucking *on*.

I stop dead in my tracks. There he is at the bar with his back to me. That's his hair, black and glossy, slick and shiny as tar. And his worn leather jacket with studs on. I remember it well: the Marlboro Red smell. The silver bits glint in the lamplight. That's his ass, no question, his taut, tight butt, it looks great in those dark suit trousers. One hundred per cent muscle, no trace of fat. I remember his glutes, the muscles in his back. The heat that rose from his skin like a furnace . . . It feels like *yesterday*. He's standing, drinking alone, a short glass tumbler in his hand. It's filled with something like whisky; the liquid's a dark amber-gold.

No ice. No straw. I wish I had cyanide. I'd slip some in there. I wonder what his last words will be. '*I am justly killed with mine own treachery*'?

I check the time: 20.51. I've got nine minutes . . . shit.

I stand up tall and walk over.

'Hey, Nino,' I say, like we're chill. Like we haven't spent the past week trying to kill each other. 'You gonna buy me a drink?'

If Nino is surprised to see me, he doesn't let it show. He turns to me with a slight tilt of the head. 'Betta,' he says. '*Ciao.*'

Oh my God, he's *gorgeous*. Even better close up like this, life-size and Technicolor, definitely real, not a ghost. Or a fantasy. Or hallucination. His skin is dark with a five o'clock shadow. His eyes glint like onyx and flame.

I see you, Dark Prince. Yes, you, big daddy. If he was on *America's Next Top Model*, he would definitely win.

Candles flicker on the bar, shadows dancing on polished mahogany.

How can he look like an angel when he is Lucifer?

Death is too good for this motherfucker. I'm going to blow him to hell.

He turns back towards the bar and sets his glass down on the wood.

'*Un altro whisky,*' he says to the barman. That sandpaper voice. That coarse baritone. I haven't heard it since the metro and his answerphone.

'Actually, I'll have a Malibu. A Malibu and Coke,' I say.

Nino turns and gives me a look.

'*Fat* Coke,' I say to the barman. 'With ice and lemon. And a straw.'

The barman nods. '*Sì, certo.*'

'*Un altro whisky,*' Nino says, pushing his empty glass across the bar.

'*Sì*, Signor Nino. *Prego.*'

We glare at one another.

He'll be mince beef, duck-liver pâté, fucking steak tartare.

I have sworn't.

Wait and see.

Nino downs the rest of his drink and slams the glass down hard. I study his scuffed-up nails, his blood-red signet ring.

Nino sighs then turns to me. 'So,' he says, '*I'm impressed.*'

'You are?'

'Yeah. You finally caught me.'

I study the furrows that crease his brow, as deep and dark as the Grand Canyon. I read his poker face.

'Yeah, well, you should be impressed. You fucked off with my car. My money. My *clothes*. I didn't have any knickers for nearly a week. It's amazing I found you at all.'

I smooth the hand grenade in my pocket, finger the silver ring . . .

Nino shakes his head. Shakes it off. Like Taylor Swift does in that song. Oh man, I miss her. I used to tweet her several times (at least) each day. But now I'm on the run I can't do it. I hope she'll remember me.

He reaches for a pitted black olive in a little silver dish and skewers it with a cocktail stick. His hand isn't even trembling. He's beautiful from this angle. The angel of light. Beelzebub. Lord of the flies.

'Betta,' he says, 'you'd have done the same thing. If you'd thought of it first.' Yes, well, to be fair that *is* true. But damn it, that isn't the point.

'No, I wouldn't.'

'Yes you would.'

I'm going to turn him to *jam*. Especially if he calls me Betta one more time. Goddamn. I am Alvie Knightly. Alvie Knightly for ever.

He turns and looks me in the eye, calling bullshit on my lie.

I hope he hasn't spotted the wire underneath my clothes.

'Your Malibu and Coke, *signorina*.'

The barman sets my drink down on a black paper napkin. He's served it in a Martini glass with a mini parasol. I pick up my drink and sniff it. Coconut. Cola. Bitter lemon. I take a sip through the straw.

'It's nice,' I say. 'You wanna try?' He could do with sweetening up.

'*Un altro whisky*, Signor Nino,' the barman says, setting down his drink. '*Con i nostri complimenti.*'

Nino nods and picks up his glass. I watch him as he swallows: his angular jaw, his Adam's apple, the short black stubble on his throat. He reaches for another olive.

Doesn't he know he's about to die?

This is it, his last supper.

We make eye contact for a second. He's the first to look away.

'Where's my suitcase with my money?' (Good to know before I kill him.)

'Domenico took it. And the car.'

'What?' No way. He's lying. 'The money's gone?'

'*Sì*,' he says.

'All of it?'

He nods.

I am going to fuck him up.

'No, I don't believe it.'

Nino turns and looks at me as though seeing me for the very first time.

'But . . . what have you done to yourself?'

He takes my hand and pulls me towards him, takes my face into his hands. His lips are so close I can almost taste him. I look into his eyes. He cups my chin and frowns.

'I had a nose job,' I say.

'I liked you better before.'

'You did?' WTF? He's *definitely* lying.

'Betta, you didn't need to do this. I like you just the way you are.'

Nino looks hurt, almost offended.

The way I am? Like Colin Firth/Mr Darcy? Who the hell is he? Timbaland?

'I didn't do it for you, you knob. This is my master disguise.'

He strokes my cheek.

I don't care what he thinks. But – hang on a minute – maybe I do. Now that he's touching me, I really want him. I'm getting hot just standing here. I want to take him straight to bed. I want this shit to get triple-X-rated. I'm sure *everything* he just said is bullshit, but you know what? He's *trying*.

I want to have one final shag before I blow his brains out.

'Did you sleep with anyone?' he says. 'While we were on a break?'

'I wasn't on a break,' I say.

'I was.'

What the fuck? Now he's Ross from *Friends*?

'Well, I was not. Did *you* sleep with anyone?' I ask.

'No. Did *you*?'

'No. Maybe. A woman.'

Alessandro doesn't count. That was business, not pleasure.

'You slept with a woman?' he says. 'Nice.'

'Nice? Nice? She was better than *nice*. The one you shot. She was gorgeous.'

I think of the cops who are listening to our final conversation. We've gone off on a bit of a tangent, not that I give a shit. I get a twinge of something – what is it, apprehension? regret? – deep down in my stomach. I know what it is: dread. I don't want to kill those policemen. They haven't done anything wrong. If anything, they have helped me. I think about the nun.

'I'm glad you caught me,' he says.

I glare at him. He's on thin ice . . . I grip the bomb and hold it tight.

'*Hurry up, Alvie,*' says Beth in my head. '*Pull the goddamn ring.*'

'I left you the diamonds. Did you get the flowers?' Nino says, his hands round my waist.

'What? Did you *miss me?*' I doubt it.

He turns away. He picks up his glass, then he puts it down again. 'Didn't you get my note? The card? Of course I missed you,' he says.

God. This guy. He's such a head-fuck. Why do guys mess with your mind like that? He's hot then he's cold. It's off then it's on. Up then down again.

'You said you wanted to work with me.'

Oh yeah, I did say that.

'I know I said it was a bad idea. But then . . . I thought about it.'

'Oh, you did?' I say.

'I thought to myself, you know, this girl, she is really something. She's got potential. Maybe it could work.'

My heart stops beating in my chest. My lungs forget to breathe.

What the hell is he talking about?

'Like Mr and Mrs Smith?'

'But you were so green; I had to test you. And, like I said, I'm impressed you caught me. I didn't think you would.'

'*Test* me?'

How dare he? The fucking nerve.

Beth laughs.

I clench my jaw. I feel the blood rush to my cheeks. I am going to lose it. But then it hits me like a double-decker: ever since school, no, scratch that, kindergarten, guys act mean when they really like you. Oh my God, Nino's *in love*. And maybe . . . just *maybe* . . . I am too? (It's a thin line between love and blowing someone up with a hand grenade.)

Right. That's it. I've been an idiot. Who am I kidding? I can't kill him. Not now. I'll give him a chance . . . I'll save his life. But if he screws up *one* more time, he is Pedigree Chum.

I grab my phone and check the time. It's already 20.59. I have one minute before the cops storm in. What am I going to do? I picture them all in my mind's eye, waiting, *armed*, out in the hall. Guns at the ready. Ready to shoot. They'll come in here and arrest him. I may never see him again. We don't have time for this conversation. *Talking* was never part of the plan. I was just supposed to get his confession. I was going to blow him to shreds.

'*What are you doing?*' says Beth. '*Why aren't you killing him?*'

Shut up, Beth. I know what I'm doing. Whose side are you on anyway?

'*Your side, Alvie. I know you killed me, but you're still my sister. And this is it. Your chance to get even. You have been through hell this week, but finally you did it. You've outsmarted him. I refuse to sit back and watch you throw it all away.*'

Oh man. What if she's right?

It cannot be but I am pigeon-livered and lack gall.

Urgh. You can fuck off, Hamlet.

No. I'm not listening to either of them. I'm going to rescue him.

I reach up under my top and flick the switch on the wire. I hear the click as the line goes dead.

'Nino,' I say, leaning towards him. 'Listen, do you trust me?'

He pauses.

'OK. Fine. Whatever. We can discuss that later. But right now . . . we have to go.' I scan the bar. 'Is there another way out of here? Apart from through that door?'

'*Sì. Sì.* The roof terrace.'

He gestures towards the French windows; they lead out to a rooftop bar: palm trees and wrought-iron tables. A killer view of central Rome.

'OK. Great.' I down my drink. 'Now you come with me.'

'What are you doing?'

'*Just trust me,*' I say. I lean in and kiss him. His warm lips, his hot tongue.

All of this danger is turning me on. Fuck, I really want him.

I take his hand and look into his eyes. 'Ready? Follow me.'

Chapter Twenty-eight

Nino and I burst through the French windows and out on to the roof terrace.

'The cops,' I say. 'We gotta run.'

But it's too late. They're coming.

I hear gunshots blast behind us. The stench of gunpowder, fear.

KA-POW. KA-POW.

'*Move*,' I say.

I grab Nino's hand again and pull him. We fly across the patio. Jump down to a lower terrace then scale an iron fence.

KA-POW.

'BETTA, WHAT THE FUCK DID YOU DO?'

I can't hear him. I read his lips. The blasts are deafening. I can only hear a tinny sound like static or white noise.

'I HAD TO. FUCKING MOVE.'

Nino pulls me to the ground; I scrape my knee against the tiles. We crouch down low behind a wall, Nino's body pressed up against mine. He pulls his gun out from his trousers. Oh my God, it's *massive*. It's a shiny new Glock 40 (much bigger than mine). I watch him take aim, his finger on the trigger. We keep our eyes on the hotel door.

Alessandro runs out.

He looks hot, I have to admit, but not as hot as Nino.

'Signorina? Where are you? Are you all right?'

Aww, bless. He's got a crush.

KA-POW. KA-POW, goes Nino's gun.

I peer over the wall. Somewhere inside the hotel somebody is screaming. Alessandro lies limp and motionless on the tiled floor. Nino shot him in the neck. Blood floods from his jugular. It makes a real mess. I study his lifeless figure, his face, his hands, his arms and legs. I get a twinge of sympathy. Poor Alessandro, but that could have been Nino or me.

'Let's go,' I say.

I reach for his hand. Nino's palm is rough and calloused and his skin is warm. I get a rush through the whole of my body. I feel magic. I'm special. Alive. He squeezes my hand with a vice-like grip, holding it really fucking tight. We leap over the edge of the terrace on to a sloping roof. The tiles are too-smooth terracotta. My new Prada pumps slip and slide. I look out and see the Colosseum and the dome of St Peter's Basilica. An Italian flag flies high in the distance. There's the crumbling Roman Forum. Starlings swirl in thick black clouds. The sky is pink and orange. Everything is blurring past us, the city distorting as we rush by.

KA-POW. KA-POW.

I look behind us. Three or four more cops run out.

We sprint over the rooftops. This is such a rush.

My pussy aches. I'm hot. I'm wet. I can't wait for the make-up sex.

I follow Nino along drainpipes. It's a sheer drop to the ground. Shit. Fuck. Do not look down. Everything looks small from up here. Ant-like people, tiny cars. Rome is a miniature village.

There's a gap of two or three metres between this building and the next. We're going to have to jump it. My stomach churns and flips.

'Come on. Come with me,' Nino says, and he's flying – soaring in mid-air – his leather jacket streaming out behind him like the wings of a bat. He looks like Batman (but with a horseshoe moustache). He lands with a crash on the red-tiled roof, slips and then grabs on (less like Batman, I guess). One of the tiles slides, tumbling down, down, down, down, down, down. CRASH.

Nino gets up and turns to me. 'Come on, jump,' he says.

He reaches out his hand.

I close my eyes and take a deep breath. This is it. I've got no choice. I can't go back to that hotel.

KA-POW. KA-POW.

They're closing in.

Oh shit, what if I fall?

That roof looks really far away. I'm not sure if I'll make it. I look up and see Nino. *My Nino.* I take a run up and just leap . . .

My stomach sinks.

And I'm falling.

Falling.

I lurch for the roof, but I miss.

'SHIT. SHIT.'

There's nothing. My arms windmill in the air. Nino grabs my wrist. My body slams into the wall. I'm suspended between the rooftops. I dangle and my face scrapes against bricks.

'OW. SHIT. SHIT.'

Don't look down. Oh God. Oh God.

I look up into his eyes. 'Help. Help. Please,' I say.

Is he going to drop me or pull me up? His hands grip tightly round my wrist; his knuckles are bony and white.

'Nino, please. Please.'

Nino's eyes – as black as obsidian – lock on to mine, unwavering. We share some kind of a moment but – what? Is he . . . is he hesitating? What's the fucking problem here? Is he *thinking about it*?

'Nino. Nino.' *Why is he waiting?* 'Don't just leave me hanging here.'

I was right: he is the devil.

I think I've peed my pants.

'Come on,' Nino says. He pulls me up and I stagger to my feet.

That was close.

'What took you so long?'

KA-POW. KA-POW. KA-POW.

Now the cops are gaining on us. They sprint across the roofs.

I grab the hand grenade from my pocket. Pull out the pin and throw the bomb.

'I'm sorry,' I say. 'I had no choice.' Then I scream at

Nino at the top of my lungs. 'RUN! MOVE. MOVE. MOVE.'

'*Ma cos' hai fatto?*'

BOOOOOOOOOOOOOOOOOOOOOOOOOOOOOO OOOOOOOOOOOOMMMMMM.

The rooftop shakes. Planet Earth seems to quake. I grab Nino by the hand and we throw ourselves down. I look at him as we lie here, at the fear in his eyes and the blood and dirt smeared on his face. Ooh, he looks like Rambo. I feel the heat against my back. Can taste the smoke and flames. It's just like that forest fire all over again. My eyes sting with the blaze. I try to see through the clouds of smoke. No movement. I can't see those cops. I cough and cough and cough. Then stop. I think they're dead. They're all dead and we killed them. For a moment, I worry. Was that the wrong thing to do? I'm not used to feeling guilty. But then I snap out of it. It was Nino and me. It was me and fucking *Nino*. We did this *together*. We're Juliette Lewis and Woody Harrelson. We are fucking *on fire*.

An alarm is going off.

Soon there will be firemen (sexy). *Italian* firemen, oh my God. And even more fucking cops. We need to get out of here. And fast. Now how do we get off?

Piazza Navona, Rome, Italy

'Ooh, what's *that*?'
'A Ducati *Monster*.'
'Is it yours?'

316

'It is now. Get on.'

I watch Nino hot-wire the engine. It's a beast of a bike.

'Can I drive?'

'I've seen your driving . . .'

'I'm better at bikes.'

He glares.

The engine coughs and splutters to life.

He climbs on and I get on behind.

Nino offers me the helmet. 'You want it?'

'Nah, fuck it.' He throws it away. I watch it bounce along the kerb and roll into a gutter. 'I've already survived *one* scooter crash.' That accident when I was a child. 'I still have a scar from the brain damage – and lightning never strikes twice.'

'Oh yeah? I have metal plates in my head from last time I came off one of these.'

'Do you? Oh shit. OK, you win.'

'Ready?' he says. 'Let's go.'

'Woohoo.'

I grab Nino round the waist and dig my nails deep into leather. He drives really, *really* fast through the darkening streets. There's wind in my hair and grit in my eyes and the taste of diesel. Or petrol? No one's following us, not yet. No cops. No mobsters. This is fun. We race down a dead-straight street that leads out of the city. The engine roars and snarls like a tiger. I've always wanted to fuck on a bike. I hold on tight and push into Nino, my thighs pressed up against his thighs, my tits squashed into his back. I feel the seat shake and vibrate; this thing is foreplay.

I check the speedometer: 135 mph. Not bad.

Then a Ferrari overtakes us. It's sleek and shiny. The engine purrs like Ambrogio's Lambo.

'Ooh, that's nice,' I say.

I don't think Nino can hear me, what with the wind and the engine noise.

'CAN WE STEAL THAT CAR?'

'What? No.'

'I WANT A FERRARI. IT'S FASTER,' I say.

I watch it as it speeds away. Oh well, another time.

I hear a siren getting louder. Now what?

'SHIT. THE PIGS.'

Nino accelerates and I grip tighter. Pull him closer. Adrenaline courses through my veins. I feel my cheeks warping, distorting, flapping in the wind. I turn and spot the blue lights flashing. Have they seen us? Are we screwed?

Nino swerves and takes an exit.

Our knees are an inch away from the road. I imagine our clothes and skin scraping tarmac. I wish I'd taken that helmet now. This isn't very safe. One head injury is enough for a lifetime. I eat dust, the wind in my hair as we race through a forest. I think it's the same one as before. The tall pine trees are familiar. Tree roots crack the broken road as we bounce along the surface.

A sign by the road reads *Ostia Antica*. There's a faint smell of ash. A desolate scene and blackened branches. At least that fire has gone out. It lasted less than twenty-four hours. It can't have been all that bad.

I can't hear those sirens any more.

'YES, I THINK WE LOST THEM.'

We pass a woman standing by the road.

Oh look, there's that girl. 'Hey. CHOW.'

I wave and wave, but she doesn't wave back. She flips me the bird. How rude.

I saved her life.

'You know her?' says Nino.

'YEAH, SHE'S COOL. I BURNT DOWN HER TENT.'

I can see the sea on the horizon: a vast black void of nothingness. The forest gives way to the seaside, beaches, restaurants, bars, hotels. Nino parks the bike by the strand.

Someone's playing music.

'How Deep Is Your Love' by Calvin Harris.

'Ooh, I love that song.'

It's coming from the beach.

I walk over to a metal rail and look down at the shadows moving on the sand. There's some kind of carnival down there, people drinking and kissing and smoking and fucking on the beach. I sigh and watch the partygoers, tasting sea salt and hash. There's a fire-twirler spinning wheels of dazzling yellow and white. Orange flames flicker and dance. Concentric circles flashing and blazing. Mmm, is that kerosene? I ♥ combustible hydrocarbons. I watch him throwing shapes in the sky. It's hypnotizing. Mesmerizing. I want to have a go. Someone's lit a massive bonfire. It's like a scene in a film by Fellini. It looks really fun.

'Nino, look. A beach party. Come on, I want to go.'

Nino shakes his head.

'No. We gotta steal a boat.'

He heads off down the promenade. *Why is he such a kill-joy?* I watch him as he walks away then turn back to the party. Someone *whoops*. There's the pop of a cork. What is that? Prosecco? Champagne? Fuck it. I'm going. I want to have fun. I just killed God knows how many cops. I need to let off some steam. I'll go to the pier and find Nino later. It will take him a while to steal a boat. First, I want to *dance*. Unwind. And I need a drink.

I swing my legs over the rail and jump down on to the soft sand. I can't believe Nino lost two million euros. Seriously? What a knob. After all the time I've spent looking for it I really need to drown my sorrows. Get out of my mind. Off my head. I walk over to the party and join the people in the crowd.

'Chow,' I say to whoever.

'*Ciao*,' shouts a guy. He smiles.

I pull off the wire stuck under my shirt and throw it in the fire.

The music's playing: UNTZ UNTZS UNTZS. I close my eyes and just feel it. Now it's Swedish House Mafia. I start to get my groove on, moving and bumping and grinding along in time to the fucked-up bass. I open my eyes and a man with dreadlocks offers me a spliff. He has long blond hair right down to his waist. He wears an orange Hawaiian shirt with bright purple flowers on. Nino would never wear something like that. I place the spliff between my lips. Take a nice deep drag. Mmm, skunk; it's sweet and grassy. I hold in the smoke and then blow it out.

Whoosh – it goes straight to my head; that's strong. Just what I need. A young girl standing next to me looks at the joint like she wants a go, but I'm not passing it on.

I dance closer to the bonfire, feeling its warmth against my skin. It crackles and pops and glows so bright. The flames lick at my feet. The music changes to something else with a funky rhythm. It's kinda eighties. Nice, I like it. 'Shut up and Dance' by Walk the Moon. I take another drag.

I sing and I'm floating, dancing like no one can see. I'm really going for it now, twerking and throwing my head around, and shaking my booty like Bey.

I look around for something to drink and spot some open bottles of spirits on a fold-out table. I pick one up and take a swig. Yum, is that Tia Maria?

I swirl around and around in circles, my arms stretched up above my head, the alcohol spilling and splashing my clothes, my hair, my cheek, my face. Someone grabs my arm and I drop the bottle, feeling cool liquid splashing up the inside of my leg.

'Hey. Get off.' I look up. It's Nino. 'Leave me alone. I was having fun.'

He drags me away through the writhing crowds, my feet stumbling through the sand.

'Betta, we got to move.'

The joint is dead now so I chuck it and follow Nino off the beach. We walk along the promenade to a pier with some yachts and boats.

'You could have partied with me,' I say. He doesn't reply. 'So, how the hell do you steal a boat?'

'Same way you steal a bike or a car.'

'You got one yet?' I say.

I look at the boats bobbing out on the water; there are speedboats of various sizes. They're shiny and white with girls' names on: *Lola*, *Maria*, *Esmerelda*. There are hundreds of little yachts. I spot a sleek super-yacht; it's fuck-off huge, the biggest by far. The kind of thing Russian oligarchs buy to impress prostitutes. It's totally pimp. I want it.

'That one. That one. There,' I say, pointing.

Nino walks past it towards a smaller, older, browner-looking boat. It's still a nice speedboat, but far less flashy, made entirely of polished wood.

'We're taking this one,' he says.

'Why? What's wrong with the other one?'

'This one won't have an alarm.'

The boat is called *Ofelia*. That sounds ominous. Why are they always named after women? Why aren't there any blokes? I follow Nino on to the deck. It lurches when I jump down. I grab on to the side.

'Hey. Whoa there,' I say. 'Make it stop. Make it stop.'

'Stop what?'

'The wobbling.'

'It isn't wobbling.'

'Oh.' Must be the wacky baccy. My head's on upside down.

I slump down on a bench on the deck. I cross my legs and hug my arms across my chest. The other boat was so much nicer. I light myself a fag and watch Nino's sexy back. He kicks open a cupboard door underneath the boat's controls. He bends down and fiddles with some wires. A little light flicks on.

I'm not sure this is a good idea. Me and Nino alone at sea. I'm not convinced I totally trust him. It would be way too easy to lose me. I narrow my eyes and cock my head. I'd better stay awake. Keep an eye on this mother-fucker. He might still want me dead . . .

An alarm goes off on the boat.

'*Merda.*'

'I thought you said it wouldn't . . . oh.'

Nino has pulled out his gun.

I close my eyes and tense. Oh God. Oh God. It's *over.* I'm *wasted.*

He shoots the alarm.

It stops. OK. That's good. I'm not dead.

He starts the engine and I stub out my fag.

'Can I drive the boat?'

Chapter Twenty-nine

We've been sailing for hours and hours and hours on the black and boring sea. It's freezing. Windy. The middle of the night. All I can see are the stupid stars and the tiny light on the boat. I sit on the cold hard bench and watch the nothingness. I've got the munchies from that spliff. I'm dangerously hungry. I look around for some kind of food. There's a packet of Pringles in the cupboard. BBQ flavour. It's like they knew I was coming. I crunch on them while Nino fiddles with the boat's satnav. He turns the radio up. They're playing 'Niggas in Paris' by Jay-Z and Kanye, and Nino raps along.

He's ruining it. He's tone-deaf, like my mother.

'Pringle?'

'Sure,' he says.

'So,' I say, 'Nino.' Crunch. Crunch. 'I don't believe we finished our conversation.'

'What conversation?'

'Before, in the bar.'

'Before you blew up the cops?'

'Exactly. I'm still not happy with you.'

'What were we talking about?'

'You taking off and leaving like that. Stealing the car.

The money. My *clothes*. It was really cold in Romania. I had nothing to wear.'

'Romania? What were you doing in Romania?'

'Nothing. I only stayed for eight hours. I went to meet a vampire.' I glare at him and chew. *Urgh*. He knows *exactly*, the bastard.

Nino looks at me and frowns, his face dark with shadow.

'You're a fucking idiot,' he says and he's laughing, laughing, laughing at me. I've never seen him laugh so hard.

'I didn't *kill* anyone . . .'

'You already told me you did,' he says.

'So what? Who was that guy anyway? And why the fuck did he have your phone?'

'I paid him to take the phone to Romania. He was a contact in the Romanian mob.'

'He tried to strangle me,' I say. 'He tried to steal my bag.'

Nino shakes his head. 'That wasn't the job. I was just trying to lose you. He probably improvised. Did you get my message?'

'Message? Which message? About my new hair?' I finish off the packet of Pringles and toss it in the sea.

'When I said we could work together?'

'Yeah, I did. So what?'

'I had to see if you were capable.'

Bullshit. 'Whatever.' *He's such a liar.*

'It's a dangerous job. Not for everyone.'

'Don't patronize me,' I say.

'I have to be able to trust my partner with my fucking life.'

'Yeah, me too.' I glare at him. 'What was that shit before on the roof? I thought you were going to drop me.'

'No way. I pulled you up,' he says. 'You're still here now, aren't you?'

I look out at the horizon, at the line where the black meets the black. There's nothing there. Just space. Dark matter. It's like before the Big Bang.

'So we're partners then?' he says.

'Partners.'

'Fine.'

'All right.'

Until he betrays me? Until he leaves me stranded again?

The water splashes against the hull. The only other sound is the wind.

'Where are we going anyway?'

Nino doesn't reply.

I think back over my vengeance plot. *Find a weapon. Find Nino. Get my money. Kill him.* I didn't get very far.

'So what have you been doing all week?' I say.

'Oh, the usual.'

'Which is what?'

'Bitches and cocaine,' he says.

I roll my eyes. This fucking guy. 'I thought you didn't sleep with anyone?'

'I didn't,' he says.

Bullshit.

'I can't believe you lost our money. Domenico took it?' I ask.

'Yeah,' he says. '*Brutto figlio di puttana.* Domenico found it at my flat. It was after I had to clear out when I shot Dynamite. He blew the door right off the hinges. Took the suitcase. Took the car. By the time I came back for the money he was driving away. I swear, if I ever find that guy . . .'

Yeah. Tell me about it.

'Nino . . .'

'No, it's *Luca* now. I changed my name, got new ID.'

'OK. Fine. Whatever.'

'Betta . . .'

'No, it's *Alvie* now.'

Once I've said it I regret it. But fuck it, I need to tell him. I can't stand another minute being Beth.

He holds me tight round the waist and pulls me in towards him. I brace myself for his response.

'Alvie?'

'Yes, Alvina.'

'I already knew, you idiot. You don't think I noticed what was up? You are like a different person. Nothing like Ambrogio's wife. Your sister always hated guns. And you . . . you're fucking mental.'

'I'll take that as a compliment.'

I look into his eyes. Is he bluffing?

'I don't care. Whatever,' he says. 'Alvie, Betta, Betta, Alvie. I don't really give a shit. I like the new you anyway. Your sister was a pain in the ass.'

For once in my life I'm actually speechless. I gaze out at the sea.

A weight has lifted from my shoulders. I feel free at last.

Eventually I turn to him. 'Where are we going?' I say.

'You'll see when we get there.'

'What's going on? Are you kidnapping me?'

'*Kidnapping you*. What are you? A kid? You're thirty.'

'*I am not*. I'm twenty-five. Fifteen years younger than you, in fact.'

He glares at me.

'Hang on. Wait a minute. What day is it?' I ask.

'None of your fucking business.'

I cock my head to the side. 0509: I remember the code for his phone. 'It's Saturday the fifth, isn't it? It's your birthday.'

'Yeah. Great. Another year older.'

'Happy birthday,' I say.

Nino spits into the water. We look out at the view. It's still black. There's nothing out there. You can see why they thought the Earth was flat. We're going to sail right off the edge. At least we'll both die together.

'Life begins at forty,' I say.

He lights himself a Marlboro Red and talks into his hands and the flame. 'Yeah, if you don't get me shot.'

I sigh, then my stomach rumbles.

'Man, I'm still hungry. I need to eat.'

'I just saw you eat a whole pack of Pringles.'

'No you didn't. I gave *you* one. I need to eat something else.'

'Catch a fucking fish,' he says.

'Don't be stupid. I need some carbs. A Pop-Tart or something. I'm half starved.'

'We're nearly there,' he says.

'Why are *you* in such a mood? I saved your life,' I say.

'You could have been killed or given life in prison.' He deserves it, the twat.

'What are you talking about?' he says. 'I was fine before you showed up. Now I'm Europe's most wanted man. Five dead cops? *Madonna.*'

'You'd be fucked if it wasn't for me.'

He should be grateful I didn't kill him. I was *this* close . . . I swear.

'Blowing up a fucking roof? *Sei pazza. Pazza.* Crazy.'

Silence.

'Well, *you* killed the Disney prince.'

'Who?'

'Alessandro.'

'And who the fuck is Alessandro?'

'It doesn't matter now.'

It's a shame about the Disney prince; he was really cute. He was eye candy, a sweetie. At least I got to shag him first, or that would have been a pity.

Nino takes an angry drag on his fag.

We listen to the sea.

'How did you find me anyway?'

'The pigs tracked you down,' I say. 'It wasn't that hard. There are *cameras* in Rome. Webcams? CCTV?'

'It took you long enough,' he says. 'I've been waiting all week.'

'What was all that shit in the metro?'

'I gave you a second chance. You're lucky you're cute.'

I go and sit back down on the bench and lie on the cold hard wood.

'Everyone I know wants me dead,' he says.

'Yeah, me too,' I say.

We sail further into the night.

I find a blanket under the bench and wrap myself up in a cocoon. Do not fall asleep, Alvina. Watch this predator. I'm quite concerned he has a gun and I have sweet FA. I'm still not sure if I can trust him. Or if *he* can trust *me*.

I'm just drifting off to sleep when I spot some lights up on the coast.

'What's that? Those lights? Is it a port? A city?'

'Naples,' says Nino. 'It's Napoli.'

'Great. Why don't we stop there?'

'Just a couple more hours,' Nino says. 'Why don't you go to sleep?'

Ha. Unlikely. I know his game. He'll kill me while I'm sleeping.

I rest my head on my handbag. It's probably safer to avoid big cities, especially Napoli. The police will be searching everywhere. And I've heard all about Mount Vesuvius. I've seen those people from Pompeii, literally petrified: twisted into grotesque shapes and turned to stone. *No way.* That's not happening to me. We were lucky last week with Mount Etna. I'm not taking another chance.

My eyelids are closing all by themselves . . . when I see something sparkling in the water. It's glinting, silver and spherical like a floating disco ball.

'What's that over there? An island?' I say.

'*Sì. Sì*, it's Capri.'

'That sounds nice. Shall we stop here?'

330

'No, I know where we're going.'

'Well, *I* don't. Are we nearly there?'

He doesn't reply.

I don't know how Nino knows where he's going, I can't see past the end of my nose. This place is darker than Nordic noir. For all I know we could be inside a whale. He fiddles with the satnav again and I watch the lights all fade away. I pull the blanket tight round me, lie down in the dark and fall asleep.

DAY SEVEN:

The One

TEN YEARS AGO

Sunday, 30 October 2005
Lower Slaughter, Gloucestershire

A plate smashes into the wall above my head, sending ceramic shards in every direction. I snap my eyes shut. Just in time. A splinter rebounds and sinks into my cheek. There's the smash of glass on flagstones.

'I hate you,' she says.

'*Mum.*'

'It's so unfair.'

'How can you say that to me?'

'You don't want me to be happy.' My mum's voice breaks with the threat of tears.

'Just stop throwing stuff at me. *Jesus.*'

I stand with my hands shielding my face, the sound of screeching in my ears. I open my eyes again, just a crack, to see the world through the blur of my lashes. My mother stands with her back to me, bent over the Aga. I watch her ribs expand and contract. She's breathing heavily.

'He's *half your age*,' I say at last, wiping the shard from my face, leaving a slick of warm blood on my finger. 'What does he want if it isn't our money?'

'*Our* money?'

I grit my teeth. '*Your* money. *Yours. Yours.*' He's after Nan's inheritance. It's bloody obvious.

She turns round to face me now. Squares up. Her eyes are cold. 'Maybe he loves me for who I am? Maybe he finds me *attractive*?'

'He finds the half mill in the bank attractive . . .' I mutter under my breath. So do I for that matter.

'He doesn't need the money,' she says. 'He's here on a *working* visa.'

I frown. 'But isn't actually working.'

'Neither are you.'

'I'm in *school*.'

We stand and stare at one another. I sniff. What's that? It's smoke. Another bloody barbecue? Or is there something in the Aga that's burning? I lean back against the kitchen island, my elbows resting on cool marble. I know I wanted a nice new dad, but that was ages ago. Two parents are worse than one. I realize that now.

My mother grabs a bottle of red and stabs at the top with a corkscrew. She pours herself a too-full glass. It disappears down her neck.

'I can't believe you agreed to marry him.'

She sets the glass down on the side, closes her eyes and breathes in through her nose. I know she doesn't want to hear it, but someone has to tell her.

'Rupert's a fucking loser, Mum. All he does is hang

around and play that didgeridoo. He woke me up at *dawn* today. "Tie Me Kangaroo Down, Sport"? Who the fuck does he think he is? *Rolf fucking Harris?* He still hasn't learnt my name and he's been living in this house for three months . . .'

'Of course he knows your name. Don't be stupid.'

'So why does he call me *Sheila*?'

'It's a term of endearment, Alvina.'

We glare at one another.

I see her before I hear her come in. I bet she's been watching. Listening. Beth walks over to our mum and puts an arm round her shoulder. She shoots me a reproachful glance, like *now what have you done?* Beth tops up the glass of red and helps herself to a sip. 'Well, I really like him,' she says. 'I'm happy for you, Mum. I think it's great you're getting remarried.'

'Thank you, darling Beth.'

'You've been alone for so long. You deserve another –'

'Right,' I say. 'I've had enough. Either Rupert goes, or *I do*.'

My sister turns to me and gawks.

I watch my mother falter.

No one says a fucking thing.

The tension is titanium. I eye the bottle on the counter. Oh man, I want that wine.

Rupert flings open the patio doors and stumbles into the bombsite kitchen. A thick wall of smoke wafts in after him, but he doesn't care or notice. He opens the fridge and helps himself to a can of **XXXX** Gold. 'Everything all right in here, sheilas?' He steadies himself against the wall, rubs his eyes and stretches. He says something else in thick Australian that I don't try to understand. Something about raping a koala. Something about a flaming galah.

Our fight has clearly woken him from his drunken afternoon slumber. I bet he forgot about the fire and burnt all the shrimps again.

'Alvina, apologize to your father,' my mother says. 'You woke him up.'

I glower at my mother, my cheeks flushed red. I study the poor excuse for humanity that has somehow crawled into our home.

'Fuck you. Fuck all of you. HE IS NOT MY DAD.'

'Language, Alvina,' says my mother.

My sister rolls her eyes.

'Where is my father anyway? Why don't you just admit he's dead?'

'Strewth,' Rupert says.

No one says another word. My mother sighs and shakes her head. My sister helps herself to more wine.

I storm out of the kitchen upstairs to my room. My eyes are stinging with tears. The stupid refrain from that fucking song goes around and around and around in my head.

I grab my trusty JanSport rucksack. Fucking Beth. My fucking mum. You know what? They deserve each other. If Rupert's so *great*, then they're welcome to him. They can play happy families without me. He'll never replace my dad. Whatever happened to him. He didn't go and live in America. No, do you know what I think? I think our mother killed him. Fifteen years ago or so, she hit the roof. She flipped. She knocked him over the head with a frozen leg of lamb, killed him, then ate the proof. The murder weapon was consumed, roasted with mint sauce and potatoes. Who knows?

I need to find out.

I grab some ties to wear as belts, my old camouflage jacket, my pair of shiny cargo pants and some sexy fishnet stockings. I find my favourite beaded bracelet, choker and matching hairband, a cowgirl shirt, some gold-mesh tank tops and a pair of corduroy flares. I sit on the bed. I think I'm packed. That's my whole world right there in my backpack. That night, I run away from home and hitch-hike to central London. I sleep rough in the rain in Leicester Square and never fucking look back.

Chapter Thirty

Sunday, 6 September 2015
Tyrrhenian Sea

The boat lurches and I wake up as the force throws me on to the deck. I sit up and rub my eyes. Where are we? What's going on? I should have stayed awake all night. I shouldn't have fallen asleep. I could have been sleeping with the fishes. That was a lucky escape. I remember my first night sleeping rough alone in Leicester Square. The terror gripped me like a paralysis, keeping me awake. The cold sank deep into my bones and the damp clung to my skin. Every noise was a predator, every man was a killer. I was convinced that that night was my last. The dawn was a miracle.

I watch as Nino steers the boat on to a pebble beach. It's tiny, no more than a hundred metres wide with steep cliffs all around. It's dark, so I can make out rocks and very little else.

'What is this place?' I ask.

'Castiglione, Ravello. This is the Amalfi coast. Come on, get up,' he says.

I yawn and stretch. My back is stiff. I throw the blanket on the deck, grab my bag and follow Nino. We jump out of the boat into icy water. We're waist deep and it's freezing. Urgh, at least that woke me up. It's so cold I can hardly breathe. The ground is soft and strewn with rocks and slippery seaweed. We stagger up on to the beach.

'Grab some rocks,' he says.

'What? Why?'

'Gotta sink the boat.'

'Why the hell would we do that? It's a nice boat. We could use it.'

'We don't want anyone to see it.'

'Well, I want to keep it,' I say. 'Just leave it here. Leave it up on the beach.' I could use it later on if I need to escape.

'I thought you didn't like it?' he says. 'You wanted that other yacht.'

'A crap boat is better than no boat.'

He bends to grab some rocks.

I dump my handbag on the beach and hear the crunch of shells and pebbles. He stops and turns to me.

'Oh *Madonna*. *Listen*. We stole the boat; they'll be looking for it. We are wanted for multiple murders. For killing a bunch of fucking cops. The whole of Italy's looking for us. We need to cover our tracks.'

'OK. Fine. When you put it like *that* . . .'

So melodramatic.

I stagger up the beach and grab a handful of rocks. 'OK?'

'More rocks.'

I grab some more and throw them on to the deck.

'Is that enough?'

'We need more.'

I grab some more and chuck them in.

'There now. That should do it.'

'More. More. *Mannaggia* . . . It has to fucking sink.'

'Oh no. We're out of rocks. That's it. They're all finished.'

Nino turns and studies the beach.

'There are some over there.'

Urgh, he's such a slave driver. Why do *I* do all the work?

I walk over to where he's pointing. I bend down low and grab a few.

'No more. My back hurts. I slept funny,' I say, letting rocks crash on the deck.

'*Va bene. E basta. E basta,*' he says. 'Now we push the boat.'

'Are you sure we have to –'

'*Uno, due . . .*'

'Just seems like a waste of a really cool boat.'

'*Uno, due, tre.*'

We stagger through the freezing water and push the boat out to sea. The waves splash up into my eyes. I taste salt and iodine, then I'm treading water. We rock the boat, and water spills over and floods the deck. The boat wobbles and then capsizes, sinking down, down, down, down, down. There are bubbles and then nothing. The whole thing took just a couple of minutes. First there was a boat and now there's just sea. RIP *Ofelia*. Better you than me.

We swim back to the pebble beach. Wild waves crashing all around us, seaweed wrapping round my calves. My feet sink down into soft sand like the earth's trying to suck me down into the underworld.

'Hurry up,' he says.

I shiver. I'm dripping wet. There's a sharp stone in my shoe. I peel off the slimy seaweed clinging to my legs. 'Yes, yes. I'm coming,' I say. I grope around in the dark for my handbag, then follow Nino's silhouette. We climb the steps that lead from the beach.

'Don't talk. Don't make a sound.'

'*I'm not*. I didn't say anything.'

'And watch out for the *vipere*,' he says.

'Watch out for the *what*?'

'*Vipere. Sssss*. On the stairs,' he says. He moves his hand like a snake.

'*Vipers?* What are you talking about?'

'Be careful where you put your feet. Vipers are poisonous.'

I stumble about in the dark.

'What the fuck are they doing on the stairs?'

'They bask in the sun in the daytime, but sometimes they fall asleep. If you disturb them, they will bite. They'll fill your leg with venom.'

I grab my burner phone from my bag and use it to light up the stairs. They're old and overgrown with weeds and wilting flowering plants. We climb past endless lemon trees, tomato plants and olive groves – the scent of citrus and earth. The stairs are crumbling and steep, leading up into nothing. The mountain rises a mile high; I crane my neck, but I can't see the peak. It disappears into darkness.

Some rubble comes loose beneath my feet. I trip and drop my phone.

CRACK.

'Shit, I think it's broken.'

I pick it up and run my thumb across the shattered screen. A shard of glass sticks in my skin. It's smashed beyond repair.

'Nino,' I say. 'Can I have your phone? Mine is totally fucked.' I don't want to use my other one; I'd probably break that too.

'You have my phone. You bugged it, remember?'

'I didn't *bug* it.'

'You did.'

'That's not what it's called. I downloaded an app to track your location via GPS.'

'You *bugged* it,' he says.

'Whatever.'

We keep on climbing in the dark. Nino won't give me his phone. He wants us to be invisible. He thinks the dark is good. The stairs are never-fucking-ending. I didn't sign up for this *mountain climbing*. Who am I? His Sherpa? A yak? A dog barks and scares the shit out of me. He's a yappy little fucker, a hellhound. He jumps up against a wire fence, his eyes flashing bright in the darkness. On second thoughts, I don't like dogs, especially not dachshunds. Or this one.

I see something long and thin and curving out of the corner of my eye.

'NINO. LOOK. A VIPER,' I say.

Nino stops and turns round, then runs down the stairs towards me.

'What? This? It's a *hosepipe*.'

'Oh. It looked like a snake.'

We keep on climbing for what feels like for ever until the air is thin. I'm getting altitude sickness from the lack of oxygen. My chest heaves, my lungs wheeze. I light myself a fag. I hear my glutes and hamstrings scream: *WHAT THE HELL DO YOU THINK YOU ARE DOING? HAVE YOU LOST YOUR MIND?*

I feel a sharp pain on my ankle.

'ARGH. Something bit me. It bit me, the fucker.'

'What? Where?' Nino says.

'Here. Here. On my foot.' He turns back and runs towards me again, bending down to take a look. 'Oh no, wait. It's a stinging nettle.'

He stands. 'A fucking *plant*?'

'I need to find a dock leaf,' I say. 'There's got to be one around here somewhere.'

'I told you to be quiet.'

I follow Nino up again. He's not being very sweet. I'm being attacked from every direction. Some sympathy would be nice.

I sing 'Poison' by Rita Ora just to pass the time . . .

'*SHHHHHHH,*' he says.

'Oh my God, are we nearly there yet? How many more steps?'

'It's just at the top of this hill,' he says, 'and then round the corner.'

I can't sing any more anyway. I am out of breath. I just sing inside my head. We climb some more stairs. We turn a corner: shadows, demons, earth, trees, rocks and yet more stairs.

'Is *this* where we're going?' I say. 'We're in the middle of nowhere.'

'*Yeah. That's the point.*'

I wish we'd stayed at the beach party. No one would have found us there . . . Actually, what are we doing here? A tall cliff. A sheer drop. The sea and the rocks crash far below us. Is he . . . Will he push me off?

Nino stops and turns round. He walks up to me. It's dark; I can't read his expression. Oh shit. What now? Is he going to kill me? I knew it. He *is* Satan.

I run at him. I'll get him first. Prevention is better than cure.

'RAAAAAAAAGH.'

I'll knee him in the balls. It's my killer move.

Nino grabs me round the waist. 'Hey. What are you doing?'

'Nothing. OW. Get off.'

He twists my arm and holds it behind my back.

'Why did you do that?' he says.

'I don't know. I thought . . . I thought.'

I look out over the edge of the cliff.

'I'm not going to push you off. If I wanted to kill you, you'd be dead by now.'

He sighs and lets me go.

I sit down. Spark another fag. 'I'm tired. I've had enough.'

I refuse to play his mind-fuck game. 'I want to know what's going on. I want to know where I am.'

'I already told you. Ravello,' he says. He kicks me. 'Get up.'

'I can't. I give up.' My lungs are bursting. My heart is racing. My clothes are drenched with sea and sweat. I lie back and study the stars. Oh look, is that Orion? 'Just let me die alone.'

'If someone sees you, we are fucked. We'll be all over the news on TV: Italy's most wanted criminals. You're not supposed to kill the police.'

'Well, my legs are knackered,' I say. 'This mountain is way too steep.'

'*Minchia*. Fucking move.'

He pulls out his gun and sticks it in my neck.

'There's no need to be like *that*.'

'I told you: get up,' he says. He pulls my arm and hauls me up.

I fall into him. 'So, you *are* kidnapping me.'

'No, I am not.'

'You're *protecting* me? How sweet. How very romantic.'

This guy. I swear. He's driving me *nuts*. But Nino is super hot when he's angry. And I do like his big gun.

'If you get caught, then they'll find me. You're a liability.'

He shoves his gun in the back of my neck. The metal's cold against my skin. 'Fucking move, before it gets light.'

I feel his hand round my waist. I like it when Nino gets cross.

'Where are we going anyway?' *This had better be good . . .*

'You see that balcony on the hill? The one with all the white statues? That's where we're going,' he says.

Villa Cimbrone, Ravello, Italy

I've pulled all the muscles in my legs and I think I've slipped a disc, but I stop and peer through the iron gates. 'Wow. What is this place?'

'It's a hotel,' he says.

'Oh my God, it's amazing,' I say as I step through the gates.

'I know. Try not to blow it up.'

Old-fashioned lanterns illuminate a garden with a golden yellow glow. Palm trees tower high above and cast wild shadows on the lawn. Ivy climbs and covers the walls. There's an ancient tower with crumbling brickwork and steps leading up to a wooden door. I follow the path through the beautiful gardens, my fingertips brushing the powder-soft petals and the leaves of tropical plants. This place is fairy-tale. Unreal. There's a fountain with flying cherubs. Lilies and roses and jasmine flowers. The air smells sweet like Woolies' pick-and-mix. A bird in a tree sings a song.

'Oh, Nino, I love it. But . . . why did we come here?'

'Pietro, he works here. He's an old friend. He can get us a room on the quiet.'

'Have you been here before?' I ask.

'It's a good place to hide out.'

We break into the staff quarters. Nino picks the lock on the door. We find a bedroom down the hall, step inside and flick on the light.

'Oi. *Stronzo. Sono io.*'

Someone's sleeping in the bed.

'*Che cazzo?* Nino? *Vaffanculo. Mamma mia. Che vuoi?*' Pietro wakes up and is blinded. Half naked.

'*Una camera,*' Nino says.

Pietro sits up. He looks at me. Then looks at Nino. They embrace.

He rubs his eyes. '*Per due persone?*'

'*Sì. Sì. E' per la mia luna di miele,*' Nino says.

'*Perché non puoi prenotare una stanza come tutti gli altri?*'

Pietro gets up and walks over to me. He holds out his hand and I shake it.

'*Ciao. Piacere. Auguri,*' he says. He kisses me on both cheeks.

'Oh. Chow, Chow, Chow,' I say.

Pietro pulls on a T-shirt and trousers, then leads us to our room; he says it's the nicest and the biggest. He unlocks the door and I step inside. I gasp. Oh sweet Jesus. It's even better than I'd imagined. The room is vast and palatial. Stunning. There's a grand and concave blue painted ceiling. An enormous marble fireplace. There are beautiful ceramic tiles on the polished floor. A black-and-white photo of Greta Garbo hangs on the living-room wall.

'It's just dreamy,' I say.

Pietro bows out of the room.

'What is "*auguri*"?' I ask Nino when he's gone.

'*Auguri* means *congratulations.*'

'Oh. Right. I see.' I study the paintings on the wall. 'So, why did he congratulate me?'

Because I'm still alive?

'I told him we got married,' says Nino. 'And it was our honeymoon.'

'Aww. That's sweet.' I sit down on the bed. 'Is Pietro Cosa Nostra too?'

'No, he just works in the hotel. He's the only person I know who doesn't want to kill me.'

'I don't want to kill you,' I say.

Not any more anyway. I feel a bit safer now we're here. Perhaps I was paranoid before? Fretting over nothing. Nino likes me, I can tell. He really did miss me this week. Was it really all just some Mafia test? A penance or initiation? Like the labours of Hercules, to see if I was badass. I breathe a long, deep sigh of relief and spread out like a starfish on the bed.

Nino turns on the TV news.

I sit up and blink.

Footage of Domenico in handcuffs surrounded by Italian police appears on screen. He's walking through a crowd of hacks and flashing lights and cameras. There's a police station. A female reporter. Nino turns the volume up.

'What are they saying?' I ask.

He turns to me and shakes his head. 'That fucking idiot. The cops caught him with Ambrogio's car. They found the suitcase with the money. Our two million euros. His DNA matches DNA found at the scene of Salvo's grave as well as your sister's.'

'So what . . . they think *he* did it? Ace.'

'They haven't got a clue. Domenico has been arrested. Triple homicide.'

Beth, Salvatore, Ambrogio . . .

'This is great. This is *awesome*.'

Nino and I do a high five.

Oh my God, I could kiss him.

I pause and look into his eyes.

'Have you got any coke?' I say. 'We should celebrate.'

'*Sì*,' he says. 'We should.'

He reaches into his jacket pocket and pulls out a see-through bag. It's filled with snow-white powder.

I look up and frown.

'You mean you had all this cocaine the whole time I was *dying* out there. Climbing all those fucking stairs and you didn't give me any?'

I *am* going to kill this guy. I wish the cops hadn't stolen my gun.

'You didn't ask,' he says.

Nino slams the bag of blow on the bedside table. He racks up two long lines with his card, then rolls up a €100 note.

Oh my God, I've missed it.

Then I remember my tiny new nose. I haven't really tried it out. It's still recovering from that surgery. It hasn't even been a week. That Romanian mobster punched me in the face. It's been through the wars, to be honest. I'm not sure if it will work. What if the coke gets stuck? What if my nose is broken?

'Nino,' I say, 'can you blow some coke up my ass, like in that scene in *The Wolf of Wall Street*?'

'What?' he says. 'No fucking way. You can stick it up your nose like everyone else.'

'Urgh, you're so boring,' I say with a sigh.

'Me? Boring?'

'Uh-huh. *Oh, Alvie, don't blow up the cops. Oh, Alvie, don't steal the Ferrari. Don't go to the beach party. Don't make a noise. Don't blow coke up your ass. Blah, blah, blah.*'

We do our lines. Mmm, powdered *awesome*. My brain lights up like a mega-watt bulb at the top of a Christmas tree.

'You think I'm boring?' Nino asks.

'Yes.'

'You come with me.'

'What is it *now*?' I ask, standing up. My face has gone numb, like at the dentist's. At least my nose still functions.

He grabs my hand and leads me out of the room and outside to the garden. He takes me to the back of the hotel to a turquoise swimming pool.

'Oh wow. It's *stunning*,' I say. 'Even nicer than Beth's.'

It's a pretty kidney shape all lit up with floodlights. It's surrounded by gardens and palm trees and flowers. The pool looks out over a cliff with a Mediterranean view. It's super cool and glamorous: the cover of a Hedkandi album.

Nino rips off all his clothes and jumps into the water. A tanned back. A white bum. A cock like an anaconda. He dives down deep into the water, then pops back up again.

'Is *this* boring?'

'This is incredible.'

I like him better naked.

We're Steve McQueen and Ali MacGraw in that summer lake in *The Getaway.*

'Come on. Get in,' he says.

I peel off my clothes and walk to the steps. They're sparkling silver in the light, shining bright like platinum jewels. I dip in a toe. It's cool and refreshing. I glide down the stairs and into the water. Swim a few strokes. It's lovely. The water feels soft against my body, skimming my skin like silk bed sheets. I can feel the drugs pulse in waves through my bloodstream. A growing smile plays on my lips.

Nino's on the far side of the pool, watching me. I feel his gaze. I swim towards him. Now I really want him. Like I've never wanted anyone so much in my life. Butterflies are swirling around in my stomach like I'm thirteen again. You know what, I'm glad I didn't kill him. It would have been such a waste.

Nino dives under the water. His dark form moves across the pool, menacing and dangerous, like a shark or a man-eating fish. Bubbles rise to the surface, then he comes up in front of me. I look into his eyes. They're dark and flashing. He holds me tight against the edge and finally we kiss. I taste his tongue, his salty lips. I pull his head towards me. His fingers gripping in my hair. His mouth is hungry, eating me. I bite his bottom lip. A warm hand slides along my hip and reaches down towards my clit. The heat from his body is warm on my skin. I moan. It's been a *week.*

Then he pulls away.

He spins me round and grabs me from behind. He bites

me on the back of my neck. A shiver runs up and down my spine. My cunt is hot and wet. I lean my head back on his shoulder. He reaches round and cups my breasts, my nipples hard, erect. I moan as his hands slide down my belly and I feel rough fingers inside me.

'Is *this* boring?' he says.

Chapter Thirty-one

Nino enters me from behind.

'A condom,' I say. 'I've got some ribbed raspberry-ripple flavour . . .'

'You can't get pregnant if you fuck in the water.'

'What?' I'm not sure that's true . . .

'Swear to God,' he says.

He fucks me over the edge of the pool. It's fine. I'm on the pill. I sink down further on his dick, our bodies pressing tight like glue. The tiles dig into my chest. His dick is pure perfection. I love his cock. I love his smell. Marlboros and chlorine and sweat. *Oh yeah.*

'Still bored?' he whispers in my ear.

'Oh my fucking God.'

I feel his cock deep, deep inside me. Feel his hot breath on my neck. His strong arms grip my waist like he is never letting go.

'Oh, baby,' he says.

'Say my name.'

'Which one do you prefer?'

'*Alvie*,' I say.

'Alvie.'

'Nino.'

'Alvie.'

'Nino. *Nino.*'

I claw at the tiles with my nails like a cat, stretching and rushing and high. My head is floating far away. Oh man, I love cocaine. Nino pulls me from the edge and pushes my head down underwater. He bends me so my head's by my knees and I can't breathe and *what*?

What the hell is he doing now? Why's he holding me down? He's going to drown me, isn't he? I'll die, like my twin, at the bottom of a pool.

He keeps on pounding me.

Oh my God, I'm going to die.

I —

I —

I —

I —

I'm going to come so hard.

I try to swim above the water, but I'm stuck firm. He pins me down. I struggle and strain, and feel the air leave my lungs and the oxygen floating away. He pounds me and pounds me and *fuck*. I'm dizzy and light-headed. My vision's a blur. I open my eyes, but all I see is blue. I feel his cock against my G spot. I'm going to faint. I can't take much more. My eyes are closing by themselves.

There's no more air.

I come.

A flash of dazzling light and I'm blinded. My brain explodes. Ignites.

We come together over and over, again and again and again. My body shakes. I'm *gone*. I'm wasted. Time and space dissolve, collapse. I watch us as we float away, rising up like phantoms or angels. We dance and glide and soar so high. There's a light. And a tunnel.

Then nothing.

Nino pulls out – I'm draped over the edge of the pool – gasping, gasping, gasping for breath. I feel my cheek slam into the tiles. My face lies flat on ceramic.

'NINO, WHAT THE ACTUAL FUCK?

'You like?' he says.

'I could have *died*.'

'That's a risk I was willing to take.'

I consider this for a split second.

'Fuck you,' I say. 'That was ace.'

A lack of oxygen to the brain . . . I already have enough brain damage. I don't need any more.

The garden spins around and around, blue then green then red. Classical music begins to play. The air is filled with beautiful arias, a crescendo of cellos and violins.

'Where is that music coming from?'

For a second I think I'm dreaming.

'Ravello Festival,' he says.

I look around. We're still in the pool, our bodies entwined in one another's. We are still alive. Everything is perfect. I look at his arms wrapped round my shoulders, as bronzed as a god's, his muscles defined. Nobody makes me come like that. Nino's the man of my dreams.

We lean over the edge of the pool side by side and look out at the Earth-porn view. The first light of day bleeds over black mountains; the sky's a vibrant warning red. We watch the sunrise together and listen to the music. It's magical, ethereal, like they're playing just for us. I look around the garden; it's Eden, everything bathed in golden light. This place is paradise.

'OK,' I say. 'Sometimes you're not boring.'

'*Bene.*'

'When you make an effort.'

'*Mortacci tua.*'

Ha ha. Now he's *cross*.

I splash and crash out of the water. Nino follows and chases me around the garden. I'm laughing and laughing, so high.

I sprint along an avenue enveloped with sweet-smelling flowers: purple blossoms, bougainvillea. Ancient terra-cotta vases. The milky marble of a nude. I skip into a rose garden. Trip and roll on the soft grass. Nino falls on top on me.

'Hey, what's that? On your butt?'

'What's what?'

'That tattoo? "Die Nemo"?'

'Oh yeah,' I say. I'd forgotten about that. 'I need to go on *Tattoo Fixers* and get it covered up. Have you ever seen that show?'

'No, I haven't. So what does it mean?'

'It means . . . You know I can't remember. I was really drunk when I got it. But at the time it was meaningful. You know, that cartoon fish?'

We lie naked on our backs and watch the dawn sky.

'Oh, look. A shooting star.'

Nino turns to me and says, 'You gotta make a wish.'

I think I know what I want . . .

'Why did you say that before?' I ask. 'About our honeymoon?'

'I don't know,' Nino replies, stretching. 'Just something to say. I couldn't tell him the truth. He wouldn't have let us stay.'

'I thought you'd stayed here before?'

'I never killed a fucking *cop*.'

'OK. Good point,' I say.

'So, you wanna hear my plan?' he asks. His voice is excited now. 'The plan that will make us fucking rich?' He pulls me up to lie on his chest. He smiles and his dark eyes sparkle.

'Hell yeah. What plan is this?' I rest my cheek against his pecs. I feel his heart beat through his chest.

'We're gonna work together,' he says. 'I've been figuring it all out. You remember the English guy I told you about? The one who killed my father?'

'No.'

'He's a billionaire art dealer. And he lives in London. His name is Ed Forbes. Total cunt.'

'So, what about him?' I say. I stroke the hair on his chest with my fingers. I kiss him. He's still wet.

'He stole from me, from my father,' he says. 'It's time we got revenge. You and me together, baby. We're gonna take him down.'

A billionaire sounds promising. 'I like the sound of that.'

'Yeah, I love fucking cunts.'

Nino stands and seizes my hand.

'Come on, there's something I want to show you.'

'Now where are we going? Not London already?'

'Shut up. You'll like it,' he says.

We walk through the gardens hand in hand, butt naked like Adam and Eve. A long, straight path surrounded by flowers leads through a pagoda to a cliffside terrace.

'*Guarda che bella vista*,' Nino says. 'The terrace of infinity.'

'Wow, now that's a view.'

I look out over the sea. The land slides down into the ocean. The mountains are covered in citrus groves with pops of yellow and gold. Villages cling to the craggy cliffs among dark green trees and azure blue. The air fills once more with the beautiful music. Now I want to dance.

'It's incredible,' I breathe. 'This would be a great place to propose.'

'I can't propose. I don't have a ring.'

He smiles a mischievous smile. And suddenly it all makes sense. This was all just meant to be. Nino is my Mr Right. No one else could handle me. He is *perfect*. He's The One.

'I do. I have two rings,' I say. 'Just wait here, don't move . . .'

I sprint back through the garden to the hotel and up the stairs to our room. My feet slip and slide on the dewy grass, my heartbeat *molto allegro*. The music's still playing, something triumphant. Cymbals crashing. A crescendo. I look around for my handbag and find it lying on the bed. I grab it and run back to Nino.

Oh my God, I hope he's still there. What if he's gone again?

He's standing with his back to me, looking out at the view from the balcony. I take it all in, that ass. That *view*. He was worth all the hard work.

'Look, I say, 'two rings. I told you.'

I rummage around inside my bag – damn, I can never find *anything*.

'Oh, look, your hat. Do you want it back?'

He pulls on the fedora.

Eventually I find the rings; the silver ring from the hand grenade (I kept it as a souvenir) and the vibrating cock ring. (Ooh, we can use that later.)

'What the hell is *that*?' he says. He looks at the cock ring in my hand. Perhaps he's not into sex toys?

I get down – quickly – on one knee.

'Nino,' I say, 'will you marry me?'

'If I say yes, will you shut up?'

'Yes,' I say.

'Yes,' he says.

I jump up and push the cock ring on his finger; it's pink and stretchy like jelly.

'Yippee,' I squeal. 'Now you ask me.'

I give him the ring from the grenade.

Nino gets down on one knee. 'Alvie, will you marry me?' He slides the ring on my finger.

'Yes, I will,' I reply.

'*Congratulations*,' says Beth in my head.

Then we kiss.

Nino and Alvie
Together for ever. His
Balls belong to me ☺

I skip and Nino walks back to the swimming pool. We pick up our crumpled clothes and head inside to our room. I'm so happy I could explode. I do one line after another until my brain is a snow globe.

Nino crashes out, exhausted, on the king-size bed. But I don't want to sleep; I'm too excited. I've got a wedding to plan.

'Nino? Do you want some?' I ask.

Oh, he's started to snore.

I'll just have both of these lines to myself . . . Waste not, want not. Sniff, sniff, sniff. Twice the fun and double the trouble. I'm too young for a heart attack.

I turn on the TV for some company. I want to watch the news. Perhaps there's more on Domenico's story? That would crack me up. I do the other line. Whoop! Whoop! Now I can't stop smiling. It's all I can do to stop myself from bouncing on the bed like a kid. The TV's showing scenes of some cloisters. A church or a convent. A solemn crowd. An Italian nun's being interviewed. I don't know what she is talking about; it's probably very dull. They overlay a photo of an elderly-looking nun. Not *any* nun. MY NUN. 'Sorella Francesca di Marzo, 71, also known as Teresa di Gesù.' Shit fuck shit fuck shit. A presenter speaks in hurried Italian. His face is sombre and sincere. The camera moves to zoom in on a road. Streaks of red.

Those are bloodstains. Of course, that's where I ran her over. Where is this going? What does it mean? Have they found her body? Another scene. The charred remains of the Cinquecento. Blackened branches. Broken trees. Scenes of sylvan carnage. Burnt grass and singed leaves. The camera zooms in on the car. Don't. Don't. Don't open it. Don't look inside, please. They spare us the sight of the nun's charred body, but I can see her in my mind's eye. Gross and haggard, her skin melted off. Grey hair turned to charcoal. Her clothes just threads . . . I close my eyes and shake my head.

'No, no, no.'

Another photo. It's that man! 'Lorenzo Mancini, 51'. I recognize him straight away. I stole his car. That was his rusty old Cinquecento. I remember his red face pressed up to the window. I remember that thick roll of fat. He looks bemused, beyond baffled. He is standing outside a court-room. Police vans and bustling crowds. I watch as the man cowers under his coat, trying to avoid reporters.

'Signor Mancini,' call the hacks. '*Signor, é stato lei?*'

The man is ushered past the crowds in handcuffs. There's a group of angry nuns. Placards. A solemn-looking priest. And not any priest, it's *my* priest. The one I rescued from the forest and who gave me a lift. My brain whirs and whirs and tries to compute, but I'm so high now that I can't think. I try to work it all out. Someone interviews the priest. I don't know what he is saying, but it looks like some kind of eulogy. I guess he's talking about that nun, Sorella Francesca Di Marzo. He's probably saying it's sad

363

she's dead. That people shouldn't kill nuns . . . The police must have arrested that man on suspicion of murdering the nun. Is *that* what's going on here? I can't believe it. There is a god. I stare at the screen for a couple more minutes. Then the story changes to something else.

I run over to Nino on the bed. I want to wake him. I have to tell him. I can't believe my luck. But it wouldn't make any sense to Nino. He doesn't know who that nun was. He doesn't know I killed her. I guess it isn't really that urgent. I'll let him sleep a little bit more. It can wait until morning. See? I'm a sweet, considerate soul. I'm a thoughtful girl. I'm going to make a wonderful wife. Nino is a lucky man. Doesn't know how lucky he is.

I watch him sleep. I could watch him for hours and listen to him breathing. It's dark in the bedroom; the curtains are drawn and shadows form a chiaroscuro that accentuates his features. My eyes rest on his beautiful face. The portrait of a Roman god. An Italian supermodel. He could be an angel by Caravaggio. He could play Ciro in *Gomorrah*.

I light myself one of his cigs and stand at the window, beaming. I am so goddamn good at this. I am getting away with *murder*. I don't even know how many that is, but that's a fuck-ton of bodies. We're going to be the best assassins that the world has ever seen. We'll go down in history as the maddest and the baddest. Nino's my king and I'll be his queen.

I smile at the sparkling sea. The sun is rising over the water. It's going to be a beautiful day. There's not a single cloud in the sky. I love it when it's like this. The pink of dawn evaporates into a blue as pale and clear as Dynamite's eyes. I've forgiven Nino for killing her. He did what he had to do. I've forgiven myself for killing those cops. Alessandro too. I've all but forgotten about that mugger, and my twin had it coming to tell you the truth. The nun was . . . regrettable. But you can't be a pussy in my line of work. The minute you catch the feels, you lose. You falter and you die. I stub the fag out on the tiles and flick it out to the garden below. I turn back into the bedroom. Nino is still sleeping.

I sit down on the edge of the bed and stroke his raven hair. Nino's snores are soft and low, as sweet as baby Ernie's. They're not monster snores like Domenico's. (He'll be popular in jail.) Nino stirs and moves in his sleep. He mutters something, 'Alvie?' He's dreaming about sex with me, I can guarantee it. There's a flicker of a smile at the edges of his lips. I lean in and kiss him. My partner. My lover. My husband-to-be. I can't believe he wants to marry me.

The bag of coke is lying open. Just one more bump — what harm can it do? I lick my finger and stick it in the pure white powder. I rub the drug into my gums. Mmm, that's proper lovely. Nino's gun is lying on the little bedside table, beside the lamp and his engagement ring. Oh. Why has he taken that off? I'm still wearing the silver ring from the hand grenade. But the cock ring isn't on his finger; it's right there on the table. That's strange. I'm not sure if I like it. What the fuck does it mean? My heartbeat quickens. Is that the coke? Or something else? But it's cool. It's OK. Chill out, babe. I stand up and stretch it out. Perhaps some chamomile tea?

I look in the bedroom mirror. It's dark, but I can see my eyes are like two flying saucers. I've never seen my pupils so wide. My jaw is set and rigid. I rub my cheeks hard up and down and slap myself in the face three times. I grind my teeth. Oh man, I'm on edge. I can't feel my chin or lips.

I see Nino stir in the bed just behind me. He reaches out his hand through the shadows. I watch his fingers inch towards something on the bedside table.

'*The gun,*' says Beth. '*He's going to shoot you.*'

I sprint back across the room. My heart is pounding double time. I get tunnel vision. Everything goes black beyond the gun. I grab the Glock, but just in time – Nino's fingers brushing mine – then I pull the trigger.

KA-POW.

Splattered blood and floating feathers.

I'm deafened. Hands shaking. Palms sweating.

Shit.

Then I drop the gun.

What just happened?

What the fuck did I do?

Beth laughs in my head. '*I win,*' she says.

I slump – heavy – against the wall and sink down slowly to the floor.

'No,' I say. 'What the fuck did you do?'

I watch the red seep through the cotton. Smell the carnal stench of blood.

'*He was reaching for the lamp,*' says Beth. '*You just killed your soulmate.*'

'No. No. The gun,' I say.

'*The lamp.*'

'The gun.'

'*The lamp.*'

'The gun.'

'*The lamp.*'

'The gun. The *gun.*'

I look at Nino, at the hole in his forehead filling up with something black. Everything is in slow motion. My vision is blurry with tears. His beautiful face is stained with blood. My stomach churns. I retch. I vomit again and again and again all over the blue tiled floor.

'*I told you I'd get my revenge,*' she says.

'No, no, no.'

Oh my God, *Beth.* I could kill her again. And that fucking clown. She's been out to get me all along. She hates me. She hates me. *I hate me?* I cry hot tears. He's dead. He's gone. What have I done? What did I do? I kiss him on his still warm lips. I taste hot iron: his blood.

I reach out my trembling hand and feel his wrist for a pulse. I wait.

And wait.

And wait.

Come on.

Come on.

Nino.

Nino.

Please.

I gently pull his eyelid open. His pupil is wide. Dilated. It doesn't shrink when exposed to light. I let it close. That confirms it.

Now cracks a noble heart. Good night, sweet prince, and flights of angels sing thee to thy rest.

I lie down next to him on the bed.

Mr Bubbles laughs in my head.

And . . .

The rest is silence.

Epilogue

My Samsung rings: 'Unidentified caller'.

'Yes? Hello? What is it?'

'Alvina, darling, is that you?'

'Huh?' Don't fucking *darling* me. It's Mavis. Why is she being so *nice*? Someone must be listening. 'Yes, it's me. What do you want?' Money for a retirement home? A live-in nurse/carer?

'I'll keep this brief, my angel,' she says.

'Good. Why's that then?' Unusual.

'I only have a minute, you see, before they cut me off. They're very strict about personal calls in these police-cell-prison-office things.'

'In what? Where are you? What's going on?' I glare at the phone, but it isn't FaceTime.

'Yes, that's why I'm calling, dear. I'm at the station here in Rome. It turns out the authorities in the UK have *finally* found your father. Can you believe it? After all these years. *Twenty-five* to be precise . . .'

'What the hell are you talking about?'

'Some police officers in Lower Slaughter found your father in the garden shed.'

'Why was my father in a shed?'

'Ah, now *that is the question*.'

'The million-fucking-dollar question. Who am I? Chris Tarrant?'

'What? Who? No. Don't swear. Anyway, the point, my dear, is *I have been arrested*. On suspicion of first-degree murder. Have you ever heard anything so utterly absurd? Anyway, I very much doubt they'll have enough evidence to convict me, what with the time span and the maggots. To be honest, I'd almost forgotten about him. Half expected he'd have disappeared or, you know, biodegraded. I was actually calling you to say *do come and get Ernesto*. I left him with Riccardo and Giuseppe, which is not ideal . . .'

'WHAT THE FUCK? MY FATHER IS DEAD?' First it's Nino then my dad.

'Will you come and babysit?'

'You killed him?'

'Alvina. Let me be clear: that's for the *jury* to decide.'

'I knew it. I knew it. You did.'

I bet it wasn't Nan's inheritance, that half a mill Mum had in the bank. Nana never had any cash. It was all my dad's. Now that's a motive if ever I heard one.

'Anyway, do you want their number? I have Riccardo's details here.'

'I don't need Riccardo's number.' I'm not going to babysit.

'I would have asked Domenico, but he seems to have disappeared. Actually, now I've got you, darling, have you got any money? I need ten thousand just for bail –'

The line goes dead. They've cut her off. I sit down on the bed in stunned silence. My head flops on the pillow by Nino's. I let the phone fall from my hand. Oh my God, my mother's a *murderer*. I don't know why I'm so surprised. Where did I think *I* got it from? Ha. It's clearly in my genes. Now there's nothing special about me. That was my one USP. She's a killer. I'm a killer. Everyone's killing *everybody*. But the difference is I'm not going to get caught. I'm next generation. 2.0. New and improved. *Advanced*.

I look down at Nino's body lying helpless on the bed. The smell of vomit wafts from the floor. There's the drip, drip, drip of his blood. He was never going to marry me. How could I be so naive? He wore that ring for less than an hour. It's what I *wanted* to believe. He said so himself; this whole week was a test. Well, *you* failed my test, asshole. I'm the one in the driver's seat now. I am the one in control. I wanted him dead. Of course I did. That was the plan all along. It was never my sister's voice in my head. What am I? Insane? Schizophrenic? That was my subconscious talking. It was just my fucked-up conscience. I knew what I had to do. I knew what was needed . . .

If anyone asks about that bomb, if anyone finds this corpse, I'll tell them that Nino pulled the ring and then he took me hostage. It's *perfect*. I killed him in self-defence. I had no other option. Who do you think they are going to believe? The *girl* or the dead fucking *hitman*?

If I can kill this ruthless mobster, if I can kill *the love of*

371

my life, then I'm more hardcore than I thought. I can kill *anyone* dead.

Yes. Yes, I'm Alvina Knightly.

That Ed Forbes had better be scared.

So put on your big boy pants, Mr Forbes.

I'm coming for you next.

Acknowledgements

*B*AD was the difficult second novel, but writing this book was so much fun. My deepest thanks go to the following for their incredible support: Paolo Esposito, Lisa Taleb, Richard Skinner, Matilda McDonald, Jessica Leeke and the team at Michael Joseph, Maya Ziv and the team at Dutton, Simon Trewin, Anna Dixon and the team at WME, Tim Bonsor, Claudette Bonsor, Lydia Ruffles, Felicia Yap, Michael Dias, Ilana Lindsey, Helen Allen, Emma Vandor, Issy Mahmoud, Maria Ghibu, Yasmeen Westwood-Ali, David Westwood, Chris Elvidge, Johnny Pariseau and Mike Deluca and Michael De Luca Productions, Chloe Yellin at Universal Studios, Senja Andrejevic-Bullock, Matilda Munro, Victoria Leung, Charlotte Murray, Andrea Vasiliou, Vanya Mavrodieva . . . I am sure there are many, many more that I am forgetting and for that I apologise! But I couldn't write this trilogy without you. You make everything possible. All my love, Chloé xxx